Never Had a Love Like This

Never Had a Love Like This

Shelli Marie

www.urbanbooks.net

Urban Books, LLC
114 Norman Ave.
Amityville, NY 11701

ISBN 13: 978-1-64556-729-5
EBOOK ISBN: 978-1-64556-741-7

First Trade Paperback Printing June 2026
Printed in the United States of America

10 9 8 7 6 5 4 3 2 1

Distributed by Kensington Publishing Corp.
Submit Orders to:
Customer Service
400 Hahn Road
Westminster, MD 21157-4627
Phone: 1-800-733-3000
Fax: 1-800-659-2436

The authorized representative in the EU for product safety and compliance
Is eucomply OU, Parnu mnt 139b-14, Apt 123
Tallinn, Berlin 11317, hello@eucompliancepartner.com

Acknowledgments

To God Almighty, I give the glory.

To my family support team:

My children: Jeremy & Tiffany, Jessica & Daqwan, Danielle, Vassie Jr. & Maya. My grandkids (The Diamond Dozen): Jaden, Tianna, Kaylen, Journey, Thalia, DJ, JaKoby, Marlee, Wynter, Deklen, Kairo, and Sofia.

Thanks for all your encouragement. I love you guys! Always!

To the rest of the Dishman clan: Jennifer Dishman, Kim Dishman (R.I.L.), Marlo and Devin Dishman, Daddy and Genora Dishman

I love you all dearly!

To my extended support team: My sissy Teruka B, my sis Lady Lissa, my sis Sheila James, my sis Summer Grant, my sis Cyndy, my bff TonYelle Reese, my sis Jeanida Luckie Weatherall (R.I.L.), Andrea, Quaran, Tierra, Jasmin, Michaele, Regina, Priscilla Cole, Lenwand, Kendra, Tanya Gary, Helen, and all the rest of the Rose City Readers group!

I love you all!

AND A SPECIAL THANKS TO ALL MY DEDICATED READERS!

Never Had a Love Like This

"Family Over Everything"

Prologue

Constance ("Connie")

"Get the fuck off me, Ricky!" I screamed, attempting to prevent my clothes from being ripped off my small-framed body.

My limbs shook from fear. My fate was unknown, and just the thought of this caused me to panic. There I was, fighting for my life, along with exercising my right to say no. That shit wasn't working.

Ricky was a high school dropout who had turned into the local neighborhood hustler in Portland, Oregon. He sold drugs in order to provide for himself and his family. I didn't have a problem with it as long as he kept the shit away from me. Since I had never seen that side of him, to me, it didn't exist. I guess you could say I was in denial. That was just how I fell into his trap and opened up to him once he began to pursue me persistently.

First, he started waiting for me every day after school. It began with him parking his car and walking me home, but things changed as soon as I gave him my very first kiss. Ricky became obsessed with me, and I was intrigued about him as well.

Against my better judgment, I began to spend more time with him. Things never went beyond first base because we never had any privacy. I was thankful for that, because even at seventeen, I was nowhere near ready for sexual relations. I had been raised sheltered and had never hung out.

"Why don't you let me give you a ride today?" Ricky offered one day after school.

"Nah, I better not," I said, refusing to take him up on his offer, since I knew that if my mother found out, she would go insane. There was no way I was gonna get into his vehicle.

Thankfully, after begging me for twenty minutes or so, Ricky gave up and agreed to walk me home instead. The entire stroll he talked about us having a more intimate relationship. Feeling uncomfortable, I downplayed his comments and then left him at my front door with a kiss. Yes, he was disappointed, but I didn't have nothing for his ass.

The following day, a Saturday, Ricky called me and apologized. It really didn't faze me, because I didn't take his advances that seriously. They were just words, and I could shake them off. He never tried to touch me other than giving me a simple hug or a kiss. If he did some other shit, it would be a whole different story.

"Please forgive me, Connie. It's just that my feelings for you are very strong. I want you around me all the time," Ricky said, trying to woo me.

Yeah, that nigga had game.

"It's okay," I whined, starting to feel shy.

"Will you come and meet me so that I can at least see your beautiful face?"

This boy was saying all the right shit to get me to respond. Knowing good and damn well that nigga was way out of my league, I nonetheless considered it. The only thing that kept from agreeing to meet him was the idea of being alone with him. That shit made me hesitant.

"Why can't you just see me after school on Monday?" I suggested, trying to stall until I made up my mind about seeing him before then. I couldn't just say no and fuck up everything.

"It's the weekend, and I don't wanna have to wait that long to see you," Ricky insisted. "Besides, I got something for you."

"You do?" I asked excitedly, ignoring any type of warning signs.

"Yeah, I went to the mall and picked you up a little something, and I don't wanna wait to give it to you."

"What is it, Ricky?" I asked eagerly, trying to get it out of him.

"You gotta meet me to see. You do want it, right?"

"Yeah, I guess . . ."

My nosy ass finally agreed to meet up with him, but only because the meeting place was near my school, in an open field. After quickly hanging up, I rushed to my closet and scanned my wardrobe. Seeing that it was a Saturday, Ricky would be able to view me without my Catholic school uniform on for the very first time. I had to be on point.

What I really wanted to sport was one of my cute sundresses, but that shit was out of the question. It was way too cold for all that shit. I had to opt for something a bit warmer. By the time I finished dressing, I was covered up from head to toe.

After putting on my final touches, I grabbed my keys, headed out the door, and proceeded to walk to the field where I was to meet up with Ricky. As I trod lightly in the direction of my school, my heart began pounding with anticipation, and tiny beads of perspiration formed on my palms.

What the hell am I doing? I silently questioned myself as I neared the abandoned small outbuildings that lined the near side of the field. Just as I reached the outbuildings, my ears suddenly tingled from someone whispering of my name.

"Connie, I'm over here."

Following the voice, I gradually crept around the last outbuilding, a shedlike structure, and couldn't help thinking that I had entered an eerie zone. As a chill crept aggressively up my spine, Ricky, along with his close friends June and Harrison, jumped out of the bushes, grabbed my arms, and hauled me into the shed. Without any warning, the three guys began violently ripping off my pink puffy jacket, my knitted hat, scarf, and my black-and-pink cheetah-print boots with the fur.

"What are you doing!" I screamed before getting a hand placed over my mouth and nose as my half-naked body shivered. It was freezing outside, and it seemed at least ten degrees colder inside this shed. The filthy concrete surface on which they held me down was even colder. My entire being shook violently as my mind grasped the gravity of my predicament.

When I calmed down momentarily to assess the situation, Ricky removed his hand from my mouth and nose, allowing me to breathe. The stench that immediately filled my nose was one that was indescribable. It was a stink unlike anything I had ever smelled. It was so strong that it made my eyes water and my stomach turn sour. When I spoke, I tried to breathe only out of my mouth.

"I thought you liked me!" I cried, feeling betrayed and scared. "You asked me here to do this to me?"

The sweat on my neck and forehead trickled downward as I envisioned just what was about to happen to me. I was scared shitless and couldn't even think about fighting back. All that mess I had always thought I would do if I ever found myself in harm's way went all out the window. This shit right here was serious!

"Shut the fuck up and take this shit off!" Ricky snarled.

They had already stripped me down to my underclothes, and I desperately attempted to grab ahold of my panties to prevent Ricky from snatching them off. Hell, they were already nearly torn to pieces, but I was determined not to give up. I didn't give a damn if there was nothing but one small shred to cover up my opening!

"You guys are fucking sick! Are you bastards really gonna do this!" I gasped before a gritty hand covered my mouth.

The three dirty muthafuckas began laughing, and it was clear to me that they were intent on stealing my innocence. Hope gradually slipped from my grip, but I would not allow myself to break.

Closing my eyes tightly, I prayed as their filthy hands touched and probed every sacred inch of my body. Some of those hands were cold and clammy, while others were rough, cracked, and dry and scratched my delicate skin.

Suddenly, I felt a warm mouth on my left breast, then a cold tongue, and then a set of teeth bit my right breast hard. That made me squirm more.

After several seconds, I reached down deep within and retrieved a bit of courage. I decided to let go of my restraint and fight, not at all considering the consequences.

Balling up my small fists, I began to swing wildly, in hopes of hitting anything or anyone within arm's reach. That shit lasted all of five seconds. Right up until Harrison removed his hand from my lips, whipped out a blade, and held it close to my throat.

"Bitch, even think about doing something stupid, like screaming, biting, spitting, or hitting, and ya ass is maggot food!" he barked. "And, y'all, shut the fuck up, so we can get some of this sweet virgin pussy." Ricky was no longer the ringleader. It was Harrison giving the orders now.

"No!" I gasped, tears streaming down my face.

Giving me a gaze of death and desperation, Harrison applied a bit more pressure to my esophagus with the sharp blade. I immediately stiffened up, in terror, preparing for the violent penetration, but to my surprise, he offered me to his friends first.

Ricky hurried to have his way with me while the other two held me down. Their fingers were embedded in my wrists, triggering excruciating shots of pain up my arms. I couldn't put up much of a fight, because every time I squirmed, I could feel Harrison's knife piercing my neck, going deeper and deeper, allowing the blood to seep down my neck.

Staring down at me, Ricky forced his dick in and out until he came to the peak of his pleasure. Lucky for me, it took only seconds.

Next up was June. The sight of his gruesome face covered in acne, along with his dirty nose, was fucking sickening. I quickly shut my eyes and squeezed them as he placed his hand over my mouth and shoved his little peter into me. After Ricky's fat one, I barely felt June. It was just as humiliating and quick.

While lying there, in tears, I was already plotting how I pay back those bitch-ass niggas. Sure, I was only seventeen and a senior in high school, but I had one mad connection in the hood. I promised myself if I survived this brutal attack, then I would have hood connection deal with them one by one.

"Go ahead on, Harrison! It's your turn, man!" June said, egging him on. "Tear that shit up! That pussy was on hit!"

"Well, wait till I get up in that!" Harrison boasted.

After switching positions with June, Harrison smiled wickedly down at me, causing me to glared fiercely at him, an expression of hatred on my face. It didn't intimidate him at all. In fact, Harrison returned the look and also added a terrorizing grin.

I wanted so badly to scream and plead for mercy. *Fuck it! I'm taking my chances*! I thought to myself a split second after opening my mouth. As my lips separated, June shoved a grimy rag he had just blown his nose with in my mouth.

"You slimy muthafucka!" I mumbled through my tears, causing me to taste his disgusting snot.

"Did you wanna say something?" he taunted, a smug look spread across his ugly-ass face.

My insides turned over, and the vomit came up, but June continued to hold the rag in my mouth. Now I had two choices. *Choke to death or swallow.* I hurried to do the second one, causing me to become more nauseous than before.

Please, please, Lord, help me! I begged in a silent prayer, hoping that God would hear my cries, though I was undeserving of mercy. I had no business being out here!

As I watched Harrison remove his boxers, it became very clear to me that I wouldn't receive any type of compassion. Not even a little . . .

Shit!

That was my first thought when I viewed Harrison's personal package below. I couldn't believe the size of his dick! There was no way that I would allow him to put that monstrous tool in me! *Fuck the knife. Fuck my life!* I was damned if he thought he was going to enter me with that Mandingo muthafucka, and raw at that!

"Let me go!" I wanted to holler as the knife went deeper, causing me more pain than I could handle.

"Keep still, Connie! You always walking around here, wearing those little skimpy-ass clothes. You were asking for this right here!" Harrison snapped, panting heavily as he stuck me below with his lethal weapon made of flesh. "You tried to deny my boy Ricky, and now you got to get penalized by this!"

No, no, no! I hollered in my mind as I felt my opening below being torn open sadistically.

"Damn, y'all didn't tell me it was gon' be like this!" Harrison moaned and grunted as he thrust in and out of me over and over. "Oh, oh, yeah, yeah! This shit right here, guys! This shit right here!"

Harrison continued on his mission, and unlike the others, he managed to last for at least five minutes. It was the longest, most painful experience of my short life.

The other two guys stood there with their little dicks out, stroking them as they watched. Even fully erect, both them uncircumcised penises couldn't have been longer than five inches in length. I was truly disgusted.

"Yesss!" Harrison shouted after finally ejaculating a huge load inside me. He climbed off slowly and left me sprawled out on the hard concrete, bleeding profusely between my legs and from my neck. The shock my body was experiencing left me motionless as Ricky and June glanced down at me in horror.

"Let's get up outta here, dude! You really fucked her up, Harrison!" Ricky stuttered, as if his conscience was messing with him. "Why'd you have to do her all like that?"

"Get ya bitch ass up out of my damn face, bruh! Just be glad I didn't tap that ass first, because it wouldn't have been shit left to fuck!" Harrison began laughing, and then he spit on me. "Nasty-ass tramp! At least she didn't stink," he added with a smirk.

"That shit was good!" June grunted as he jumped back on me. He plunged into me with all his weight. This time was just as quick and appalling as the first. The only difference was that when he got up off me this time, his knife dropped out of his pocket.

As soon as I eyed it, I went for it. Once I had it tightly in my grip, I made a bloody mess as I jabbed it into

June's side over and over until he was no longer moving. Harrison and Ricky didn't even try to help him, either. *Ole punk-ass cowards!* Instead, they shot out of the shed quick, fast, and in a hurry! I swear, I wanted to chase them both down and kill them, too, but the chilly air reminded me that I was butt-ass naked!

Exhausted from the fight, I sluggishly searched for my backpack, and when I found it, I pulled out my bottled water and pour it on my tank top, then wiped the blood from my face and body. I then put my clothes back on, retrieved my cell phone from the side pocket of my backpack, and dialed my brother California. We called him Cal for short.

The first thing he told me when I got him on the line and explained what had happened was not to call the police. He assured me that everything would be taken care of and that I had no reason not to believe him.

"Those muthafuckas will be dealt with, sis! Believe that shit!"

Cal was my brother from another mother, so very few people knew about him. He was known to wreak havoc in the streets, but he could also be a silent creeper. His cover was his job. He always kept one.

"Sis, don't say shit about this to no fucking body. You know how I work. I won't even have to tell you shit. I'll just show you," he went on. "Now, I'm gonna send Stacey to come pick you up and take ya ass to the medical clinic on Central Avenue. They know me by my government name, so be sure to tell them California sent you. They will take good care of you. Connie, you know I would come get you myself, sis, but I don't wanna be seen with you, just in case."

"I don't think I can wait," I sobbed. "I'm in pain and can barely walk. Plus, I think I may need stitches in my neck."

"Damn! I'm so sorry, sis, but don't worry. She's in ya hood, so it shouldn't take her but a few. Hold tight." He took a deep breath. "About those bitches, though . . . I'm gonna put those muthafuckas in the dirt!" he promised, his words laced with fury. "Don't trip about shit, sis. I love you, and I'll see you real soon."

"Love you too, Cal," I responded. "Be careful."

"At all times!"

"Wait, Cal! What about this body?"

"Leave it there, and I'll take care of all that. You cool?"

"I will be. Thanks, Cal."

We hung up, and within minutes, Stacey arrived at the shed. She took me straight to the neighborhood medical clinic so that my injuries got treated. Too bad the doctor didn't have anything to cure my hunger for revenge.

When I made it home from the clinic Stacey had taken me to, I found my mom in the kitchen, cooking and drinking. She was drunk, so I didn't even bother covering up my bruises and bandages.

Drinking had become the norm for her ever since my father left her to go back to California's mother, Florida. She wasn't even aware that I had a relationship with my brother. If she knew, she would probably disown me. That was just how she was.

"Where have you been, Connie?"

"With Lydia," I lied, mentioning my best friend.

When I uttered the fib, my mother turned around and gave me an angry look. I flinched instantly and prepared my body for a blow.

"You ought to pray to God for forgiveness for lying right this second, young lady," my mother yelled as she raised her fist to strike me. "Lydia just left here, looking for you. Now, where have you been?"

She snatched me up by my jacket and immediately noticed that it was ripped and dirty. Then all her attention went to the bandages on my neck.

"What on God's green earth happened to you, baby?" she cried. Frantic, she grabbed her keys and started dragging me by my arm toward the front door.

"Let me go, Mom!" I shouted as I tried, unsuccessfully, to pry her fingers from my arm. "I'm okay!"

"Well, let the doctor tell me that!" she hollered, still holding on to me and pulling me so hard that I was damn near tripping as I tried to hold my ground. "Now, let's go!" She yanked me out the front door, pulled me over to her car, and ordered me to get in the front seat.

"Mom, you don't need to drive," I whispered as she got behind the wheel. Ignoring my plea, she placed the key into the ignition. "Please, Mom! Are you listening to me? You don't need to drive!"

My chest heaved up and down from fear. I knew that if I had even tried to take the keys from her, she would have tried to fight me. She was heavy-handed and quick to get me in line by using physical force. I didn't want to challenge her now, but at that moment I felt I had no choice.

"Mom, please, just pull over and call the ambulance," I said emphatically. "They will take us. You don't need to drive."

Suddenly, my mother turned toward me and slapped the shit out of me. The force of her hand was so strong that it twisted my neck sideways, leaving me staring out my window. That was why I saw the truck that was headed right at us and was about to hit us.

"Mom, watch out!"

Before the semi could hit my side of the car, a small white sedan nicked our tail end and sent us spinning. At that very second, the odds of my being hit turned completely around. A second later the semi plowed into my mother's side of the car.

"No, no!" I screamed.

Our large vehicle went tumbling, and when we landed, we were right side up. I turned to check on my mother and noticed that she was bleeding from several different areas. I immediately attempted to reach for her, but I couldn't. My right leg was pinned under the dash, and I couldn't get to her.

"Mom, can you hear me?"

When she didn't answer me, I began to panic. No matter how hard I tried, I couldn't get her to respond.

Stretching my arm out for the third time, I was finally able to reach her hand. I held on to it and prayed out loud until I heard people outside trying to help. They were unable to open the car doors.

"Did someone call nine-one-one?"

"Yeah, they're on the way."

"How many people are in the car? Are there any kids?"

While I listened to the people talk, I yelled out for help. That was when I smelled the gas.

"Wait, get back! That car is about to catch fire!" someone shouted.

As the bystanders began to back up, I could hear the sirens getting louder. It didn't stop my panic, because my mother still wasn't responding. I needed them to hurry.

It seemed like a whole hour had passed before firefighters arrived at the scene, but I knew it was only a matter of minutes.

"Move back!" one bystander yelled as a firefighter approached my side of the car. Working with a crowbar, he managed to pry open my door about a foot.

He leaned down to talk to me. "Are you okay?" he asked.

"Yes, but my leg is stuck. Can you get my mom first?"

The clean-shaven, blue-eyed firefighter called for another guy to check on my mother, then set to work prying my door open wider. The whole time I kept my eyes on the man who was on the other side of the car, trying to open the driver's door.

Just as the blue-eyed firefighter was pulling me to safety, the firefighter working to help my mother stood up and looked over at us, a hint of sadness spread across his face. After slowly nodding his head no, he turned away, and so did I.

"It's gonna blow!" a lady suddenly shouted.

Seconds later the car went up in flames.

"My mom! Get my mother out!" I sobbed loudly, nearly losing it. "Get my mom!"

All my cries went unheard, and I watched our car continue to burn.

Boom!

There was a big explosion, and it blew our vehicle to pieces. My breath became short, and my head began spinning. Before I knew it, everything went black.

By the time I came to, I was at the hospital, in the recovery room, with my leg in a cast. I was so doped up on medicine that I could barely focus.

"Connie, I'm right here," I heard my grandmother whisper. "Everything is gonna be okay. I'm here for you, baby."

The doctor came in before I could respond. He informed my grandmother that a woman would be there to talk with her shortly. He told her that after she was done, she could take me home with her. I didn't want to go. I wanted my mother.

No matter what Grandma Betsy or my best friend, Lydia, might do or say, nothing could make me feel better. Nothing but writing.

I began by jotting down thoughts down in my journal. Then, before I knew it, I was rewriting my whole life story and giving it a "happily ever after" ending. It was the only thing that kept me sane over the next week. That was when another tragedy struck.

My grandmother had a fatal heart attack a couple of months before I graduated high school. My heart was totally broken, right along with my spirit.

They said that tragedies traveled in threes. I just never thought that they would hit my circle like that.

Chapter 1

Constance ("Connie")

Seven years later . . .

"I'll be glad when I can live a normal life," I sighed as I observed two squirrels playing through the double-paned window in my bedroom.

I had been reflecting on the past lately and had realized that the past seven years, which had slowly crept by, were restorative but still not enough time to heal emotionally from the tragic ordeal I had endured. I had been doing my very best to put it all behind me but had been struggling something terrible.

Thankfully, Lydia and her mother had been there for me, allowing me to stay with them until my life insurance check for Grandma Betsy came. Good thing it did, too, because due to my mother's drinking and driving, I couldn't cash in on her policy.

Using a big chunk of the large check I received, I renovated the old house my grandmother had left me and paid my way through college. Submerging myself in my studies, I spent all my time reading and writing. I even obtained an associate of arts degree in less than two years.

Although I kept myself as busy as possible with school and martial arts, I couldn't help but worry about Harrison being out there somewhere, lurking. You see, my brother California was able to murk only Ricky. Unluckily for me, Harrison was on the run. He was last seen in Arizona, but he had family all over the West Coast, so it was impossible to pinpoint his location. It was driving me crazy!

Ever since the brutal attack, my life had been a total wreck as far as relationships went. I had serious trust issues, so instead of seeking lasting commitments, I resorted to taking my chances at dating every so often.

I'm so sick of being lonely.

Complaining to myself, I finished making my bed, drawing the bright yellow down comforter up over the pastel-colored printed top sheet. Today was another day of waking up alone. Yes, I had my fair share of male friends at the moment, but we engaged in nothing physical, and I definitely had no overnighters.

Thing was, any shallow encounters I had had in recent years had got old quickly. Right along with my battery-operated buddy. My body craved to be touched all over, by hands. Hell, I needed a man!

So far, I had failed miserably at having even one single serious, steady relationship. Most of my budding relationships had ended with me being asked, "Can we just be friends with benefits?" And the remainder had fizzled when an old girlfriend or a baby mama suddenly appeared out of nowhere, bringing drama with her.

Shit, I'm twenty-four years old! I'm at a point in my life where I want to settle down and have a family.

I had started to feel the pressures of my biological clock. I had realized the clock was ticking. I still had to find my soulmate, date him for a while, and then marry him, and all that had to happen *before* I could even consider having kids!

I want it, though! I want that shit bad!

The past few weeks I had been dreaming about my "happily ever after." I was beginning to crave it, but I had to keep telling myself to be patient. I had dared go looking for love and had gotten nowhere, so I decided to wait until it came to me.

The first candidate that came along who could actually stimulate my mind and body with words was Sean. He was a sexy something with a great gift of gab. But before long, Sean began pushing for more, but I definitely wasn't trying to take it there with him too quickly. I was glad I didn't take it beyond dinner and a movie, either, because after just a couple of dates, he thought I was his woman and started becoming aggressive out of the blue. I had to back his tail up and set him straight. He didn't take that shit too well, either. Matter of fact, he tried to buck up on me, until I backed his ass up with a frying pan. Yeah, he received that message loud and clear, then got his ass up out of my house quick, fast, and in a hurry.

I had to nod and laugh at myself when I thought back to that day. I never ceased to amaze myself.

"I'm going back to church, and I'm gonna renew my library card!" I promised myself, uttering the words aloud, as I gathered my things, preparing to leave my quiet, lifeless apartment. After lifting my handbag from the lounge chair, I proceeded to find my keys. Once I was together, I headed out.

Enjoying the beautiful sunshine and the smell of the crisp, clean air, I decided to stop by and pick up my homegirl, Lydia. I knew she would be down to get out the house. I just wasn't too sure if she would agree with my destination.

She didn't. But my persistent ass just kept at her until she gave in. She wasn't too happy. I could tell when I looked over at her and noticed her wrinkled-up forehead before we hopped in the car.

As I glanced over at Lydia once we were on the road, I noticed that we had a lot of physical similarities. The only major difference was she was a few shades darker than my caramel complexion and her bra size was a bit bigger. We both stood at five and a half feet. We wore the same size clothes and shoes. Plus, we both wore our hair naturally and kept it at shoulder length.

That's my rider, I thought silently.

As we made our way up the road, I began contemplating which library we would go to. When I asked Lydia which branch she preferred, she quickly chose the Albina Branch, on Killingsworth Street in northeast Portland. Although it was in the neighborhood, I hadn't been there in quite some time.

Now, Lydia, she loved the public library in the hood, and I couldn't blame her, because the historic building was beautiful and made me feel right at home. Since it was the first time in years that I had been to that branch, I was anxious to go inside and see what changes had been made.

It had been way too long since I stepped my ass up in a library. I had been missing a good paperback and the smell of crisp pages turning. Since everything seemed to be coming out in digital form, I hadn't had the chance to hold an actual book in my hand and enjoy it in months.

"See, this is my shit! I love this place!" Lydia gasped quietly as soon as she opened the front door. As we stepped in, I took in my surroundings. The setup was the same, but the displays were much more colorful and inviting.

Trailing behind my friend Lydia as she made her way to the urban fiction section, I became easily distracted by a familiar book cover. I gasped in excitement.

"Damn, Connie! You see Ashley & JaQuavis got their own publishing company?" Lydia screamed, clutching a novel while pointing out the owl symbol on the cover.

I quickly hushed her and grabbed up books in "The Circle" series, then looked to see what Racquel Williams had out, leaving Lydia behind. I had been hearing that chick's name and was anxious to read *The Faithful Side Chick*.

Once we both had our works of fiction in hand, we checked them out and then went down the street to the little publishing office space/bookstore I was leasing. I had to pick up a contract there on my way home.

"Why don't you browse the Rose City Ink books box and see what came out recently?" I suggested to Lydia before I ran to the back to grab the documents.

When I returned, Lydia was assisting an unfamiliar, handsome-looking man. He was attempting to locate a read by Shorty, who was a new urban author. I had been hearing a lot of good things about his new book. I'd been upset when this Hispanic chick beat me to his publishing contract! I loved his work and couldn't wait to get lost in another one of his sensual journeys filled with words of ecstasy. I was getting moist at just the thought.

"We carry his book. It's right here, on the new-releases shelf," I informed Lydia as I escorted her and the nice-looking patron to the appropriate wall of shelves.

As I took a closer look at the guy, I noticed it was Shorty himself. Swiftly taking the opportunity, I introduced myself without being a little over the top with it.

"I loved your erotic novel *Bump and Grind*," I confessed. "I'm Constance Bell. I write a little and read a lot, but my main profession is putting out good books right here at Portland Publishing."

"I thought you looked familiar!" Shorty laughed. "I was just checking out your Amazon page over there on the computer."

"You live in Portland?" I asked.

"Yeah, born and raised!"

"Small world," Lydia smirked and pointed at one of the shelves. "Well, here's your book. Did you just wanna see it? Because I'm sure you have a million copies at home."

I picked it up first and read the synopsis. I hadn't had a chance to do any of that before I stuck the last shipment of books on the shelves.

"Oh, hell yeah, I'm checking this shit out," I shouted when I finished skimming over the synopsis. I then quickly covered my mouth, feeling embarrassed.

"Hold up, Constance. You mind if I take a picture of you holding my book?" Shorty requested.

"No, I would be honored."

Shorty stepped back, smiled, then snapped several shots before sliding beside me and requesting that Lydia take one of him with me. I was so flattered that I couldn't stop grinning.

After the mini photo shoot, Shorty stated that he had an interest in my work. Although we didn't make any plans to get together to discuss things, I still left my office on cloud nine, thinking about a bunch of what-ifs.

Could he be the one?

There I went, jumping the gun! I couldn't help it. Shit! I was anxious to have a man. I was tired of going home and doing nothing but spending my time there all alone.

Chapter 2

Dasio Vazquez

Man! This day couldn't have been more fucked up. I swear, at twenty-eight years of age, I should have had my own damn spot. The only reason I still stayed at my parents' house was that I didn't want to leave my mother alone with my father. That fool had been putting hands on her since I was younger.

My dad used to do that shit in front of me all the time. Only back then I was too small and frail to do anything about it. But as soon as I got older, I started hitting the gym on the regular, and I continued this until I got my weight up. That was when he stopped testing me and we had our first real altercation. It was right after I graduated high school when I had to step to him.

Yeah, he chilled for a while after that, but it didn't take long before I noticed bruises and cuts on my mother once again. The shit was becoming ridiculous.

"*Madre*, why you let that nigga hit you like that?"

Smack!

My mother's hand came across my face so hard that it stunned me for a minute. There was no way that I would ever raise my hand to her, but I couldn't resist hitting her ass with a verbal assault.

"Damn! Why you don't hit ya husband like that?" I spat, with a shake of my head. "If you did, I bet he'd back the fuck off you!"

“Where the hell did you learn to talk like that, Dasio?” she yelled. “I can’t believe you’re speaking to me like that!”

“I can’t believe you are still lettin’ that sorry-ass muthafucka put his hands on you!” I shouted as I raised my hands and stormed out of the raggedy-ass shack we stayed in and headed to my girl’s.

Yes, Puerto Rico was my home, but my mother’s family was from the US mainland. When I was growing up, my father spoke Spanish, while my mother insisted on me speaking proper English. I never understood it, but I obeyed. The rest of my friends were fluent in English, so it felt natural for me to speak it as well.

As far as our lifestyle went, we lived over an hour away from San Juan, in a run-down small town where everyone knew each other. So, you knew you couldn’t get away with shit there. You had to stay clean and keep a job if you wanted to stay out of jail. The cops there didn’t have shit to do but fuck with folks.

A majority of the houses in our town were poorly made and barely standing. The way we were living was beyond unacceptable in my eyes, and I despised it on a daily basis. It irritated me majorly that everyone around me seemed to be so content with their life. Even my girl, Carla . . .

“What’s up, baby?” she greeted as I exited my ride. I walked up onto her property. She and her homegirls were sitting out front, drinking, like always. “Damn, who popped ya *globo*, *papí*?”

My ass had to take a couple of breaths before approaching Carla. I loved her deeply, but she was so fucking narrow minded. All that bitch thought about was fashion and sex. She didn’t know about anything outside that.

“Hey, *papí*. Are you okay?” Carla asked, snapping me out of my thoughts.

"Yeah, ya man is stressed the fuck out, so bring ya ass in the house so you can do something about the shit!" I demanded.

Carla jumped to her feet and did as I had told her ass. I did the shit only because she allowed me to. She never fought back, with her passive ass. She was nothing like the rest of her wild family. They were all street hustlers and thugs with no fucking morals.

"*Puta*, take yo' ass in there and suck it *muy bueno*! *Mamabicho*!" one of her friends joked.

All I could do was shake my head while her friends were clowning her. The shit was funny, and I couldn't help but laugh too.

"What's wrong, *papí*?" Carla asked as soon as we got in her bedroom and she closed the door.

"Talkin' is not on the fuckin' menu right now, baby," I whispered as I motioned her to get on her knees. "I just need you to dust me off right quick."

"Really, Dasio?" she huffed.

All I had to do was give her that look. She quickly took heed and dropped to the floor to perform her duties. She had a nigga topped off within minutes.

"Did you have to fuckin' bust in my mouth, Dasio?" Carla spat.

"Here you go," I replied as I tucked my dick in and zipped up my pants.

"I know you ain't gonna just leave now that you got yours," she whined, on the verge of tears. That shit wasn't about to work with me.

"Go 'head on with that bullshit, Carla," I laughed as I crossed her room. "I'm up out of here." I stalked out of her room.

"Go then, Dasio!" she cried, trying to save face, but it was too late. All her friends had peeped the scene, and now they clowned her ass even more.

Ignoring them all, I trotted off to my ride. Soon as I got near my shit, that bitch Carla came outside, like she had grown a pair of balls. She was equipped with a forty-ounce bottle and didn't hesitate to throw it at me. Now, maybe if I had seen that shit coming, I could have ducked or something, but I didn't. The muthafucka hit me right on my left temple, drawing blood instantly.

"*Puta*, is you fuckin' loco?" I hollered.

"Ooh," everyone shouted in unison as I ran up and caught her ass by the neck.

"Do you have a fuckin' death wish? If you eva do some dumb shit like that again, it's gonna be a rap!" I spat, dropping her limp body to the ground. "Matter of fact, stay the fuck away from me, and we ain't never got to say shit to one another ever again! You got that shit?"

"Yeah, you piece of shit!" Carla yelled, but I didn't entertain it. *"Vete al carajo!"*

"Did this bitch just tell me to go fuck myself?" I huffed but kept it moving.

As I drove back home, Carla called my cell back-to-back. I powered that shit off after the third time. Shit, she had me heated, and lucky for her ass, the fresh air helped me calm my temper, because I was seriously thinking about turning around to go fuck her ass up.

"Damn, back to this muthafucka!" I sighed when I caught sight of my house.

I parked my car and headed to the front door. When I stepped onto the dirt porch, I heard yelling, followed by crying. It was my mother.

Rushing inside, I found my father holding his gun up to my mother's head. I froze in my fucking tracks, scared to make the next move. I had to act with precision in order to take him down without endangering her life.

"Stay back, Dasio, *por favor*," my mother pleaded, tears streaming down her face. Her eyes begged me not to get involved, but her cries gave me no other choice.

"Let her go!" I stated calmly but firmly.

"This ain't ya business, Dasio," my father, José, warned as he cocked the pistol to release a bullet into the chamber. "Go back outside and let us handle it! You better tell him, Mary!"

"I can't do that, *papí*," I smirked as I headed to my room. As soon as crossed the threshold, I hurriedly got my little deuce-deuce. I would have used my nine, but I didn't want the security company that had issued it to me to get involved.

Without hesitation, I left my room, went around through the kitchen, and snuck up behind my father. Before he had a chance to respond, there was a loud pop, and then his body dropped to the floor.

A brief moment of silence followed. Right after that, my mother became hysterical.

"You killed him!" she screamed. "You fuckin' killed your father, Dasio!"

I was sickened by how my mother was acting. She dropped to the floor, hugged her husband's body, and rocked him back and forth. Brain fragments leaked onto her clothing and onto the carpet. This didn't stop her, though; she continued to hold him in her arms.

"Just go, Dasio!" she ordered. "The police will be here soon, and I don't want you here! Go far away and never come back!"

"Are you fuckin' kidding me, *mamá*?"

"No! I'm serious. Now go!"

"Where the hell am I gonna go?"

She gently placed my father's lifeless head and shoulders down and rushed to her room. She came back holding a wooden box.

"Take this and go to the mainland. Go to Portland. Go to my sister May's house. Her and Carlos are our *familia*."

"*Mamá*, I don't know them like that!"

"You talk to Carlos all the time! Now go!"

"I don't even have a passport!"

"You don't need one! Besides, that's where you were born. Your birth certificate and all the information are in here, along with enough money to last for a long time."

"I don't know what you're talking about, *mamá*! I don't understand!"

"Just go!"

My mother grabbed a roll of tape from a drawer in the kitchen, then taped the box shut. After handing it to me, she gave me a kiss on my forehead. She then clenched my arm and led me to the door.

"I love you, Dasio, but you have to leave," she cried as she opened the door.

She tried to push me outside, but I snatched my arm away and ran back to my room to pack a couple of bags right quick. I didn't know when and if I would return, so I gathered all my necessities and enough clothing for a few days.

By the time I reached the front door, ready to leave, I heard sirens. They were growing louder by the second, and I began to panic, but I couldn't resist taking one last look back at my house.

My heart went out to my mother. I definitely didn't want to leave her all alone, but there was nothing that I could do except obey her wishes.

Chapter 3

Constance ("Connie")

The early morning sun peeked through my partially open blinds. Rushing to pull the covers back over my head, I gently closed my eyes and wished the day away. My moping lasted all of ten minutes. The anxiety came next.

I began panting as I rolled over and dug my hand down into the bottom of my purse, which lay on the floor by my bed, and rummaged around until I located the slender item I was searching for. Once I felt it, I drew it out to look at the screen.

As I checked my phone, I realized that it had been seventy-two long hours and the fascinating author I had met had yet to call. Not wanting to be first to make contact, I slid my cell under my pillow, then relaxed for as long as I possibly could.

By noon, I was done lounging. I was ready to get things moving. I couldn't waste my time daydreaming. I needed to snap myself back to reality and get some things accomplished in my life.

Suddenly, I heard a buzz. It was an alert notifying me that I had a voicemail. I didn't even have a missed call, so I was a bit confused.

"How the hell did that happen?" I wondered aloud while listening to Shorty's message. "Well, well, well, imagine that!"

I smiled as I listened to the captivating words over again. His voice was intriguing, and my heart fluttered with anticipation. Just the thought of seeing him for a second time had my adrenaline pumping and my palms sweating. I quickly dialed him back to hear what he had on his mind.

During the conversation, Shorty began to question my future in writing.

"Why do you ask?" I said.

"I was just thinking," Shorty replied with his smooth baritone voice.

Surprisingly, he wanted to get together to discuss some future writing endeavors. He asked me if we could write a book together, a love story.

"I'll definitely consider it," I responded, caught totally off guard.

I told him all about the many stories that I had already begun. He seemed anxious to read them, so we hung up after making plans to meet up that evening. The library was the place he chose. An educational sanctuary was perfect.

As I disconnected my call, my mind began spinning off thoughts of all sorts. On this particular evening, all my energy would be directed toward a story of love that starred me and Shorty. . . .

I sprawled out on the plush cotton spread on my bed. I immediately began to imagine a magical date filled with romance and seduction. My visions were extremely sexual and explicit, bringing a new feeling to my spirit, which I freely welcomed.

The vivid fantasies that danced in my mind were so enchanting that they held me back from retrieving a pen and paper to jot my thoughts down. I didn't worry, though. I knew that the scene would play over and over in my head thereafter. That's just how powerful it was.

As I shook myself out of my fictional daze, as if giving myself a mental cold shower, my alarm began to ring nonstop. I jumped up rapidly, hit the OFF button, and proceeded to my closet. Everything in my closet was arranged by color, so immediately I began leafing through the garments in the fall floral-print section.

After carefully choosing the sexiest dress that I could find, I made certain that it would still be appropriate for the library. I wanted to be very careful not to send the wrong message.

The afternoon flew by, and before I knew it, it was almost time to head to the library. At the last minute, however, I got nervous and called Lydia and asked her to meet me at the library. After promising me that she would beat me there, I was very disappointed when I pulled into the partially empty lot and didn't see her vehicle.

After parking near the entrance, I climbed out and embraced the amazing weather. It was nice out, and the sun was still shining brightly. Glancing upward, I smiled, feeling thankful. It was definitely a blessing.

"Amen!" I chanted before stepping inside the library and flipping my sunglasses to the top of my head. I didn't want to break my neck in the darkness by trying to be cute.

"Here it goes," I whispered aloud nervously after spotting my friend Shorty right as I reached the romance section. Just the sight of him sent the butterflies soaring inside my stomach. I prayed my anxiousness didn't show.

"Hello, Constance." Shorty greeted me with a warm embrace, and I inhaled the sweet smell of his unfamiliar cologne. It was so enticing that it drew me right in and had me gone.

"Hello, Shorty," I chanted rhythmically. I giggled at the way his name flowed from my lips. I was blushing nonstop and hated that I couldn't control it.

"You are so beautiful. I love your dimples. You should always be wearing a smile," he told me, flirting with me.

"Well, thank you," I said and blushed even harder when I looked over and noticed Lydia standing over in the cut. She stayed put and listened and observed while the smooth-operating, attractive author wasted no time getting down to business. This totally threw off my intimate mood and shifted things up a few levels on my body until they reached my head.

Shorty began with questions pertaining to my writing and my goals. He asked me nothing personal, and that was definitely a pleasant change from the guys I was used to dealing with. The interest he took in my mind sent chills throughout my inner being. No one had ever made me feel so important, so special.

"Look, I'm just starting this company. Why don't you let me rerelease that book you self-published a while back called *Repercussions of Love*? I read it last night, and it seems to have real potential to be a best seller," he said, getting down to business. "How about I come by tonight and we can get the ball rolling?"

Without hesitation, I took Shorty up on his offer. I mean, why not? He was already well established in the industry, and I was still a little fish trying to swim her way to the top. I thought this idea of his would be a good way for me to get my name out there. Plus, he was a very good-looking businessman, and he seemed to possess a great deal of intelligence, along with a strong sensual swagg. I felt as if I had nothing to lose.

After quickly jotting down my address on a blank piece of paper that I retrieved from my notebook, I passed it to him and smiled. I knew that I was taking a chance, and I promised myself that I would take the necessary precautions to ensure my safety before his arrival.

"Uh, how about I swing by tomorrow instead of this evening? Let's say around sevenish?" Shorty said as I watched him peck at the keys on his cell. "Your spot, it's right by that little bar called Spirit, behind Albertsons, right?"

"Yes. I see you know the area quite well." I giggled, swinging my purse over my shoulder. "I guess I'll see you then."

Lydia at least waited for Shorty to get out of earshot before she rushed over to me and blasted me about being so forward with him. I understood her concern, but I had learned a whole lot since the last time I chose to trust a man. With Shorty, I figured that it could only be a few things that he was after.

I didn't have much money, so I deleted that from the list of possibilities. If it was sex and I wasn't a willing participant, then I had something for him that would teach him a very valuable lesson, if he even survived it. So that left us on an even playing field.

"Maybe he just wants to get to know you better," Lydia suggested. "Just be careful."

Seven o'clock on Sunday evening came swifter than I had anticipated. I found myself scurrying around with a mister, filling the air with cinnamon- and vanilla-scented spray.

If Shorty wanted an adult beverage, I had a bottle of sparkling white wine chilling in the ice bucket in the kitchen, just in case. I dared not set it out in the open or offer hard alcohol, as this might give the wrong impression.

Suddenly, the doorbell rang. "Damn, he's right on time," I said aloud. I smiled as I checked my cleavage and freshened up my gloss.

Standing by the door, I twiddled my thumbs until I calmed down, and then I opened it. I didn't want to stumble over my words and say something crazy, like I was known to do.

"You sure look nice, Constance," Shorty said, complimenting me, as he stood there holding a bundle of vibrant pink-colored carnations.

"Thank you very much. Come on in."

We briefly embraced, and like a delicate summer breeze, it was invigorating. It lasted all of five seconds, which was much too fleeting for my appetite, but I smiled and released him when he let go of me.

My senses were aroused by his fragrance, which spiraled in the air, leaving a trail to the sofa, where he took a seat. I excused myself and placed the flowers in a vase I had filled with water, then set it on the large oak table in my dining room. Stepping back a bit, I looked at the arrangement and then smiled on the inside.

"So, what's up?" I asked as I joined Shorty on the sofa.

He quickly explained that he had come over for business, but the vibes he was freeing caused me to believe differently. Complaining was the last thing I was about to do. At this moment, both business and pleasure were fine with me.

Although I was very excited about working alongside Shorty, my physical attraction to him was foremost in my mind right now. I had to get my emotions in check.

"Did you want something to drink?" I offered.

"Sure. What do you have?"

"Well, I have water, orange juice, apple juice, soda, wine, tequila, Jack, and Courvoisier." I grinned as I ran down the selections. "I don't really drink too often, but I like to stay stocked up for when my girls come through."

"Check you out, Constance. Quite the little hostess, and a gorgeous one at that," Shorty said, flirting, with an expression of desire in his eyes. "I'll take a shot of Courvoisier and a slice of lemon, if you have it. If not, some water will suffice."

"Coming right up," I replied as I stood and twisted my hips.

I hurried into the kitchen, poured both of us double shots, sliced the lemon, and placed the slices on a small ceramic plate. I downed my drink, then took a slice of the sour fruit and bit into it to calm the sting of the cognac. Right after that, I quickly refilled my drink, placed everything on a small tray, and returned to the living room.

"Damn, you were even a beautiful child," Shorty complimented as he stood admiring my pictures hanging on the eggshell-colored wall across from the sofa.

I thanked him and eased back down in the spot where I'd sat before. I placed his glass on a coaster and placed the dish with the lemon slices in the middle of the coffee table. Then I picked up my glass and took a sip. When I glanced up, I noticed that Shorty was still standing there. Now he was staring at my high school graduation picture. It was one of my favorites, despite the tragedies that surrounded that time in my life.

Next, he scanned the room and began asking me all types of questions. What started out as general inquiries quickly turned into much more personal ones. I should have known these questions would come sooner or later. . . .

"Are you seeing anyone right now?" he inquired as he walked over to the coffee table and lifted his glass from the rose-print coaster.

"Not at the moment," I told him and smiled as I set down my glass.

Shorty tilted his drink to his mouth and drank until the contents of the glass were gone. Immediately afterward, he placed his glass down, then took several large slices of lemon and squeezed the juice into his empty glass on the table. He removed the seeds and drank the juice.

"The reason why I asked is because I find myself growing a serious attraction to you. I realize we just met and all, but that's where my feelings are, and I'm gonna be a man about mine."

That was all the confirmation my body needed to respond when Shorty pulled me up from the sofa and came in for the first kiss. It was perfect. The pressure he applied, the amount of tongue, the taste of the tangy fruit, and his firm, strong arms around me were the right combination to raise the fire in me.

"Please tell me if I'm overstepping my boundaries, Constance," he whispered in between wet, passionate kisses. "Tell me, because I'm far from being finished. Actually, I'm just getting started."

Shorty backed up a bit, then lowered his eyes and gazed in my direction. He stared at me with his eyes tightened, then bit down on his lip. "Stay right there," he instructed.

After walking over to one corner of the room, he shut the lamp off and twisted open the blinds to allow a small amount of the streetlight glow inside. It was so quiet in the room, you could hear a pin drop. I wanted desperately to turn on some music, but I didn't want to interrupt the mood that he had set so precisely.

Shorty slowly came back to me, nudged me gently down onto the sofa, then placed his hand under my thigh and gently moved me forward. Before I knew it, I was on my back, the perfect position for him when he kneeled before me.

Looking me in the face, Shorty searched for a sign of my approval, which I quickly gave him by opening my legs and palming his head. Within seconds I was trembling and finding it hard to contain the orgasm that was wildly attempting to escape from my sweet spot. Pausing for a brief moment, I tightened up. It had been a while since I had let someone go down on me. The last time it happened, I had to beat dude's ass with a bat to get him up off me, because I wouldn't fuck him afterward.

Shorty must have sensed hesitation on my part, because he began to increase the depth to which his tongue went, as well as his oral pull. The moaning and smacking did it. That was all I could take.

"Oh, my! Oh shit!" I yelled out, in ecstasy.

Wasting no time, Shorty let loose and gave my body everything it craved. I had never been so sexually satisfied in my entire life, and we didn't even have sex. My mind was actually blown that he didn't even try!

Ignoring all my insecurities, I snuggled up in the strong, passionate author's arms as we lay together on the sofa, and as I drifted off, I wondered what tomorrow would bring.

Chapter 4

Dasio Vazquez

When I got to the airport, ready to leave, I realized I had lost my driver's license. Luckily, I had the box with my birth certificate in it, right? Hell nah! Come to find out that shit had been forged by my mother. The only truth to my identity was my name, my mother's name, and my date of birth. My father's name wasn't even given. I didn't know what that was all about, but that shit delayed me in Puerto Rico for two extra days. Then, to make it worse, they had me wasting my money on a damn hotel. The shit was ridiculous.

Once they finally got all my documents straight and I thought I was cleared to leave Puerto Rico, they hit me with a physical. I knew that shit wasn't routine, and they were just looking for a reason to fuck with me after I had cussed everybody out in the fucking building, but I went with it.

I was cool, too, until these muthafuckas took me to the homemade clinic in the basement and tested me for everything from TB to HIV. They even checked my heart. To add to things, they made me pay for that shit too.

Since the ten-thousand-dollar banded stack I had was stitched inside the waist of my jeans, I couldn't get to it until I got to the US mainland. I was now down to twenty-two hundred dollars of my own money, and I still had to pay for my ticket.

"One thousand two hundred ten dollars? Are you kidding?" I yelled at the agent at the United Airlines ticket counter.

"No, sir. That's the final charge, and the last flight leaves at five forty this evening. With this flight, you'll have only one layover, which is in Houston, Texas."

"How long will I be there?" I was worried, thinking about having to spend more money on another hotel. I would be on the mainland then, and I had no idea what a hotel room would cost me.

"Only one hour, and the flights look like they're on time so far."

"Okay, let me get one please," I requested as I broke bread once again.

I got my ticket and checked my bags. Before I strolled my ass through security, I veered off to the side and dialed my cousin Carlos up. I had to make sure he was going to be able to scoop me up at the airport. Especially since my flight wasn't due to arrive in Portland until after midnight the next evening.

Carlos, my mother's sister May's son, and I were about the same age. We had lost touch when he started his musical career, but I had found out that he still had the same number.

"Hey, cuz. What's good?" I said when he answered.

"Hey, Dasio. Your mom called and told me that I should be hearing from you. Are you here already?"

"I'm on my way to you, *primo*," I informed him as I stood there and watched the line for security get longer. It didn't faze me, because I still had time. Plus, I had to give Carlos my flight information.

"Damn, I can't wait to see you, fam!" Carlos shouted excitedly. "I'll be there to scoop you at the airport at midnight."

"Cool!"

Once we hung up, I called my mother. Her first question was, "Are you in Portland?"

"No, I'm at the airport, on my way. What happened?"

"I told them that I did it. They have ruled it self-defense so far. They have to go through some legal technicalities, though, before they close the case. I will let you know when they do. Then you can come home. Maybe soon."

"Well, that shouldn't take long. Maybe I should just stay. I can get a hotel and lay low until then. I really don't wanna just leave you like this, *mamí*."

"I'm fine. You just go!" she urged with a stern tone.

I just shrugged it off, told her I loved her, and hung up. Something didn't sound right, but I didn't have time to call her back. I had to get my ass through security with my money.

When my last flight landed in Portland, I purchased a prepaid cell phone inside the terminal and called up my cousin.

"Hey, Carlos," I huffed, trying to get my bag over my head to rest it on my shoulder.

"What's up, cuddy? You here?"

"Yeah, I just got in. I'm at the airport."

"I'm right down the street, cuz," he laughed. "I'll be there in about ten minutes. Hang tight."

When we hung up, I went to the bathroom and locked myself in a stall. I checked on my hidden ends and then counted what I had left of my loose money. I didn't want to be nowhere leaking. In order to keep my paper, I knew that my first priority had to be getting a damn job. I had always kept one of those.

Before I left Puerto Rico, I did the bookkeeping for two different strip clubs since I was a whiz at numbers. That was how I spent my days. At night I did armed security.

There was never a dull moment, but I was ready for a change. I was ready for something more laid back.

Let me get my ass outside, I thought silently as I flushed the toilet. I left the stall and went to wash my hands.

As I bent down, I could smell my own breath. I couldn't go out there and greet my cousin with my breath all tart and shit, so I took care of it.

When I came out of the men's room, I ran smack-dab into a fine-ass brown-skinned girl with a fat ass. I wanted to holler at her, but I wasn't too familiar with mainland chicks.

"What's up?" she asked, smiling. "What's your name?"

"Nothin' much, *chica*," I replied with a lick of my lips. I couldn't help flirting with her. "My name is Dasio."

"Oh shit," she giggled. "You're not from around here, huh?"

"Why you say that?"

"Because of your strong-ass accent!" she exclaimed. "That shit is sexy as hell!"

"Oh, it is, huh?"

"Hell yeah," she teased, coming closer. "My name is Christy. Good to meet you, Dasio. Are you here to stay or just here on a brief visit?"

Damn, this bitch is bold! I thought to myself as she brushed her hand across my manhood.

"I may be here to stay," I replied cutting her short. "My *primo* is on his way to *scoop* me now."

"Well, I'm waiting for a ride, too, so I'll just walk out with you."

I couldn't shake the bitch if I wanted to. She was already being too damn clingy, and that was definitely a turnoff for me.

When we went through the glass revolving door, and as soon as we were outside, I heard some music blaring.

It was so loud, it was shaking the windows on the cars that were idling along the curb.

As the volume of the tunes increased, I saw an all-chromed-out black Hummer pull up. At the same time my cell rang.

"Hey, cuz. This me right here!" Carlos yelled as he held his hand out the window and waved. I swear, that peanut-colored nigga looked more Puerto Rican than I did with that curly hair all over his head. Although we both were mixed with African American, I was darker, and my hair was short and wavy.

As Carlos pulled up, this Christy chick began smiling and pointing. I looked at her and then at my cousin's whip.

"Los is your cousin?" she asked, in shock.

"Yeah. I gotta go," I replied in a rush. "I guess I'll see you around."

After I slapped hands with Carlos, I threw my bag in his ride and hopped inside. The first thing he did was clown me about talking to that Christy chick.

"Man, that skank-ass trick," Carlos laughed as he swerved all the way into the left lane to avoid the congested traffic at the airport. "Stay far away from that one, cuddy."

"Point well taken, *primo*." I nodded affirmatively and began bobbing my head to the beat of some banger my cousin had beating up in his whip. I was getting all into the shit when he turned it down and told me that we were about to pick his boy up.

"Yeah, I gotta go by the spot and get Harrison. He's my father's brother's son, so he's family, but I don't claim that fool," Carlos explained. "He's always fuckin' with a scandalous-ass bitch who he winds up putting his hands on. Then the muthafucka wants me to come to the rescue. That dummy stays in jail. I swear, if it wasn't for hearing my uncle Larry's mouth, I would leave the fool where he lays!"

The more that Carlos told me about Harrison, the more I didn't care for his ass. I just prayed he got in the car and acted like he had some damn sense. I had zero tolerance for the bullshit. . . .

About ten minutes later, we were pulling up to a large Victorian-style house. A tall, goofy-looking dude was standing out front.

"What's up, fam?" Harrison greeted us as he threw his hands up and rushed the car.

I could tell that he was a little surprised to see me sitting up front, but once he did, he hopped his ass right on in the back. I heard his little smirk when he did so, but I ignored that shit and took a mental note to chin check him if he disrespected me again.

"This is my cousin Dasio," Carlos said, introducing me, as he fired up a blunt and passed it back to Harrison. "You smoke, cuddy?"

"Yeah, but y'all do all this shit while riding down the street?" I questioned him, in disbelief. "You get caught doing this shit in public in Puerto Rico, you could get two to four years, especially if you don't have a medical card."

"Yeah, this shit legal here, cousin," Carlos said as Harrison gave him the blunt. Carlos took a hit and smiled before damn near coughing up one of his lungs. "You ain't, ain't . . . supposed to smoke and drive, but fuck . . . it!"

Hell, I wanted to reach over and pat my cousin on his back to help him get it together. I quickly decided against this when I saw him hitting it again. *Hardheaded-ass fool* . . .

"You a'ight?" I asked.

Carlos nodded. "I'm straight . . ."

"Nah, you ain't, nigga," Harrison said, clowning. "Pass that shit back here to a real man and let me show you how us grown folks do."

Carlos passed the blunt back to Harrison, and that dummy did the exact same thing. They had me leery about even hitting that shit.

"Damn, what the fuck is y'all smokin' on?" I inquired with a frown and then took the blunt from Harrison.

"This shit right here is some Headband," Carlos revealed as I slowly inhaled.

After I blew that shit, I could see just why they called it that. I had to take my time with that shit and take a light draw. The taste was smooth, and I was surprised.

By the time I took a second hit, we were already pulling up to my cousin's spot. It was a nice two-story brick house, with stairs leading up to a secured large porch.

My muthafuckin' head was tied the fuck up, and I had to regroup before stepping out of the car. Instead of going into the house, like I had expected we would, we went into his garage, which he had converted into a nice-ass studio.

When we entered, my eyes widened. I wasn't expecting to see all this state-of-the-art musical equipment. I was very impressed.

"Damn, fam. You got this shit hooked up!" I gasped as I checked out all the instruments he had set up on one side of the room.

"You know I have to stay close to Moms. Ever since she had that stroke, I've been here," Carlos explained. "I leave only when I have an engagement out of town, and when I do, I come right back."

"I feel you, cuz," I acknowledged, with mad respect for his loyalty to and love for his mother. "When was the last time you had a performance out of town?"

"Funny you ask that shit, cuddy. I got this gig hooked up in the Bay Area this weekend. You gotta roll out there with me!" Carlos responded as he stroked the keys on the electronic piano. "The shit is gonna be hot, and you know it's gonna be bitches galore!"

"Oh, hell yeah, I'm down!" Harrison shouted, inviting himself.

"Pump ya brakes, young blood," Carlos uttered, frowning. "I ain't got time for ya shit, fool. I gotta think about that one."

"What the fuck that's supposed to mean, cuz?" Harrison snapped, with an attitude.

"Just what the fuck I said," Carlos stated firmly as he lit the blunt back up. "Accept it or reject the shit."

"Don't come at me with all that sideways shit, fam," Harrison replied, growing angrier by the second.

I was paying closer attention to their exchange now, as I felt a serious confrontation was about to erupt. At the time I didn't give a fuck if Harrison was Carlos's folks or not. If he laid hands on my cousin, I was going to have to get involved.

"Nigga, what?" Carlos smirked as he approached Harrison and served him with a cold right hook.

It was on from there. Hell, I didn't even have to get in it. Carlos whupped Harrison's ass so fast and had him storming out the door within two minutes. I couldn't help but laugh.

"Damn, cuddy," I teased. "I thought you was about to beat the brakes off that nigga!"

"You stupid, Dasio," Carlos laughed as he dusted his pants off, picked the blunt back up, and relit it. "I ain't got time for that shit. That nigga should've already known how I got down."

I guess he knows now, I thought as I sat back and listened to my cousin's latest single.

That shit was on hit.

Chapter 5

Constance ("Connie")

"Where is he?" I said aloud after I woke up in an empty bed.

Noticing Shorty's pants on the floor, I figured that he was in the bathroom. After lying there for a few, I began to hear a faint noise. It sounded a lot like fingers stroking a keyboard. I didn't remember him bringing in a laptop, so he had to be in the spare room, which I had made into my office.

My heart sank in disappointment from the thought of him snooping around without my permission. Testing him, like I would any other person I had over for the first time, I had purposely unlocked my laptop and transferred all my important information onto my external hard drive. I'd left only unfinished portions of a few unworkable stories I had written and decided not to use, along with miscellaneous statements from bank accounts that had been previously closed.

Slipping on my robe, I tiptoed into to my office door. Just as I had thought, he was tapping away on my laptop. When I cleared my throat, Shorty briefly fumbled around.

"What the hell are you doing on my computer?" I snapped without a second thought as I popped him in the back of his head.

"Hey, chill. I was just online, looking for some tickets to Oakland. You know they're having the Urban Book Fair down there next week. These last-minute tickets are ridiculous," he explained as he switched the screen to the Southwest Airlines website. "You made me click off the page, sneaking up on me like that."

The odd feeling in the pit of my stomach made me consider throwing his ass out right then for invading my privacy. Lucky for him, he was able to dismiss himself before I got the chance.

Lifting himself up onto his feet, Shorty rubbed his head and informed me that he had a meeting to get to by seven. It was already after four in the morning.

We went back to my bedroom, where he retrieved his pants and slid them on. I watched his every move with his sneaky ass.

Suddenly, Shorty clenched my hand and held on to it as he led me to the front door. I gracefully slid my hand right back out of his grip and hurried him along before I let him have it verbally.

"Thank you for the wonderful evening. We didn't get any work done, but I definitely enjoyed myself," he said and chuckled, pulling me close to him. "We have to do this again real soon, Constance."

Although I agreed half-heartedly, I knew deep down that there was not a chance in hell that would happen if he did anything to betray my trust. Anything.

After closing the door behind him, I returned to my office and pulled up the browser history on my laptop, just to make certain that Shorty had done nothing foul. With three clicks, all my darkest thoughts came to fruition. A terrible sadness shot through my body, one that I could not quite explain. The anger came next. I wanted to call him right back over and crack his ass a couple of times with the bat I had sitting next to my bed, but I knew he wouldn't come back here. Not after the deceptive move he had made.

Refusing to beat myself up about it, I chose to put the whole affair on the back burner until I had the chance to think of the proper way to address it. No need to give him a heads-up that I was onto him. At least not yet.

I climbed back in bed and curled up with my king-size overstuffed pillow. I clutched it securely and rocked myself until I fell back asleep, hoping that when I woke up, I would have a different outlook on the entire situation.

Well, I was correct. Daylight came, and I rose, feeling energized. Being able to swallow my indiscretions from the night before was a simple task once I had convinced myself it was nothing.

Yes, he may have attempted to snoop in my files, but he couldn't have stolen anything, because there wasn't any email activity, and he didn't have a memory stick. At least I didn't see him with one.

Still, Shorty's actions proved to me what type of man I was dealing with. And this enlightened me on how to handle him. Even though he had crossed the line as far as trust went, I still wanted to have the option of using him in the publishing industry. I mean . . . he did have mad ties.

"Ugh, it's so ugly outside," I complained as I peeked out the window.

It was a dreary Monday, and once again, the weather was nothing nice. The wind was blowing something fierce, and rain was falling at an abnormal rate.

Sitting at home, bored, I called my homegirl. After getting her on the phone, I somehow convinced her to come through, since she didn't go to work today.

Lydia was employed by Portland Public Schools as a substitute teacher, so she had the option of working only on the days she wanted. She was amazing with kids, so I could just imagine how she would be with children of her own.

"Hey, girl, you need to get out of this house," she said, clowning, the moment she walked in the door, shaking her umbrella. She removed her raincoat. "You stay up in here all day, writing, becoming different crazy-ass characters. By the way, what's gonna happen to fine-ass Tyshaun? Shawnda's naïve ass don't deserve him! Is Redd really pregnant by him? That broad is crazy!"

"Oh, and you're teasing *me* about getting all wrapped up in my characters?" I laughed loudly. "You need to snap up out of it. You know you have to wait, just like the rest of the readers."

"That's your phone," Lydia chanted.

Yes, it was my cell was going off. It was nobody other than my brother California calling me.

"Hey, Cal. What's up, bro?" I said when I took the call.

"Is that your brother? Let me talk to Mr. Handsome," Lydia teased as she puckered her lips to kiss the phone. "Am I ever gonna get to make his acquaintance?"

I shooed her away and asked California where he had been. I hadn't heard from him in quite some time. Although disappearing acts were typical of him, I found this unsettling.

"I'm straight. I'm out here in Oakland, sis. You know, they're having some type of fair for black writers out here this weekend coming up. I got this promoting gig, and I'm here now, helping to set things up. You want me to reserve you a table? Soon as I got this contract, I thought of you. I know you got those two books out. You wanna come out here and get them off and maybe network a little? You know authors are always looking for a great publisher."

"Yeah, I could use some extra clients. How much is the table to reserve?" I asked, knowing that I couldn't afford either that or the trip to get there. Not when the rest of the insurance money from my grandmother's death wouldn't be released until I was twenty-five, so I had almost a year to wait.

"Do you wanna come or not?"

"Of course, but I don't want to come out there by myself. Let me see if I can borrow some money from my friend Lydia. I know she would wanna come with me."

"Say less, sis," California told me. "Text me her full name, and I will send you the confirmation codes for your airline tickets and hotel reservations."

"Are you serious, bruh?"

I was hopping around from excitement. When I glanced over, I saw that Lydia was more overjoyed than I was! Her ass was over there hitting the running man while she held one ankle!

"If that's what it takes to see my little sister and help her promote her work, of course," he insisted. "I'll talk to you soon, sis. Let me go handle this business. Love you."

"Love you more."

Lydia waited not one second after I hung up from the call to hit me with a bunch of questions all at once. It was like she had won the lottery and needed specific instructions on how to cash in the ticket.

I took my time to explain word for word what my brother had said, and Lydia had me repeat it a couple more times before she started crying.

"I've never been anywhere without my mother, Connie! This is gonna be the first time I've left the state as a grown-up! I can't believe it," Lydia said, weeping. "I need a drink right now to celebrate. Are you not happy?"

"Shorty is gonna be there," I blurted out unexpectedly.

"That's even better! He will never expect to see you there!"

Before I could respond to her, my cell rang. "Dang, Cal didn't even give me a chance to text him the information," I giggled, thinking it was my brother calling back. Answering the call without checking the screen, I blurted out that I was doing it right now.

"You're doing what right now?" Shorty asked.

After quickly covering up the phone, I whispered to Lydia that it was the author on the line. She began laughing and teasing me as I tried to calm her down without cackling my own self.

"Constance, are you there?" said Shorty.

"Yes. How can I help you?" I replied in a fake-ass tone.

"I'm sorry, babe. Please forgive me," he said, apologizing. "I know that I said I would call you last night, after I left, but I left to come to this book fair early this morning. I'm already here in Oakland."

Not wanting to expose my plans to be there also, I didn't mention anything about going. Instead, I wanted to sneak up on him and peep his reaction.

"Damn. So you're already there, and it isn't until Saturday?"

"Yep. I had some things to take care of ahead of time."

"I'm jealous. I really wish I could go," I whined, pretending to be disappointed.

"So, you're not coming?" he quickly said, probing.

"No. Maybe next year," I replied with a hint of sadness to appear convincing.

"Well, maybe I can see you when I get back to Portland?"

"We'll see," I responded dryly. "Have a good time in Oakland."

"I'll have a better time with you when I get back. That's when the fun begins," Shorty replied, flirting with me. "I'll talk to you soon."

When I hung up, Lydia gave me a look of displeasure. She stated that she did not want to come along if I was going to spend all my time with Shorty. She had a point, and it was well taken.

"I will keep it up front with you, Lydia. When and if I see him again, it will be strictly business. That's it. I have no intentions on starting or being in a committed relationship with Shorty," I informed her boldly. "I don't like him like that at all, so you don't have to worry about that shit. Trust me."

"So, you're saying that you're not gonna kick it with him at all while we're there?"

"Nope."

"Why?"

"Because I didn't tell you what the fool did," I responded, now feeling a bit of embarrassment. "Don't judge me please."

Lydia held back her words briefly. The moment of silence was followed by a bunch of questions pertaining to exactly what had happened. She wanted detailed information. I gave it to her. When I finished, she was through with him too.

"Fuck that snooping-ass creep! Just ignore him, and let's focus on going to the Bay Area and having some fun!" Lydia declared happily. "What are we gonna do for four whole days, Connie?"

Before I could answer, she hopped onto her cell and began to search for some exciting activities that we could indulge in once we made it to Oakland. I was thrilled that she had turned her attention to our trip, because I did not feel like discussing Shorty anymore. Instead, I wanted to begin preparing for our trip.

"Look at this shit right here, Connie!" she shouted, then showed me a video of people on Jet Skis.

After discovering several tourist attractions that she was just dying to visit, her eagerness got the best of her. "I can't wait to leave. Let me get out of here. I have a million and one things to do before wheels up."

Lydia, unlike her usual self, had only one quick drink, then hurried off to get packed. Yes, we had a whole three days before we left, but I knew it would take that long for her to have her shit in order.

Chapter 6

Dasio Vazquez

During my first few days in Portland, Carlos showed me all around what they called the City of Roses. It was totally different than Puerto Rico, especially the weather. One minute it would be pouring down rain, and the next it would be sunny and warm.

"You know what time it is, yo?" Carlos shouted, waking me from a deep sleep. It was Thursday, and it was the day we were leaving for Oakland.

I squinted while I wiped the drool that was leaking out of the corner of my mouth. My head was still banging from the previous night of drinking shots of Jack Daniel's with Carlos and his homeboys.

"How long I got?"

"We're leaving at five, so you have about forty-five minutes or so."

"Damn, the sun ain't even up yet," I sighed as I forced myself up out of the bed.

After dipping through the shower and packing a bag, I met my cousin downstairs. He was with Auntie May, who was wearing a big grin when she saw me.

"You look just like your mother," she said and sniffled. "I miss her. I wanna go see her."

Carlos looked at his mother and patted her on her back. "Maybe we can all plan a trip soon. If not, I'll send for her."

"You promise, baby?" my auntie whined while facing her son. "I need to see her before I leave this earth. It's been much too long, and we are all we got, son."

"I know, Mom. I'll make it happen."

Carlos kissed his mother on her forehead and told her goodbye before handing her caregiver, Mrs. Brown, specific instructions. I could tell he hated to leave his mother. He really loved her, and seeing their bond only made me miss my mother more.

"Let's roll," Carlos laughed, breaking the emotional moment.

He and I picked up our bags and walked out the front door. After placing our bags on the back seat, we climbed into his SUV and headed to the gas station.

"Soon as we fill up, we're hittin' the highway. I-Five by five," he told as he put gas in the tank.

On the long drive to Oakland, Carlos and I got caught up. We talked for hours and hours while we rolled over the mountains and through a whole lot of greenery. The view was incredible and made it hard for me to concentrate on what my cousin was saying . . . until the conversation got deep.

Carlos began to fill me in on what had been going on there on the US mainland. The secrets that he revealed were so mind-blowing that after a while I felt comfortable enough to confess what had happened back in Puerto Rico.

"Man, that ain't shit," Carlos laughed. "I know that nigga had that shit coming! If someone did that shit to Moms, I would've done the same thing, fam, for real."

"Man, you just don't know," I sighed and rubbed my head, trying to dispel the gruesome memories that I had worked so hard, to no avail, to erase from my brain.

"That ain't shit, cuddy," Carlos laughed, trying to lighten the mood. "Wait until I tell you about Uncle Miguel murking Auntie Carlita. Don't nobody else know about that shit to this day, fam."

Just as he began to tell me the story from the very beginning, the GPS chimed, alerting us that our exit was coming up in half a mile. That cut our conversation short, leaving me hanging on the outcome of that situation. We took the exit and drove about a mile.

"Here this shit is," Carlos informed me when we arrived at our hotel. He checked his watch. "Good thing the club I'm singing at is up in here."

We were already running behind and had a whole lot of shit to do. By the time we checked in to the penthouse suite and got dressed, we had only a couple of hours before Carlos had to perform.

I didn't even get to suck up the luxurious perks of the plush two-bedroom suite we were staying in before I noticed Carlos pacing the floor. The fidgeting he was doing gave me the impression that he was a little nervous.

"Let's go on down there," he suggested before I could ask him if he was all right. "They're having spoken word first, and I need a couple of drinks before I take my ass up there and perform this new single."

"Is this your first show, cuddy?"

"Nah," Carlos laughed as we left the suite. "Shit, I stopped counting after about twenty. It's just that I haven't let anyone hear this song before."

"Let's go, cuz," I said when we reached the elevator. I hit the button. "You know you got this. I don' heard you sing that muthafucka a million times, and you'll be fine. Stop trippin'." The elevator arrived on our floor, and we stepped in.

"Thanks, cuz," Carlos replied with a pound of his fist as we descended to the first floor. "I'm glad you're here. Ain't nothin' like family."

"You sho' right," I acknowledged with a smile, knowing he was absolutely correct.

We stepped out of the elevator and took a long, dimly lit corridor to the back entrance that led to the club.

When we entered the club, I saw that it was much bigger than I had expected.

My senses became heightened immediately, and my eyes bulged when I stepped all the way inside and saw so many beautiful ladies. It felt like I was in heaven, or at least close to it. It wasn't like back home in Puerto Rico. The females that I was now viewing were some grown-ass women that appeared to have some class. That made me want to bring my A game and be the gentleman I knew how to be.

Good thing I got cleaned up!

I smiled as I glanced down at my dark gray suit and my white dress shirt. I had left the shirt unbuttoned at the top a bit in order to show off my defined chest. I knew that was one of my great physical assets.

As we made our way to the bar, several chicks stopped my cousin and asked for his autograph. That shit had me bugging for real, but it didn't seem like a big deal to Carlos. He was humble, and I respected that shit.

"Yo, you don't trip off all them groupies and shit, fam?" I asked ten minutes later, as I sipped on my double shot of Crown on the rocks while sitting across from Carlos at a small table.

"Nah, I ain't never liked the spotlight like that. I just have mad love for those that have love for what I do."

"That's what's real," I said and nodded affirmatively. Then I continued to enjoy the scenery, along with the smooth R & B that was playing. I sat there and got comfortable as they began to play this jam by Kendrick Lamar. The shit was hot.

"Hey, cuddy, I gotta go to the back and get ready," Carlos informed me as he stood up and finished the last of his drink. "You cool out here?"

"Yeah, believe it or not, I'm enjoying myself," I admitted, with no shame. "I'm cool."

Chapter 7

Constance ("Connie")

Boy, oh boy, the next few days were crazy. I wasn't stupid, though. I knew how to handle business before leaving.

The first thing I did was meet all my deadlines and decline all new projects. I wanted to be able to relax the entire time I was in California. I desperately needed the change of scenery, not to mention a change in the weather.

"All done!"

The minute I turned in my last document, I called Lydia. I knew she wanted to go out and do some last-minute shopping. We both needed outfits to wear to the writers' conference and a couple to wear out. Cal had promised to show us around the Bay Area while we were there. I already had picked out several spots I wanted to check out.

"You ready?" I asked when she picked up.

"I stay ready," Lydia answered, clowning. "I wanna go to Jantzen Beach Center, to go to Ross. They have this pair of peep-toe leather wedges that I have to cop."

"All right, girl," I said, laughing, then remembered that I had to change my clothes. "I'll be there within the hour."

"Cool!"

We hung up, and I hurried into my bedroom to get ready. I knew that Lydia could be a little impatient, especially when she was anxious about something. I didn't blame her, though. I was excited as well.

Within the allotted time, I pulled up to Lydia's place and honked my horn. I knew she hated when I did that shit, but I was in a hurry.

"Come on. Shit," I huffed when she didn't come outside right away.

I waited three minutes, and when there was still no sign of her, I parked the car and went up to the door to knock. Her mother opened it and greeted me.

"Hello there, Connie. Don't you look beautiful today," Mrs. Stewart complimented as she ushered me into the kitchen. "Lydia is up in the bathroom. Would you like something to drink while you wait?"

"No thank you, Mrs. Stewart."

"You know I'm so proud of you, Connie," she began as she sat down and sipped on her coffee. "I've seen you grow up through more heartbreaks than someone three times your age. Still, look at you. You still stand strong and push forward. You have style, grace, and brains, like no other young woman I have ever known."

"Even me, Ma?" Lydia teased as she stepped into the kitchen. She kissed her mother's cheek.

"Even your spoiled tail, child," her mother replied with a smirk. "I still love you, though."

"Love you, too, and we'll be back later!" Lydia yelled as she dragged me out of the kitchen before her mother could lecture me some more.

"I love the relationship you have with your mother," I sighed as Lydia pulled me through the front door.

"Thanks, Connie, but you know she loves you just like a daughter too, right?"

"Yeah, I know," I replied, thinking about the loss of my mother. "I'm grateful for everything she's done for me." By now we had reached my car. We got in, and I started the engine.

"We are grateful to have you, Connie," Lydia told me as I pulled off.

As we continued to chat, we rolled down Alberta Street, heading toward Martin Luther King Jr. Boulevard. That was when my friend began to get amped up about the trip all over again.

"I'm so ready to leave!" Lydia smiled from ear to ear, bouncing in her seat. "I've been online the past couple of days, buying clothes and having them sent to this store. I hope everything is in."

"Why didn't you tell me!" I fussed. "Now I have to search all around to find what I'm gonna buy, while you have everything picked out already for yourself."

"No, now I'll have time to help you," Lydia told me. "You know I can't wait to hook you up with some shit that's out of your comfort zone. Don't say a word either. We will be in a place where no one will know us or will ever see us again, so we can wear whatever we want. I say let's get real classy while keeping it sexy."

"I like that. I'm game. Let's just make it quick. I wanna get home and get some rest before our early flight tomorrow."

"Yeah, me, too, because when we get there, I'm gonna be Team No Sleep. I wanna kick it!"

"Me too," I answered honestly.

We made it to Jantzen Beach Center, took our time shopping, and were leaving by the time the last store closed. Our hands were full of bags, and my feet were hurting. All I wanted to do was go home and soak my weary body.

"My mother is gonna drop us off at the airport tomorrow, so you can leave your car at my house while we're away."

"Okay. I'll be here at five," I said as I pulled up in her driveway.

"Okay. I'm about to go inside and finish packing now. With all the rules and regulations after nine-eleven, I don't wanna get embarrassed at the security checkpoint about what I can and cannot bring aboard. I ain't got time for all that," Lydia told me as she gathered all her bags, then climbed out of my car. "Anyway, I'll call you later to check on you."

After she closed my car door with her hip, I waved and drove off. After traveling directly home, I stuck to the game plan and was packed and in bed by ten. Six hours later I was waking up to my alarm.

Feeling drowsy, I took a quick shower before getting dressed. It did the trick, and I was at my destination at five. I had parked my car on one side of the driveway and was grabbing my bag when Lydia and her mother stepped out of the house.

We piled into Mrs. Stewart's car, and she drove us to the airport. After cruising through security and waiting a little while at the gate, we boarded the plane, and we were in the air right on time. When we touched down in Oakland less than two hours later, I began to get anxious all over again. I was ready to get into something. It was only Thursday, and so I had plenty of time to hang out before the function on Saturday.

We rushed to get to the car rental place and chose a nice late-model ride, then shot on over to the hotel that my brother had reserved and paid for us. It wasn't too far a drive.

"This is nice," I gasped as we entered the lobby. I immediately identified a few authors from pics I'd seen on social media. "Glad Cal booked us here."

This hotel was much nicer than I had imagined. The décor had an Egyptian theme. There were faux statues of great pharaohs on one side of the lobby, and gold accents sparkled from every angle. I paused a moment to take in the magnificent scenery.

"Come on, girl!" Lydia whispered, stealing my attention, as she nudged me toward the counter.

We quickly checked in and went directly up to our suite. It was small, but we each had our own private room. After Lydia chose which one she wanted, we hurried off to our separate areas to nap until evening came.

Well, my slumber lasted until 7:00 p.m. When awoke, I didn't hear Lydia stirring around, so I decided to go ahead and shower and change. When I finally came out into the living room, she was just coming back in the suite. This surprised me because I hadn't even noticed that she had left.

"I heard some chicks downstairs talking about going to this nice lounge down the street. They are having open mic for poetry, which they now call 'spoken word.' Plus, they have some R & B fella performing. I didn't catch his name, but you wanna go?"

"Yes, I do. That sounds like a whole lot of fun. I have several new pieces I wanna share," I said with a giggle. "They're very explicit, so I may need a drink or two first."

After Lydia showered and changed, we made our way a couple of blocks north to the nice-sized lounge. From the moment we walked in, we really felt the crowd. They were giving off a positive energy, which was inviting. It relaxed me just enough for me to consider getting up on the stage with the very attractive saxophone player. His mellow tunes were enticing and had me mesmerized, triggering obvious surveillance by yours truly.

"I'm going to sign you up on the list," Lydia announced. "Let's sit right here, and if the waitress comes before I get back, order my favorite drink."

Nodding my head affirmatively, I sat down at the table and focused my attention right back on the guy on the stage playing the sax. The tune he blew while the woman spoke her words was fucking magical.

“Snap out of it, Connie,” Lydia teased as she plopped down in the seat next to me minutes later. “He *can* play that horn, though!”

“Yeah, he can,” I agreed, sitting up at full attention as the next performer got up there.

Patiently awaiting my turn, I watched the free-flowing woman finally wrap up her set, then begin blowing kisses. I was amused at her candor and tipped my glass upward to pour some of my sweet Moscato into my mouth before rising to my feet.

“Connie? We got a Connie up in here?”

“I’m ready,” I announced as I stepped forward. I took my spot beside the gorgeous musician on the stage.

The smooth jazzy melody he released from his brass instrument permitted every muscle inside my frame to relax fully. After a few moments, he offered me a smile and a wink, which was a clear cue to join in.

“Attractive . . . Attractive is the way a man carries himself, the way he dips a bit when he walks, and the way he smiles and compliments when he talks. That’s an attractive man to me . . .

“Loyalty . . . Loyalty is an unspoken faithfulness. For it, you don’t have to ask . . . It is being true to me and removing your mask. It is like an ‘on-call’ job, being available at all times, regardless of what is going on in your hectic life. That’s a loyal man to me . . .

“Sexy . . . Sexy is the look in his eyes when they meet mine. The way he licks his lips before he whispers promises of sensual pleasures while tracing my spine. That’s a sexy man to me . . .

“Love . . . Well, love is a very complicated thing . . . It is something I wish for and often dream about. It is like a slippery tangible substance that is not easily gripped, but if you're ever able to grasp it, I heard it is a spectacular trip. Love is something I am still trying to figure out. It is something I am still chasing, if only I could locate the route. To be away from that someone and being barely able to breathe, to have that someone make me a priority, that's what love is to me . . ."

My words left the crowd cheering, especially the men. They were yelling at me, trying to get my attention. I smiled, waved, then hurried to join Lydia at the table.

After greeting me with a hug, Lydia told me how much she had enjoyed the way I delivered my words. She described my show as erotic and inviting. I guessed the tall, handsome, well-groomed brown-skinned guy who was approaching our table at that very moment thought so too.

He had my full attention right from that moment he began to introduce himself.

Chapter 8

Dasio Vazquez

Carlos and I dapped each other up, and just as he walked off to go backstage, this beautiful woman took the mic. Her caramel skin was glowing under the lights as her wide hips swayed while she delivered her spicy poem.

I eased a little closer to the stage to get a better view. I was taken by her every move, by her every word.

When she was done, the folks went wild, and this seemed to embarrass the beautiful young lady. She brushed her hair from her face with her perfectly manicured hands before covering it and walking carefully off the stage. She then returned to the table she was sharing with another chick.

I just had to go over there and get her name. If I was lucky, her number too . . .

"Excuse me," I whispered as I bent down between the two women and focused on the one that had just performed. "My name is Dasio, and ya spill was . . . I mean, I really like how you did ya thing up there."

"Thank you," she replied shyly. "My name is Constance, and this is my really good friend Lydia."

"Damn, you have a strong accent!" her homegirl blurted out. "Where are you from? Do you wanna have a seat?"

Before I had a chance to answer, she was pulling out a chair and sliding it between herself and Constance. I sat my ass down and laughed to myself.

They weren't as proper as I had expected them to be, but they were definitely well educated. That made me a little more relaxed. I was so used to the hoodrat chicks back home that I didn't really know how to converse with these real women.

"I'm from Puerto Rico, from right outside San Juan. I just moved to Portland, Oregon, with my cousin Carlos. He's about to perform next," I told them.

"Los?" Lydia screamed. "Your cousin is Los?"

"Yeah," I declared and shook my head.

"You live in Portland?" Constance asked, sounding shocked.

"Yeah, you ain't heard of it before, huh?" I said, clowning, and then flagged down the waitress so that I could buy us a round of drinks. "I thought that same shit when my moms told me that it was where her family was from."

"That's where we live too," Constance said in a low tone, avoiding direct eye contact.

"Forget all that shy shit you're doing right now, Connie! I wanna know what this man just said. Shit, did you just say that Los is your cousin?" Lydia blurted out, causing us all to laugh.

"Yeah, he is," I replied, then looked over at Constance. "But seriously, though? Y'all live in Portland too?"

"Yeah, small world!" Lydia said, answering my question for her friend. Then she continued to interrogate me about my cousin.

"Lydia!" Constance exclaimed, trying to hush her, and then laughed. "Cut that shit out!"

"Quiet. Los is about to come on now!" Lydia whispered as she made a downward motion with her hands.

The place went almost completely dark, the only light coming from the candles that flickered on the tables. This set the right mood. At that moment, I realized I was sitting precisely that a right angle to get a good view of Constance without making it too obvious.

Suddenly the bass kicked in and threw my thoughts off. At the same time, the spotlight hit the stage. There sat Carlos at the piano. Everyone present went wild when he began to play.

My eyes traveled all around, and I noticed that the place was now filled to capacity. There was standing room only. Everyone in the crowd was bobbing their head to the music. They were really feeling my cousin's new tune.

I laughed to myself as I watched Constance and Lydia dancing in their chairs while waving their hands in the air. All the while, their eyes were glued to my cousin. They stayed that way until the song ended.

"Oh, shit!" Constance screamed after she checked her cell. "We are way late to meet Cal at the hotel! We are supposed to check in and get our table assignments for the book fair. I forgot all about that shit!"

They both jumped up and began to excuse themselves. Standing to my feet, I offered to walk them out. I hated to leave during the middle of my cousin's set, but I couldn't miss out on getting Constance's digits.

"So, where's the book fair?" I asked, finding myself beating around the fucking bush, as we walked out of the club.

In the past I never had to worry about rejection, but right then I found that I was treading hard in uncharted waters. I had to pull it together and come at her correctly.

"It's right down the street from the hotel we're staying at, but it's not until Saturday," Lydia responded before Constance could, and then told me the exact location. "Why don't you come on over after the show? And please bring your cousin with you. We can all hang out or something."

Before I could get Constance's number, her homegirl was dragging her away. I stared at her silhouette until it faded into the darkness.

"Damn!" Caught totally off guard, I found myself getting into my feelings. "Why am I trippin'?" I questioned myself aloud as I went back into the crowded club and made my way to the bar.

I had to down a few more shots to deal with all the people that were now damn near shoulder to shoulder. I could barely breathe.

After finding a spot in the back, I slid my chair over to the wall and chilled until I was interrupted by the first set of females. There were many more after that too.

I couldn't lie. I was a little flattered by all the chicks that came for me. By the time my cousin's set was over, I even had a few numbers.

The women were fine and all, but not one of them could touch what I had seen in Constance. Everything about that female, from her beauty to her charm, most certainly had me captivated. For me, that was rare.

"Aye, who was ole girl you was hollerin' at inside the spot?" Carlos inquired as we snuck out the back door. We were heading out to get some food.

As we climbed into his ride, I said, "Oh, just this chick, but what I wanna know is why we didn't just get something to eat at the hotel?"

"Did you see how many muthafuckas were up in there, Dasio? We weren't even about to make it upstairs. I gotta get some security."

"Yeah, you seem like you need some help. You tryna juggle your career and taking care of your mother. That shit is a lot, fam."

"Tell me about it, cuz," Carlos huffed. "I can't wait to get up out of that house!"

"Have you thought about moving out of the hood?" I asked him.

"Hell, yeah. I think about that shit every day."

"So why haven't you?"

"Because that is the house that Moms and Pops bought together, and she doesn't wanna leave it. I've tried to bribe her with everything in the book, and her ass still won't budge."

"Damn, I feel her, though." I sighed as I thought about my parents. Carlos was lucky.

Not ready to get all into my feelings, I changed the vibe by asking my cousin why we drove here instead of flying. That fool had me dying.

"I don't do planes. Ever since that nine-eleven shit, I'm cool."

I looked at him and laughed. "Ole scary ass."

"Whatever!" Carlos replied and started laughing with me.

"Hey, while we're right here, can we swing by this hotel right quick?"

"Yeah. Where is it?"

I instructed Carlos on where to go. Once we arrived at the hotel, I had him park in the side lot, which was where I saw the WRITERS' CONFERENCE/BOOK FAIR signs.

When we got out of his ride, I noticed that he had put on his Portland Trailblazer cap and some dark shades. As we walked, he tucked his chain into his shirt, took his bracelet off, and slid it in his pocket.

"Damn, cuz, you gonna change ya clothes too?" I remarked, clowning, as I opened the door to enter the large auditorium that was connected to the hotel.

It was a little after eleven, and nearly everyone had left. The only people there were the ones who were setting up tables and decorating. I hurriedly searched around to make sure that I didn't miss Constance.

"You must be really feeling this chick, huh?" Carlos teased.

"I just wanna get her number and see what she's about."

"Well . . ." Carlos smiled as he tugged on my shirt and pointed. "She seems like she's about her business to me."

Glancing over to the left, I saw Constance. She was bending down, autographing a book. When she finished, she took a picture with the girl standing beside her.

"Shit. She write books?" Carlos asked.

"Hell, I didn't know, but I guess so," I admitted truthfully.

"That means she's pretty smart," my cousin replied, trailing behind me to the table where Constance and Lydia were standing.

"Glad you could stop by. Connie is almost done filling out her paperwork to get her spot on Saturday for the book fair. She was the last one in line," Lydia informed me, then swung all her attention toward Carlos. "Hey, Los! I just wanted to tell you that I love your music."

"Shhh," he whispered as he took Lydia in an embrace, catching her totally off guard. "I don't want anyone to know it's me."

"Oh, okay. I'll keep it on the low," she promised as she pulled away, looking dazed and shit.

"Snap out of it," Constance told her friend, embarrassing her even more.

"Carlos, this is Constance," I said, introducing her.

"And I'm Lydia," her homegirl added, flirting playfully.

"You can call me Connie," Constance stated, clarifying matters, as she shook Carlos's hand and smiled.

When she let go, she stared me straight in the face and grinned bashfully. That shit had me stuck. She was so beautiful, and I couldn't take my eyes off her.

"Stop staring!" Carlos said in a hushed tone and dug his elbow into my side.

Everybody fell silent.

"So, what are you ladies doing after this?" he asked them, interrupting the brief moment of awkward silence.

"Going back to the room," Lydia replied, pouting, as a tall, muscular guy approached the table.

"Hey, what's up, Cal?" Connie greeted him with a hug.

I couldn't tell if that was her man or not, so I fell back until I could find out. I guessed Carlos couldn't wait. He went straight to asking Lydia.

"Is that her dude?"

"Nah, that's her brother," she answered and then gave Cal a hug too.

"Hey, y'all. This is Cal," Connie said moments later. "This is my brother, and he helped set all this up for Saturday."

"You do promotions?" Carlos asked him.

"Yeah, I've been doing it for a few years," Cal explained, and before I knew it, Carlos was offering dude a job.

"Good looking out." Cal smiled excitedly. "I thought I recognized you. I just didn't wanna say shit and be looking all stupid if it wasn't you."

While Cal and Carlos were talking business, I slid to the side and began chatting it up with Connie. I could tell she was uncomfortable, so I tried to make small talk.

"So how long have you been writing?"

Connie got quiet, as if she went into deep thought, then whispered, "I guess since my senior year in high school."

"What made you wanna write?"

After taking a deep sigh, she answered me. She was hesitant, but I waited patiently to hear what she had to say, only to be disappointed.

"It's a long story. Maybe I'll tell you one day when we have more time."

"How about tonight?" I asked, hoping that she would say yes and that we could continue our conversation.

"Yes," she answered with a smile.

Shit . . . Lucky me!

Chapter 9

Constance ("Connie")

When I met Dasio at the lounge, I knew he was going to be different. At least I prayed he would be. After dealing with Shorty, I couldn't be too sure.

As a matter of fact, until I discovered exactly who I was getting involved with, I decided to take my time. Even if it *was* hard, and by the looks of things . . . namely, him . . . I knew that it would be.

"Let me help you carry your stuff to the car," Dasio offered, picking up the large box and the bag that sat next to it.

"It's okay," Cal said, intervening. "I'll have everything taken up to your room, sis. If y'all wanna kick it, here's the keys to my car."

"We got a rental, but we'll roll the Benz?" Lydia asked him, clowning, before we left the table.

"Yeah, but y'all be careful and at least check in, so I know y'all straight," Cal responded as he tossed the keys to me.

"Hey, let me buy a couple of those books before we leave," Dasio said, digging in his pocket for his wallet.

"How many do you want?" I smiled and reached into the box.

"How many do you have?"

I slowly counted them. "I have a hundred," I informed him.

"I'll take them all."

"I'm gonna need some for the book fair," I remarked playfully, with my hand on my hip.

"Okay, let me get twenty of them," Dasio said, bargaining with me.

"Nah, let me get ten of his twenty, cuz," Carlos said, butting in. "I can give them away as gifts."

"They're fifteen dollars apiece," I informed them. They both counted out one hundred and fifty dollars and handed me the money.

"Yes!" Lydia shouted and gave me a high five. "Get ya grind on, girl. You gotcha ends. Now let's go."

"Y'all comin' with us, right?" Dasio asked, checking.

"We'll follow you to your hotel," I suggested in order to avoid going to our small room.

"All right, cool," Carlos stated, giving Dasio the green light for Lydia to come along.

Soon as we got into my brother's whip, my friend began screaming at the top of her lungs. She was so excited that she wanted to tell the world. Hell, I had to stop her from posting our every move on a social network.

"At least wait for Los to give you the okay before you start tagging him in stuff," I suggested, trying to tease her but knowing she didn't care one bit.

"Okay," Lydia huffed. "Don't be a party pooper, though, Connie."

"I won't."

"You promise?"

"I really do."

I knew what she was getting at, and she was right. I was already feeling some type of way after Dasio had asked me why I started writing. My mind instantly went back to that horrible day when I was gang raped. That was something I didn't want to think about, let alone talk about, especially on this night.

"Let's go in here and have a good time, okay?" Lydia reminded me as we pulled up to the valet. "Just relax and enjoy. I'm sure you won't do anything you don't want to, because I sure hate for you to have to karate chop a muthafucka!"

"You got jokes, girl!"

"Nah, you got lethal hands, girl! You know that, right?"

I nodded, with a smile, at Lydia's jokes. She always clowned me about my martial art skills.

"We're right back where the show was," Lydia shouted as we parked and got out. "Why didn't they just tell us they were staying at this fly-ass hotel?"

"Hush. They're right in front of us," I whispered while attempting to calm the butterflies that were fluttering inside my stomach. With each step, I took a deep breath. I could even feel my palms sweating.

I need a drink! I thought before having a silent pep talk with myself. *I need to calm down. This is ridiculous*.

As I continued to mentally pump myself up, I followed carefully behind Lydia, Carlos, and Dasio, who kept looking back at me and smiling, causing me to shy away. I couldn't help it.

Dasio stopped walking and waited for me to catch up to him. "What's up?" he asked as he slid his hand into my sweaty palm.

When he felt the wetness, he looked down at me and grinned widely. He squeezed my hand tighter and whispered, "Don't be nervous, *Constance*. I'll be on my best behavior. I promise."

The sincerity in his eyes helped to break the ice. For some reason, I believed him.

The four of us entered the hotel lobby and went right up to Carlos and Dasio's suite.

"Wow, this is nice!" Lydia complimented the second we entered the oversize two-bedroom presidential suite, equipped with a wet bar and a full kitchen.

Dasio went over to the far side of the suite and made us all some drinks as Lydia and I got cozy by the electric fireplace in the living area. It was so nice and relaxing.

Before his cousin joined us, Carlos went and got his guitar and dimmed the lights. Easing his body next to Lydia's, he asked if she had any requests.

"'Love Me Some Kinda Right'!" she replied excitedly. "That is my favorite song out of everything you've released!"

"Wow! That was the very first song I wrote," Carlos responded as he stroked the keys. "It's my favorite too."

As Carlos sang to us about a very lonely period in his life, Dasio gave us our drinks, then took the opportunity to get close enough to me to place his arm around my shoulder. It was nice. Really nice.

We sat there for a couple of hours and listened to Carlos play. He was very talented and had my friend Lydia hooked. It was so funny to see her acting that way, but it was even sweeter to watch how Carlos was treating her.

"Look at them," Dasio teased as we observed Carlos massaging Lydia's neck.

Next thing I knew, they were creeping to the room, leaving me all alone with Dasio. *Damn!* I didn't want my homegirl to be a little "jump-off groupie" who just got her turn. She was too good for that and deserved so much more, but it wasn't my decision to make. I had to allow her to make her own decisions, and I had to worry about making the right ones for myself.

"I couldn't wait for them to leave," Dasio laughed. "We couldn't even talk."

"I know, huh?" I stuttered, allowing the first words that came to mind to spew out.

"Yeah, I have a million questions to ask you," he confessed.

"Like what?" I asked, loosening up a bit.

"What trait do you like in a mate? What do you like to do for fun? What's ya favorite color? What foods do you like? Damn, were you always this damn beautiful?"

"Huh?"

We both broke out in laughter, and I became even more comfortable. I even caught myself watching his every move. How he showed his masculinity and his intelligence impressed me. He had me captured by his intriguing speech, which he flowed with an exotic accent.

Damn, he's so sexy!

My thoughts had me so distracted that I could barely answer his questions. My ass was too busy visiting la-la land.

"What trait do I like in a person?" I repeated as I searched for the right words. "Well, that's a tricky question, but if I had to answer it off the top of my head, I would say honesty."

"Hmm, that's a good one," Dasio responded with a smile.

"I like to watch movies and travel. My favorite color is orange, and my favorite food is Chinese."

"What about my last question?"

"Huh?"

"The one about you always being so beautiful," Dasio said, complimenting me again and causing me to blush a bit.

I shrugged and smiled. "I honestly have no idea."

That was when the real conversation began. Every time he asked me a question, he answered the same one himself, even when it caused him embarrassment.

After our little exchange of questions and answers, Dasio began to tell me about his upbringing in Puerto Rico. The way he described it, Puerto Rico sounded like a beautiful place.

"Why did you leave?" I asked curiously. "Don't you miss your family?"

Dasio paused for a minute or so, while he seemed to reminisce about something. Whatever it was that he was thinking about had his eyes teary. It had me regretting ever asking him those questions. I quickly attempted to retract them.

"We can talk about something else if you like," I suggested.

Right when I did, my cell rang. I ignored it the first two times it rang, but after the third time, Dasio urged me to answer it.

"Is it your boyfriend?"

"No, it's a friend of mine, Shorty. He's an author that my small publishing company is doing business with. I missed him at the book fair registration. By the time I got there, he had already signed in and was gone," I explained. "He's probably just checking on me."

"Go ahead and answer it," Dasio repeated. "I'm gonna go out on the balcony and take a smoke."

As he walked away, I connected my call.

"Yes?" I answered.

"Someone just told me that they saw you at the hotel, registering for the book expo. Are you here?"

"Yes."

"Why didn't you tell me that you were coming when I talked to you?" he huffed.

"Because it was a last-minute decision, and I was running late," I explained, feeling irritated and ready to cut him off completely. "Right now, I'm with a friend, and I don't wanna be rude."

"Well, can I see you after you leave your friend?" Shorty asked, sounding desperate. It wasn't a good look.

"Truthfully, I'm on a date, so I'll be out late," I replied, stretching the truth just a tad.

"Wow. Like that? It sho' don't sound like a last-minute trip. It sounds planned—"

Cutting Shorty off, I told him that I would talk to him some other time, then hung up. I didn't have the energy for his games. I should have left him alone when I saw him on my computer without my permission. I was being real stupid for even associating with his trifling tail. "Ugh!"

Right then I realized that I didn't have to settle for that crap. My self-worth was valued way higher than that.

To place my mind in a better space, I tilted my glass up and emptied its contents. The warm liquid stung the back of my throat as I swallowed, so I chased it with a few swigs of my bottled water.

"You cool?" Dasio asked as he came in. He went over and washed his hands in the kitchen sink.

"Yeah, I'm cool."

Rising to my feet, I went and placed my cell in my purse. When I looked up, Dasio was eyeing me as he entered the living area of the suite.

I could still smell the faint scent of weed on him, but it didn't drown out the intoxicating aroma of his cologne. The closer his body came to mine, the more my knees weakened.

Soon as he made it within arm's reach, he drew me close and held me in a warm embrace. It felt so good, so right.

"I'm sorry if I overstepped my boundaries by hugging you, but I just needed that shit right now," Dasio whispered as he wrapped his arms around me a little tighter.

"I did, too, Dasio," I confessed, inhaling the sweet fragrance coming from his shirt as I nestled into his chest.

As we broke apart, Dasio released one arm and used it to tilt my head up to face him. The jitters set in quickly as I anticipated a kiss, but he just stared at me instead. When he did, his eyes allowed me to see into his heart, and it scared me. No one had ever looked at me that way.

Damn!

Before I could turn away, Dasio took his hand and pulled my chin up until our lips met. He pressed his against mine just long enough for me to moan just a bit.

How embarrassing.

Chapter 10

Dasio Vazquez

When Constance let me kiss her, I couldn't believe that shit. I knew that we had just met, but there was no way I was about to miss that opportunity. That moment was perfect. At least it felt perfect.

"I just had to," I confessed as I held her in my arms again.

"I'm glad you did," Constance answered, blushing.

"I'm really attracted to you, and I wanna get to know you a whole lot better," I told her as I sat her down on the sofa. I got as close as I could until she leaned her head on me.

Constance sat there and began to tell me about when she used to go to Catholic school. I began to envision her with her uniform on. I knew she was sexy as hell.

After a few minutes, I heard her doze off midsentence as I stroked her hair. She was snoring lightly, and when she did, her lips poked out. I laughed before easing her down onto her side.

When I was free from her beautiful body, I went and got my cell out to catch her ass snoring on video. I knew she would get a kick out of it once we got a little closer. I wouldn't show her until that time came.

After a few minutes of capturing some pics of "Sleeping Beauty," I put my phone down and took advantage of some cuddling time while I could. I knew that if Carlos was as square as I thought he was, he and Lydia would be flying out of the room at any second.

Oh, how wrong I was. Shit, the sun was already up when my eyes opened. The clock on the table next to the brown suede lounge chair read 7:36 a.m. Constance was still sleeping, and Carlos and Lydia were still locked up in the room. After slipping out from under Constance, I went to tap on my cousin's door.

"Come in," Carlos called out.

When I opened the door and entered, I saw them hugged up on the bed, fully clothed. Lydia was still asleep, and Carlos was just lying there, chilling.

"You cool?" I teased with one hand over my mouth as I pointed toward them.

"Yeah, she cool peoples, cuz." Carlos grinned as he kissed Lydia on the forehead. "Connie still asleep?"

"Yeah, knocked the fuck out," I laughed. "What time we leavin'?"

"Well, the girls have to be back at their hotel by six tonight for some type of gathering. When they get up, we can go out to eat and kick it for a while. After that, we can drop them off at the hotel and smash it back to Portland. Cool?" he whispered before shooing my ass up out of his room.

Seeing just what he saw in Lydia, I gave him the thumbs-up and went back into the living room. Noticing that Constance was still sleep, I took advantage and rushed through the shower, then changed.

When I returned, I found her up, stirring around, trying to locate her shoes. I spotted them at the end of the sofa, so I reached down, picked them up, and handed them to her.

"Are you ready to go so soon?" I asked her, hoping she would rather stick around.

"Well, honestly I didn't expect to stay the night, and I really wanna get cleaned up and change," she replied while partially covering her mouth. "Thank goodness I have my toothbrush."

Holding her finger up, Constance excused herself without another word and headed down the short hallway. When she disappeared into the bathroom, I got on the phone and dialed my mother. She hadn't returned any of my calls, and I was starting to worry about her.

"Hey, Dasio," she greeted, sounding drowsy.

"Hey, *mamá*. Did I wake you up?"

It was after 9:00 a.m., so it was strange to think that my mother was napping. I sensed that there was something wrong.

"No, I was just relaxing. I have a little headache."

"Are you sure, mamá?"

"Yes, Dasio. I should be asking you how you are," she replied and began questioning me about what I had been up to.

No matter how many times I tried to steer the conversation back to her, my mother was ahead of the game. She sidestepped each and every inquiry I made.

After all my efforts to get answers failed, I ended the conversation on an upbeat note, hung up, and decided to call Carla. I knew her nosy ass could find out what was up with my mother. She answered on the first ring.

"Hey, Dasio. Why haven't you called me? Do you have my number on some type of block? Is this a US mainland number you're calling from? That's probably why I can't call you! You know this cheap phone won't let me dial out to the mainland! Where are you, Dasio? What's going on, *papí*?"

Carla was talking so fast that I couldn't even get in a damn word edgewise. I didn't want to snap on her ass and risk the chance of her denying me my request, so I just let her get it out.

"Oh, my fault," I laughed, playing it off. "I really need to ask you something, though."

"Oh, have you talked to *tu madre*?"

"Why? What's up?" I sighed.

I should have known that I wasn't going to have to ask her anything. If she knew something was going on, she was definitely going to fill me in, with some added dramatics.

"You haven't heard! Well, then, you need to get home, Dasio!"

"Why? What's up?"

"Your mother has shot your father and killed him!"

"I know, Carla. How did you know I was gone?"

"I rushed over there when I heard about the shooting, but you weren't there!"

"Yeah, I headed straight to San Juan right after I left your house."

"I'm sorry about throwing that bottle at you," Carla cried. "Are you coming home?"

"There's nothing I can do now. My father's dead."

"Your mother needs you! She quit her job, and she's been in the house for the past few days, without visitors."

"How do you know?"

"Because everyone in this town talks!"

"Have you seen her? Does she look sick?"

"I haven't been over there," Carla admitted and then seemed to feel bad. "I can go over there now and check on her. I will stop by the market and pick her up a little cake or something."

"Oh, hell yeah, I appreciate it, Carla. Call me as soon as you leave there."

"Didn't I just tell you that I couldn't call you?"

"Damn you got a smart-ass mouth," I huffed, ready to cuss her loopy ass out. "I'll call you back in an hour or so."

When I hung up with Carla, my mind started racing. I tried to come up with possible reasons why my mother had quit her job. The information my ex had given me had me worried, and I was ready to go back to Puerto Rico, but when Constance came back into the room and stood in front of me, I quickly changed my mind, at least for the moment.

"Carlos and Lydia haven't come out yet?" Constance asked as she stared toward the closed door.

"Nah, they're still in there," I responded with a laugh and took a seat.

Constance drew her cell out of her purse and told me that she was sending Lydia a text to see if she was awake yet.

"Just go knock on the door, like I did," I suggested while shrugging my shoulders.

"I don't wanna be rude," she sighed and sat down beside me.

"I don't know why," I said, clowning. "They ain't doin' shit."

Right as Constance was about to reply, an alert on her cell went off. She hurried to open the text and read it. A big smile spread across her face before she turned to me and spoke.

"Humph! That's not what she says!" she laughed and slid her phone back into her purse.

My mind went in a dozen different directions, but I shook them off quickly and laughed with Constance. I didn't know exactly what was going down, but I wasn't about to interrupt.

"Are you hungry?" I asked.

"Yeah, but I don't wanna just leave without Lydia. Let me text her and ask if she wants to go."

Within seconds, both Lydia and Carlos came out of the room, grinning. They were dressed and ready to go. I was glad because a brutha was starving.

Chapter 11

Constance ("Connie")

Soon as Lydia and Carlos showed their faces, I urged my friend to come back with me to our hotel room so that we could change. Everyone seemed to be really hungry, but I couldn't enjoy a meal until I washed my body.

After agreeing to follow us back to our hotel so that I could give my brother back his car, the guys hopped in Carlos's truck. We arrived there within minutes.

"After we change, we can just eat in the restaurant here," I announced once we had pulled up to the valet station and were standing on the sidewalk in front of the hotel's main entrance.

"Yeah, that's cool, but hurry up, please. We'll meet y'all in the hotel restaurant," Dasio yelled right before I gave the car keys to the valet.

My best friend threw her hand up as we hurried inside the lobby.

"So, what's up between you and Los?" I teased as we jumped in the elevator.

"He's cool, but he made it perfectly clear that he wasn't looking for a relationship."

"So, what now?"

"You know how I feel about casual dating," Lydia huffed.

"Yeah, you say that's how you always wind up getting your heart broke," I mocked her sarcastically. "Well, how will you ever know if you don't give it a try?"

"Look who's giving who advice!" Lydia laughed loudly as we entered our suite. "Girl, hush. I got this!" she added before we headed our separate ways.

Ignoring her words, I could already tell that she was a little sprung. I didn't blame her. Carlos was a popular icon in the music industry and was still down to earth, like he was one of us. Oh, not to mention he was very good looking.

"Ready, Connie?" I heard Lydia yell just as I was sliding into one of the new outfits I had gotten just for our trip.

It was hugging me in all the right places, but I still felt a little insecure wearing it. I was used to sporting an ensemble that was much more casual.

"Here I come!" I shouted as I puckered my lips and smacked my gloss. "Ready or not!"

"Look at you, girl! You are looking really sexy, *mamí*!" Lydia teased as I pranced into the living room of the suite. "You tryna make that man fall in love?"

"Nah! Hush, girl!"

"I'm just sayin'!"

We joked all the way downstairs, but we calmed ourselves as we headed to the restaurant to join Carlos and Dasio. Just as we were about to step into the restaurant, Cal caught up to us and spoke to me about possibly signing a new writer. It was an established writer from our hometown. She was a well-known author and was guaranteed to bring in at least ten thousand a month in e-books alone. Now I was anxious to speak with her.

"Here's the chick's contact information. Give her a call at the end of next week."

"At the end of the week? She ain't here?" I said.

"She was, but not for the book fair. I guess she was just here on vacation or some shit. She left already." Cal handed me a card and gave me a quick hug.

"Thanks for letting me roll your car, bro. Here's your valet ticket." I handed him the ticket.

"Cool. I'll see you guys later. I have a meeting in the conference room."

Lydia and I waved at him as he headed off, and then we proceeded into the restaurant. We spotted Dasio and Carlos sitting at a table near the windows. As we inched closer to the table, I saw that the guys had already ordered some pastries and fruit. We greeted them, sat down, and dug right in.

Within the next hour, I was full and feeling lazy. All I wanted to do was go to my room and go to sleep for a few hours before we had to go to the function taking place that evening.

"You look tired," Dasio whispered in my ear as he palmed my thigh and smiled.

"Yeah, I am a little."

"So, you guys heading back to Portland today?" Lydia blurted out.

"Yeah, I have to check on my mother, and I also have a prior engagement tomorrow afternoon," Carlos explained.

"Well, we wanted to do a little sightseeing while we're here," Lydia announced. She turned her head and met my eyes. 'We still have a few hours before you have to meet up with the other authors," Lydia reminded me.

"That's cool," Carlos commented. "We can go over to San Francisco and go to the piers. I haven't been there before."

"Yes, I wanna go!" Lydia chimed in.

"I hate to be the party pooper, but I'm gonna have to take a rain check. I think I need to get in a few hours of sleep before tonight," I stated, excluding myself from this excursion.

"Well, I guess some other time," Lydia said, pouting.

"No, no, no! You guys can go. It's totally okay," I assured them as I stood up to leave. Dasio rose as well.

"You want me to stay with you to keep you company?" Dasio whispered as he took my hand. "I promise not to disturb you."

"Y'all gonna miss out!" Carlos teased. "Lydia and I are about to do the town! Wait until you see the shit we come back with from the shops! I'm treating too!"

Knowing I needed a shopping spree, I was sadly about missing out on the fun, but I took Dasio up on his offer.

"You're probably gonna be bored," I warned him, thinking of a way to entertain him.

"We can just watch movies until you doze off. Is that cool?"

"Sure," I replied happily as we left the table, waving at Lydia and Carlos.

As we headed up to the suite, I said, "Before we went to eat, they were about to have a scary movie marathon on TV. You like thrillers?"

"Hell yeah. I hope they show *Candyman*. That movie had my ass jumpin'," he joked as we exited the elevator.

A minute later, we entered the suite. I was totally comfortable with being alone with Dasio after the previous night we'd spent together. He had been a perfect gentleman so far.

Reaching down, I grabbed the remote control off the sofa table, then tossed it to Dasio. "I'm gonna change right quick. I'll be right back. Make yourself comfortable."

After rushing in my bedroom, I threw on some leggings and a long oversize T-shirt, then tied my scarf around my hair to keep my edges straight. Afterward, I washed off the light makeup I was wearing and reapplied my gloss.

I needed to see how Dasio would react to seeing me all natural. I didn't want him to just be attracted to my "made-up" appearance. I needed him to fall in love with my mind and my natural self.

Maybe I was jumping the gun, but something kept telling me that this was just what I needed. Thing was, I was terrified of getting my heart broken after trusting someone with it.

"Did you find a movie?" I asked as I peeped the scene Dasio had set.

He had moved both of the ottomans up to the sofa, closed the curtains, and found a spare blanket and a pillow somewhere. He already had some drinks and snacks set out. I was still full, so I passed on the food.

"Come over here," Dasio urged as he held his hand out to help me down onto the sofa. He drew the blanket over my lower half and then fluffed my pillow. "Is that cool?"

"Yeah, thanks." I blushed.

"You really look good without makeup. You know you don't need that shit, right?"

"I only wear it occasionally."

"Well, for the record, you ain't ever got to wear it around me."

As Dasio pulled me nearer, he seemed to stroke my hair down at the scalp. The first thing I thought was he was feeling for tracks. I was right too.

"Damn, this is all your hair?" he blurted.

"Yeah," I laughed. "What you know about some weave? Don't all the girls over in Puerto Rico have long silky hair?"

"Hell nah," Dasio answered, clowning. "My ex, Carla, got some nappy shit and wears a weave faithfully. She pays a grip to get that fake shit sewn in. I swear, I don't know why females go through all that shit to get attention."

"Maybe she just likes it. It's fashion, you know?"

"Yeah, but that shit ain't for everybody," he commented as he turned on the television.

We both laughed as we waited for the next movie to come on.

"Yes!" Dasio shouted, pointing to the television. "They are about to show *Sinister*! Have you seen it before?"

"No. Is it that scary?"

"Well . . ."

I pretended to be very afraid just so that I could cuddle even closer to Dasio. It felt so good. So right.

Chapter 12

Dasio Vazquez

The time I spent with Constance helped me to get to know her a little better. I was glad to see her open up, and I couldn't wait to kick it with her once we got back to Portland. Our time together in Oakland flew by too damn quick. It was already time for us to leave.

"See you soon," Constance shouted and waved as Carlos and I pulled off.

"A'ight. Call me when you get a chance," I yelled back.

"I will," she promised and sealed it with a smile.

Soon as we left Constance and Lydia at their hotel, we hit the highway and headed back home. Carlos couldn't wait to start questioning me.

"So, what's up with you and Constance?" Carlos began.

"What's up with you and Lydia? While you all up in my business?" I shot back.

"Cuz, do you know that girl knows every song I ever wrote? She even knows the ones I posted on YouTube before I ever got signed to a major deal. Every single one of them joints, fam!"

"You like her, huh, *primo*?" I teased him as I looked at the smile that spread across his face.

"I told you she's cool."

"Yeah, okay. Well, you know she's feeling you, right? She made that shit very obvious, cuz."

"If I was ready to settle down, I might give her a shot, but the way this music shit is set up, I can't do it," he revealed.

"Why not, fam?"

"It wouldn't be fair to Lydia or any other female. With my lack of time, this traveling shit, studio time, and taking care of my mother, well, I can't do the shit, cuddy."

As we continued to ride, the conversation suddenly diverted to my future plans. I knew I had to get a job. I just didn't know where.

The cost of living in Portland was way higher than back home. If I got my own place right then, I would have to have a great-paying job within a couple of months. That meant I had to get on my grind.

"What did you do back in Puerto Rico?" Carlos inquired.

"I mainly did bookkeeping, but I did security on the side for extra money."

"Well, you know I can always give you a job until you get something more permanent," Carlos offered. "My mother was my manager until she got sick. I've been doing it myself ever since then, and I can surely use some help. As far as security, you can come with me when I perform and manage my other guys and keep them in line. Those niggas be off track sometimes."

"You sure, Carlos?"

"I'm positive, Dasio. That's what family is for. You know I'm gonna look out for you. Hell, if I didn't, you know my mother would have my head," he joked.

"How long has Auntie May been sick?"

"Almost a year ago she was diagnosed with a liver disease. She started drinking heavily when my father was shot by his mistress's husband."

"What?"

"Yeah, that shit right there taught me a lesson. I would never treat a woman, especially my wife, like that.

Respect, loyalty, and love are what you're supposed to give your mate. If you can't give her that, then be man enough to walk away."

I related to my cousin's story more than he realized. I hurt on the inside for him as well as for myself. There was nowhere to go but forward, and it was up to us to break the cycle of abusive men in our family.

Just as Carlos was about to speak again, he began to yawn loudly. I hurried to check on him.

"Are you tired? You want me to drive?"

"Nah, I'm straight. Let's just stop and get something cold to drink. I need to stretch my legs."

It was about nine at night, and we had driven for only five hours or so. I had no idea where we were.

"Medford is coming up. There should be a few spots to eat there," he announced, as if reading my mind.

We took the next exit, turned left to go across the overpass, and found a burger joint open. I ordered while Carlos went to the bathroom.

I picked up our order and took it to a table before Carlos reappeared, and right when I sat down, Constance was ringing my cell. I connected the call and greeted her with a friendly hello.

"I was just checking on you guys. How are the roads? I heard it was raining really heavily in Northern California."

"Yeah, we made it through there. We just got to a place called Medford, Oregon."

"What y'all doing?"

"About to get some grub."

"Okay. I won't hold you up."

"A'ight. We probably won't make it back to Portland until well after midnight. I know you'll be in dreamland by then."

"Yeah, that's late, but at least text me when you get there to let me know that you guys made it back safely."

"For sure," I promised as I glanced up to see Carlos all in my face. "I'll let you know. Bye." I ended the call.

"I assume that was *Constance*, huh?" Carlos blurted out unexpectedly.

"Yes," I laughed.

"Lydia asked about me, huh?"

"No, we didn't talk about all that," I said, clowning. "Call her, or did you even get her number?"

"Uh . . . oh. Uh, no, I didn't," Carlos confessed, a confused expression on his face. "Dasio, I haven't asked a female for her digits in years. I'm just so used to girls passing it to me without requesting the shit that I didn't even think to ask her."

"Damn, you are seriously slippin', *primo*," I laughed as we began to eat our food. "You must really like her, though. That big-ass smile on your face says it all."

"To be honest, Lydia is the first female that I've been around in a long time that wasn't just trying to fuck me or get paid. I mean, all night we were engaging in mentally stimulating conversations that had me wanting to talk to her ass for hours. Usually, I can't wait for a bitch to shut up."

"Oh yeah, well, just wait until she starts stimulating your lower head. Now, that's the game changer," I replied in between bites. "You say that you two are just friends and shit now, but just wait. Y'all about to be thick as thieves, and I can see that shit happening."

"Whatever, fam," Carlos laughed. "Don't worry about me. I got my feelings in check."

"You sure?"

"Hell yeah. Now, let's get back on the fuckin' road before I have to clown your ass about *Constance*," Carlos added. "And look who's talking. All this coming from a man with his own nose wide open. I see how you look at Connie, and I think I know why."

"Why?" I asked curiously and waited for him to explain.

"She's smart, beautiful, and she likes you. She seemed to be just the opposite of what you are used to, and that makes her intriguing to you. I say go for it."

"Are you giving me relationship advice when you're running from the shit yourself?" I asked Carlos with a frown as we walked back to his truck.

"Shut the hell up!" he told me jokingly before I climbed behind the wheel.

Once I was back in the passenger's seat, he laughed loudly before turning up the volume on the stereo to drown me out, in case I had something more to say about Lydia. Then he had the nerve to yell over the loud music, "I got almost two years on you. I do know a little somethin'."

I looked over and shook my head at my cousin as I reclined my seat, then closed my eyes. I didn't open them back up until we were pulling up to Carlos's house.

When we got inside, I went straight to the room I was staying in. I was dead-ass tired, but I gathered up enough energy to hit Constance's cell with a text message.

While I waited for her to respond, I dialed my mother. I hadn't heard back from her, and I was beginning to worry. They were three hours ahead of us. That made it after five in the morning there.

"Hey, son," she answered in an upbeat tone.

I could hear people talking loudly in the background, along with the faint sounds of music. I had called the house phone, so I knew she had to be at home.

"What's going on over there at this time of morning?"

"I'm having a little get-together. They closed the case today, and I laid your father to rest. I didn't wanna be alone, so I invited a few friends over."

"Yeah," I sighed, not quite understanding what the hell she was doing.

It was totally out of character for her, and I didn't know what to say to her. She had never been the partying type, and I barely ever saw her take a drink, so I didn't know what the hell she was up to.

Instead of questioning my mother, I told her to write down my number this time and to call me back when she had the time to talk. She agreed, and we hung up. I immediately dialed Carla to see what she knew.

"Dasio, where have you been? Why the hell haven't you called me back?"

"Damn, is that the way you answer your phone?"

"It's just that I heard your mother was having a wild party at your house. They say she was drunk and everything! Did you know *tu madre* drank?"

"Yes," I lied. "I gotta go, Carla. Find out what you can, and I'll call you back."

"But when are you coming home, Dasio?" Carla whined.

"I don't know. Now, I gotta go."

I hung up, feeling like something fucked up was going on with my mother. If I didn't hear something positive from back home soon, I was going to have to plan a trip back to Puerto Rico. I really didn't want to go back, but if I had to, I was going to be on the next plane smoking.

Chapter 13

Constance ("Connie")

The next couple of days in the Bay Area were boring without Dasio to kick it with. But the trip had been a success: I had sold all my books, signed up for a future book signing, made some important contacts, and managed to cuss Shorty out.

"I don't think I'll be hearing from him anytime soon," I said aloud and laughed as I climbed into my bed.

It felt good to be home. It was Sunday night, and I didn't have shit to do. Since I had been talking to Dasio quite often, I thought I would give him a break.

"Who is this?" I whispered aloud to myself while rolling over to the side of my bed as my cell rang. After reaching to grab it, I slid the green icon over and answered it.

"What's up, girl?" Lydia greeted. "Are you in the bed already?"

"Yeah. You too?"

"Yeah. I can't sleep, though," Lydia confessed with a sigh. "I was thinking about calling Los, but I don't have his number, and if I did, I wouldn't wanna be a fucking sweat hog anyway. We're cool, and let me leave it like that. But, anyhow, have you talked to Dasio? That was a stupid question. I'm sure you have. I'm surprised you're not talking to him right now."

As usual, my homegirl was spitting sentences out so fast that I had to play catch-up when she was finished. I swear, she always had me laughing.

"No, I haven't spoken to him." I smiled when I heard the chirping alert. "But that's him texting me now."

"Oh shit, you know these are officially booty-call hours, don't you?" Lydia said, clowning. "But we all know, Connie ain't givin' up the booty!"

Ignoring Lydia's jokes, I hit the SPEAKER button so that I could continue to listen to her chatter and read Dasio's message aloud at the same time.

Call me if you're up, *bonita*.

"*Bonita*! Who the hell is Bonita?" I huffed, irritated by the thought of Dasio texting me by mistake and calling me by some other chick's name.

"*Bonita* means 'beautiful' in Spanish, Connie." Lydia laughed loudly.

"I knew that!" I giggled, trying to save face, as I replied to his message.

I'm up . . . bored. What's up with you?

Dasio and I went back and forth for the next few minutes. I totally forgot I was even on the line with Lydia until she began screaming.

"You didn't hear shit I said, did you, Connie?"

"Ah, no, I'm sorry. What did you say, Lydia?"

"Well, damn. What did Dasio say?"

"Not much. I'm about to call him now," I told her, deciding to do this out of the blue.

"Ask about Los without bringing up my name and call me as soon as you hang up. I don't care how late it is! Don't make me blow your phone up, girl!"

"I will," I promised. "I'll call you the second I hang up with Dasio."

After hitting the END button, I scrolled through my recent call list and found the contact that I was searching for. I tapped his name and listened to two rings before hearing his sexy voice. His accent was so damn intoxicating.

"Hey, Constance," he said smoothly.

"Hey, Dasio," I answered, smiling uncontrollably. Thank goodness he couldn't see my face. I was sure it was a bright shade of red.

"I know it's late, but I'm glad you called. I really wanted to hear your voice since you wouldn't let me pick you up from the airport," he told me, teasing.

"Well, when Lydia's mom insisted, I didn't wanna be impolite. It's just that was the longest that she's been away from her daughter since outdoor school, and that was when we were twelve," I explained.

"What's outdoor school?"

"When you're in the sixth grade, you go to camp for a whole week and learn about the different natural resources," I explained briefly.

"Well, damn, we don't go to school for that," Dasio responded. "We learned about our natural resources every day, when we stepped out of our house."

Dasio went on to tell me about their poor living conditions. I couldn't believe what he was telling me until I researched his small town while we were on the phone.

"Well, you dress and present yourself as if you're well educated," I replied honestly. "You carry yourself with much confidence, as if you were raised in a strong family."

"I wouldn't say all that, but my mother made sure I had proper schooling, and I pretty much learned everything else from the streets. Not so much as what to do, but more like what not to do," Dasio explained and went on to tell me about his childhood.

"So, you said you had two jobs back home. I know about the bookkeeping, Mr. Math Wizard," I quipped. "But what was your second job?"

"I worked security."

"What type of security?"

"Mainly at the strip club I did bookkeeping for," he answered, throwing me through a loop.

"Ah . . . okay," I stuttered. "How was that?"

"Seriously, if you see one ass, you seen them all," he confessed, laughing. "I respect their hustle, but I can't respect a woman that undresses to make a buck. Your body is your sacred temple. You should always treat it as just that."

Damn! Did this man just get deep on me?

He went on. "I love a woman who respects her body and demands that everyone else does. A woman who knows what she wants and isn't afraid to go after it. A woman who knows when a man is right for her, and when she feels the same way, she allows no other person to come in between that."

"What about loyalty and trust in a relationship?" I questioned, feeling anxious for answers.

"Loyalty is a must once you create a certain bond. Although they say trust is earned, I give it freely the first time. If betrayal is the end result, then it will never be given again. From there on out, it will have to be earned," Dasio said, sounding passionate about his every word.

"I understand that but never thought about it that way," I responded as I snuggled under my blanket.

My body was shivering, and the ceiling fan that was blowing directly on me was making it worse. There was no way that I was getting out of bed in my shirt and panties and going all the way over to the opposite side of the room to shut it off.

"Are your teeth chattering?" Dasio asked, half kidding.

"Yes, I'm cold," I told him, feeling my nose start to run. I sniffled. Now I had no choice but to get up. "Ugh!"

"It sounds like you're getting a cold."

"I hope not."

I hopped up, ran, and flipped the switch to the fan, rushed into the bathroom to get tissues, and sprinted back to the bed to bundle up once again. I did it all while holding the phone up to my ear.

"Why do you sound out of breath?"

All of a sudden, I broke out in laughter. I couldn't help it as I had discovered that I barely had enough tissues to blow my nose. I had to get back up again.

"You are getting sick. I can hear it in your voice, Constance," Dasio insisted. "I can bring over something for you."

"No, I'm fine."

"Are you sure?"

"Yes, I'm just gonna go to sleep, and hopefully I'll feel better in the morning."

"How about I come over in the morning and bring you some of my special tea?" Dasio offered. "My mother used to make it for me all the time. Trust me, if anything can knock a cold out, this tea can."

"Okay, if you don't mind," I said and giggled from the thought of seeing my new friend again. I couldn't wait.

"I won't come too early, though. I'll let you sleep in, because it's already after midnight."

"I should be up by ten."

"Cool. See you then, *mamí.*"

"See you then," I said.

I didn't want to get off the phone with Dasio, but I thought it was rude to keep sniffling and sneezing the whole time I talked to him. Feeling defeated, I went ahead and hung up, then shot him a quick text with my address.

As soon as it went through, my cell rang. I knew who it was.

"Damn, you didn't give me a second to call you. I just hung up with him," I snapped, seeing that it was indeed Lydia, who was about to bug me.

"Did you ask about Los?"

"I didn't get a chance to!" I answered honestly. "I started feeling sick and had to go. I'm about to take a dose of NyQuil and call it a night. Matter of fact, I'm about to call my assistant and tell her that I will be working from home the next few days. I don't wanna chance it."

"Okay, Connie," Lydia replied, sounding concerned. "Do you have everything you need? Do you have orange juice, Kleenex, soup, and some Lysol?"

"Yes, I think I have everything I need," I said with a laugh. "Now I'm about to medicate myself into a light coma. I'll talk to you in about ten to twelve hours."

"Okay. If I don't hear from you by then, I'm coming over there," she insisted. "I hope you feel better soon. Love ya."

"Thanks, hon. Love ya too," I replied.

Then I did just as I had said I would. . . . I fell asleep within minutes.

Chapter 14

Dasio Vazquez

After getting off the line with Constance, I went downstairs to get something to drink. I was surprised to see Carlos in the kitchen. He looked like he was heated.

"What's up, *primo*?"

"This fool Harrison called, talking about some niggas rolled up on him and his homeboy and let loose on them."

"Did he get shot?"

"Nah, but his boy got popped in the chest, and they're at the emergency room up the street," he explained as he grabbed his keys off the black and silver marble countertop. "Now I gotta go get this dumb muthafucka from up at Emanuel Medical Center before the police come up there questioning him."

"Why the fool worried about that shit if he was the one getting shot at?" I asked, feeling confused by the entire ordeal.

"Knowing that nigga, he was being foul too. Guaranteed he was either fuckin' a nigga's bitch or tryna get over on a muthafucka. Either way, I know his ass was doing something he had no business doing. I'm seriously tired of running to this nigga's rescue."

"Yeah, you gotta know what the situation is before getting up in the middle of it," I commented as I retrieved a bottle of Riptide Rush Gatorade out of the fridge. "I'm rolling with you on this run, *primo*. I gotta feeling that there's more to what that nigga Harrison is saying."

While Carlos went to check on his mother, I went and grabbed my little heater. My cousin had given it to me the very day I got here. He'd said the neighborhood we were staying in wasn't to be trusted. Just like the shiesty cats that lived in it.

"You ready?" Carlos asked when he found me standing in the living room minutes later.

"Yeah. You strapped?"

"You know I am," Carlos acknowledged, lifting his shirt up to reveal his weapon. "Let's roll!"

We walked outside, hopped in his truck, and went to see what was up with Harrison. Honestly, I didn't know what to expect.

"Look at this shit right here," Carlos complained as we pulled onto the road that led to the hospital.

There were cops everywhere. There was even a line of them curbside, with their lights flashing.

"I'ma hit Harrison on his cell," Carlos whispered as he circled around the parking lot just before the emergency entrance. "Where is this nigga at?"

As he tried to get Harrison on the phone, I watched the police detain every black male that approached the hospital doors. They seemed to be looking for someone, and we weren't trying to get caught up in all that bullshit.

"Man, where the fuck are you? You got me up here in all this shit, and you ain't nowhere to be fucking seen!" Carlos shouted into his cell.

I could hear Harrison yelling through the phone. The shit he was saying was disrespectful, and I couldn't see why Carlos kept saving his ass. I would have been done stop fucking with him long ago.

"Just meet me at Kathy's Market, on the other side of Dawson Park. Now, nigga, or get yo' ass left the fuck out here!" Carlos yelled into the phone.

When Carlos hung up, I filled him in on what the police were doing. He shook his head and got even madder.

"I swear, if they're looking for this nigga, I'ma beat his ass myself! This is my last time doing this shit! I need to be thinking about my career and my fucking freedom!"

"Yo, you need to be thinking about your *life*, cuz," I told him honestly as we pulled out of the hospital parking lot.

Fifteen minutes later Carlos stopped the truck in front of Kathy's Market.

"Here come this nigga, sneaking out of the bushes and shit," Carlos said, pointing over to the side of the store. "Who is this muthafucka hiding from?"

Harrison ran over and jumped in the back seat. "Nigga, go!"

"Who the fuck you yellin' at, yo?" Carlos snapped as he put the truck in park.

"Why you playin' right now? The police are interviewing everyone fitting my profile right now!" Harrison howled.

"What profile is that?" I asked, getting all up in his business. Hell, my life was involved now as well.

"A black man," Harrison hollered and patted Carlos's shoulder. "Now will you please pull the fuck off?"

Carlos veered onto the road and headed north to his house. He cursed Harrison out all the way there and finally got the truth out of him. It was just like he had said. That fool had got caught messing around with someone's girlfriend at her crib and had been in a shoot-out.

"Why would you go over there in the first place if you knew the bitch had a man?" Carlos yelled as we sat in his truck in the driveway.

"It wasn't even her man that was poppin' his gun at us! It was her fuckin' brother!" Harrison muttered.

"Huh? Now, what kind of sense does that make? Why the fuck would he beat your ass and shoot at you for fucking his sister? That is, unless she's underage."

"Hell, nah, the bitch is older than me!" Harrison said in his own defense, getting all hyped and shit.

"Then why the hell did he try to murk you, man?" Carlos asked again and again.

Each time Harrison answered the question, he said something different. None of the shit was making sense until he said something about giving the girl a transmitted disease.

Carlos shook his head. "So what if you gave the bitch the clap? That's still not a reason to try to kill you, nigga. So what is it?"

"She's saying she's pregnant too," Harrison mumbled. The fool was definitely covering some shit up.

Carlos waved his hand at his cousin, as if he had heard enough. He didn't want to hear anything else. We all climbed out of the truck.

"You can stay here tonight, but tomorrow you gotta go. I can't have all that shit over here with my mother being sick and all. You gotta respect her as well as this house," Carlos told Harrison as we entered the house through the side door.

"Don't worry about it, cousin. I'll be out first thing," Harrison said through clenched teeth.

Soon as he got out of earshot, Carlos began venting. "That nigga is lying."

"Yeah, he's not telling everything. There is something more to his story," I mused. "Just get some rest and the truth will come to the light just as sure as his story will unravel."

We went our separate ways to go and get some sleep. It was already after three in the morning, and I was exhausted, but that didn't prevent me from getting my ass up when my alarm went off at eight. The only thing that helped me get my ass out of bed was the thought of seeing Constance. I hadn't seen her in a few days, and I was looking forward to it.

"Damn. I still gotta go to the store and get the shit for the tea," I reminded myself out loud as I got all fresh and clean.

When I came out of my room, I heard Carlos yelling. I immediately went to the front door to see what the commotion was.

"Where the fuck is Harrison?" Carlos asked when he saw me.

"I ain't seen him," I said and shrugged as I stared at the two white men in business suits standing on the porch. "What's up?"

"He is from the fucking health department," Carlos explained, pointing to the first guy. Then he did the same to the other, a taller guy. "And this right here is the police. They are both here for Harrison."

I frowned. "Huh? For what?"

"They said they have a warrant for his arrest for knowingly spreading HIV!"

Right then I knew why that dude had been shooting at Harrison's ass the night before. Carlos must have been thinking the same thing, because he looked at me and shook his head.

"That muthafucka!" Carlos spat and took the papers from the taller man. "I'll let you know as soon as I see that bastard!"

Without waiting for a response, Carlos slammed the door and began to flip out. I didn't blame him. Shit, I would have been heated too.

"That's attempted murder right there! That nigga is going to jail for the rest of his life!"

"Fuck that!" I exclaimed. "He is slowly killing muthafuckas in the street! Out there fucking carelessly and not giving a fuck who gets infected, just because his ass got caught up! I hate a muthafucka like that and on God, he's gonna get his just. That fool is reckless!" I took a deep breath and quickly calmed down. "Let me get the hell up out of here. I'm about to go check on Constance. She's not feeling good."

"A'ight, man, you do that, and I'll check with you later."

"For sure, *primo*," I replied with a pound of my fist against his. "Keep me posted on the situation with ya folks."

"I will, Dasio." Carlos nodded, then retreated to his room.

Now I was running a little late to Constance's house, but I still managed to make it there in good time. I was able to stop by three stores and find all the things I needed to treat her cold. I even picked her up an electric throw blanket.

I parked, then walked up to her door with my hands full and knocked. Nothing. I continued to knock for about three minutes or so before getting concerned. "Damn. Why ain't she answering?" I wondered aloud.

Glancing around, I saw that her car was parked out front, so I figured she had to be inside. Turning back around, I peeped through the slats in the window blind on the window closest to the front door. When I did, I could see that the television in the living room was on.

After pulling out my cell, I called her. I could hear her cell ringing inside the house, but she didn't answer.

What is she doing? I wondered, trying my hardest not to start tripping and shit. *Maybe she's in the shower*.

Waiting on the front steps, I continued to call Constance's phone. That was when her friend Lydia walked up.

"Hey, Dasio," she said, smiling, and checked her watch. "How long have you been out here?"

"What time is it?"

"Almost eleven," she told me.

"Almost an hour," I admitted shamefully, not realizing that it had been that long. "I've been knocking and calling, but she's not answering."

"Yeah, she hasn't been picking up for me either. I hope she's okay," Lydia stated like she was concerned. That shit only made me worry more.

"Why wouldn't she be?"

"Because she took some NyQuil last night, and knowing her, she took a full dose."

"What's wrong with that?" I said.

"Well, we had a few drinks last night on the plane, and sometimes that shit don't mix."

Using her key, Lydia opened the door and let us into Constance's nicely laid house. It was so clean that I didn't want to touch shit.

"You can take that stuff in the kitchen. It's right through there." Lydia pointed, showing me the way. "I'm gonna go check on Sleeping Beauty. Be on standby, though. She may need her prince to give her that special kiss to wake her ass up."

Laughing at her jokes, I went to prepare the tea. I hoped that Constance would be down soon and that Lydia would be leaving. I had a little something planned, and three would definitely be a crowd.

Chapter 15

Constance ("Connie")

"Get the fuck off me, Ricky!" I screamed as I kicked and swung my fists, only to open my eyes up to Lydia standing there.

It was too late. I had already hit her in the face and busted her nose while she was yelling for me to stop.

"I'm so sorry, Lydia!"

My vision was blurry, and I felt dizzy. Unaware of my surroundings, I blinked a few times to try to get a clear picture of things.

"What the fuck, Connie?" she cried while wiping off the blood that was trickling down into her mouth with a Kleenex. "It's me!"

"I'm so sorry, Lydia!" I cried, apologizing again, as I glanced around and noticed that I had done a lot of damage.

Everything that had been on the nightstand was now on the floor. The lamp was broken, and papers were everywhere.

All of a sudden Dasio appeared out of nowhere, with his gun drawn. "What's going on?"

"It's okay," Lydia assured him as she reached our her hand and lowered Dasio's weapon. "She was just having a nightmare."

Quickly giving Lydia the look of death, I prayed that she wouldn't reveal the details. She ignored me with a "duh" smirk and began running her mouth while I sat there, looking stupid.

"Connie's okay, but she does have these things from time to time," she explained while she got some more tissues and dabbed at the blood dripping from her nose. "Well, actually you haven't had one in over a year, huh, girl?"

"Yeah, I think it was that damn NyQuil. That shit put me in a deep one!" I downplayed the event while trying to check out Dasio's reaction to the whole episode.

"Whatever it was, know that it was just a dream and you're safe," Dasio told me. He came over to the bed, leaned down, and held me for a few seconds. "I'm gonna go back downstairs and make your tea."

I waited to thank him until he released me and stood up straight. After pausing until we had made eye contact, Dasio gave me a smile and then disappeared.

"Damn, he really likes you, Connie!" Lydia declared in a whisper as she gathered all my papers into a neat pile. "You know he's been outside waiting for you for over an hour?"

"You are lying!"

"The hell I am! What the fuck did you do to that nigga to have his ass wide open like that?"

"I didn't do shit," I answered truthfully. "Now take yo' ass downstairs and entertain him while I wash my tail. I'll be down in fifteen."

"Hurry ya ass up," she ordered, clowning.

The whole time I was getting ready, I couldn't stop sneezing. My head was hurting, and my throat was scratchy. All I wanted to do was get back in bed, but Lydia screaming my name from the kitchen prevented that from taking place.

"I'm coming. Sheesh!"

As I came down the stairs and entered the hallway, I could see the silhouette of a person opening the front door, then leaving. "Lydia?" I called out, but Dasio answered me instead.

Dasio stepped into the hallway. "She said that she had to go and that she'd check on you later."

"Oh, okay," I replied, then sneezed.

"Damn, you *are* sick!" Dasio frowned as he backed up.

"Yes, I'm probably contagious too!" I sniffled while wiping my nose for the second time. "You may not wanna come too close."

Suddenly a chill came over my body, causing it to shake. I rapidly wrapped my arms around myself and squeezed tightly.

"Are you cold?"

"Yeah. Is there a window open?" I asked. I went over to check the thermostat. It was seventy-nine degrees in the house, and I was still shivering.

When I turned around, Dasio was right behind me. He smiled and took me into his arms.

"Okay, you're gonna get sick," I warned with a giggle as I continued to sniffle.

"You know I'm not trippin' off a little cold."

"You're sayin' that shit now. Just wait until you're the one sneezing and coughing."

"I take my vitamins daily and eat pretty healthy. I should be okay."

"Are you sure, Dasio?"

"I'll take my chances," he told me while leading me into the living room, where he had a blanket and pillow all set up on the sofa.

"Thank you so much, Dasio. You know you didn't have to do all this, right?"

"Don't trip, *mamí*. I gotcha."

Dasio made sure that I was comfortable on the sofa, then handed me a box of moisturized Kleenex tissues. "I'll be right back. Let me go get your tea. It'll have you feeling better in no time."

Just as Dasio was about to run off to the kitchen, I lifted the glass of orange juice on the table next to me.

"Sip this slowly," Dasio warned. "It's a little warm, and it does have a kick, but you're over twenty-one, so it should be cool."

We both laughed as I took my first taste. "Damn!" I frowned seconds after I swallowed, but I was already able to breathe better. And the coldness of the liquid temporarily eased the pain of my irritated throat.

After the second gulp, the taste barely bothered me.

"How is it?" Dasio asked as he sat next to me and stared closely at me.

"It's actually not that bad," I lied while turning my head shyly as I set the glass down.

Removing the loose hair out of my face, Dasio kissed my forehead and caressed my cheek. As he moved away a bit, he looked at me and smiled. "Are you feeling better yet?"

"I am, but I'm getting a little sleepy," I admitted with a yawn. "Forgive me if I doze off on you. Just know it won't be on purpose."

"It's cool," he said and smiled. "You can lean back on me if you want to. That way you can put your feet up."

The way we repositioned our bodies made me totally relax. The only sounds that could be heard came from the television, and it was set on satellite radio. Soft melodic tunes filled the air, and we drifted right off.

Dasio's cell ringing pulled me right up out of my deep sleep hours later. It must have startled him as well, because he damn near jumped out of his skin.

"Hold up, *mamí*," Dasio whispered, gently lifting me up and placing my head on the pillow. "This is Carlos."

Nodding affirmatively, I closed my eyes and tried not to listen to his conversation. His loud voice made this impossible, though.

"What's up, *primo*?" Dasio answered and then waited to talk again. "Get the fuck outta here!"

Now he had my full attention. Something was going on, and my nosy ass had to find out.

"That nigga come by there again, that's gonna be lights out for his ass, cousin or not!"

My eyes opened, and I sat up. There was no sense in playing sleep now. I had a million and one questions to ask as soon as he hung up. Waiting impatiently, I continued listening.

"Is Auntie May okay?" Dasio asked, sounding concerned. "That shit is crazy. He just came up in there and took the shit?"

Who took what? I wondered silently.

"Look, *primo*, I'm on my way there now," Dasio announced. "If that fool comes by there before I get there, hit me up!" He hung up.

"What happened, Dasio?" I questioned him the moment he set his cell on the sofa.

"Carlos got this loco-ass cousin on his daddy's side that keeps getting him wrapped up in his shit. Now this fool done came over there and tried to get some money, but when Carlos wasn't giving it up, dude grabbed my auntie's jewelry box and ran."

"He had a gun?" I gasped.

"Hell yeah, stupid *cabrón*!" Dasio muttered while he grabbed his keys. "Let me go over there and see what's going on. You gonna be all right?"

"Yeah, I'll be fine. You just be careful."

"Damn. I don't wanna leave," Dasio mumbled.

"Whatcha say?"

"Nothing." He grinned. "I'll be back."

"I'll be here."

I walked Dasio to the door in hopes of getting one last embrace before he departed.

"Oh, I almost forgot to give you this," he blurted out, digging into the inside pocket of his jacket. When he handed me the envelope, I twisted my face up in confusion.

"What's this for?"

"Just open it up and read it," Dasio replied as he pulled me in for that hug that I was waiting for. "See you later."

Just like that he was gone, and I was cheesing. I couldn't wait for him to close the door behind him, so that I could rip that card wide open.

"Aww, this is so sweet," I gasped when I viewed the contents of the envelope.

The outside of the card had a picture of a teddy bear with a pink thermometer in its mouth and read "*Que se mejore pronto, mi amor.*"

I quickly pulled up Google on my cell to translate it and found out that this meant "Get well soon, my love." I placed my hand over my heart and gave a deep sigh. I was genuinely touched. Next, I opened the card to read what was written inside it.

> *Get better soon, Constance. I have so many plans for us. Although we have known each other just a short time, it only makes me look forward to the future with you.*
>
> *Dasio*

"Well, damn," I whispered to myself. "Maybe he is feeling me."

Chapter 16

Dasio Vazquez

I really hated leaving Constance like that behind some dumb shit that Carlos's cousin Harrison did. He was becoming more of a problem, and I was about to help eliminate that shit.

"What's up, cuz?" I greeted Carlos as I entered the den. "Is Auntie May all right?"

"Yeah, she's in her room, sleeping," Carlos sighed as he sat down and rubbed his goatee. "I'm really trippin' off this nigga. He is really about to make me catch a fuckin' case."

"Let's roll out and see if we can find that fool," I suggested, getting more amped by the second.

"I was thinking that same thing, but I don't wanna leave Moms here by herself."

"Where's the medical assistant you hired?"

"Mrs. Brown can't protect my mother from Harrison. If that nigga comes back here, actin' stupid and shit, he be don' gave them both a damn heart attack!"

"Yeah, you right, *primo*! Mrs. Brown is pretty old and frail," I noted as I took a seat on the stool by the corner bar. "Now, ya mama, she might be able to take him!"

"You right." Carlos laughed loudly.

"So now what? You gonna wait until they catch him to leave the house?"

"Hell nah." Carlos frowned and checked the time. "I called down to the agency and had them send a few candidates over to interview for the position."

"So, you're gonna hire a man?" I asked, assuming that he was trying to hire some male muscle.

"No, no, I'm not gonna have no nigga up in here around my mom. *Shit*, so I might have to beat his ass too? I don't trust no man outside of us to stay up in here alone with my mother. Nah, it ain't gonna happen. Not unless it's someone certified and a background check is done."

"Yeah, I feel ya on that shit, *primo*," I said, nodding, just as I heard the doorbell ring.

"That should be the first lady now," Carlos informed me anxiously with a rub of the hands. "You may wanna stay, cuz. This is about to be real interesting."

"Why you say that?" I questioned, not quite understanding.

"You'll see." He grinned sneakily. "I specifically asked for a woman with certain qualifications in my request, so I can't wait to see who shows up."

"You're hiring a chick?"

"Yep, and you already know," he teased, rubbing his hands together again.

I fell out laughing at my cousin. His ass had jokes for real.

He rushed to the front door, and from the den, I heard him say, "Hello. You must be Gloria," when he opened it. Minutes later, Carlos showed the tall, brown-skinned woman into the den.

Carlos introduced me to Gloria, and then they sat down to talk while I observed their interaction. Although she answered his questions in depth, her emotional response was shallow. I couldn't see her sincerely caring for Auntie May. If it came down to it, I would guarantee that she would saved herself first, and for me, that meant she wasn't going to work out.

I waited for Gloria to leave to discuss this with Carlos. As soon as he closed the front door behind her and turned around, he asked for my opinion. I told him just how I was feeling.

"Damn, I was thinking that same thing," he revealed before stepping right back to the door. "The next one is here already."

Now, the one that came in this time was fine as hell. She was dressed like she was going to a club, but we didn't give a damn. We were too busy checking the chick's curves out.

"Hey. My name is Generra," she said, introducing herself. She had a Southern drawl.

As Carlos was introducing himself, she suddenly recognized him and began acting all star-struck and shit. She was jumping and giggling so loud that she woke up Auntie May.

"Carlos?" my auntie yelled. "Who is that in there making all that noise, baby?"

"Here I come, Mom."

Carlos got Generra's file from her and handed it to me. "This is Dasio. He'll be interviewing you." he told her.

Well damn! I thought to myself, feeling a little out of place. Carlos had caught me totally off guard.

"Hey, Dasio," she said flirtatiously as she stood right in front of me. She was already a little too giddy for my taste, but I gave her the benefit of the doubt and looked over her credentials.

"So, Generra, you served four years in the marines?"

"Yes, I did, and I have—"

"Yes, I see all your certifications," I interrupted. "They seem impressive and all, but let me ask you this."

"Shoot," she said with a cocky grin, as if she had the job in the bag.

"If you were here alone with my aunt May and a perpetrator forced his way in here, what would you do?"

"Honestly, I would shoot first and ask questions later," she answered, smiling.

"Well, what if it was dark and you couldn't see who it was?"

"Nobody should be sneaking around in the dark. Only a stranger would do that. I stick with my first answer."

"So, you mean to tell me, if I came home late one night a l'il tipsy, knocked something over, and it broke, you would come in shooting?"

"Well, I didn't think of it like that," she replied shamefully.

"No, you didn't," I sighed as I handed her folder back to her. "Thanks for your time, though."

As I walked her to the door to see her out, I couldn't help thinking, *All that damn beauty and no damn brains*!

"She's gone?" Carlos asked when he reappeared. "I thought for sure you were gonna hire her sexy ass."

"Oh, hell nah! She wasn't the right one," I responded with a shake of the head.

"Well, I hope this one is," he said with a laugh as he headed to the door once again to let in the next potential caregiver.

"Hello. My name is Kadedra," a young female said when he opened the door.

"Come in, Kadedra," Carlos told her and then ushered her inside the house.

As he walked behind her, he childishly made faces and silent gestures like he wanted to bang her. That was until she turned around and nearly busted him.

The three of us sat down in the den, but then nobody said anything.

"Kadedra, I'm not gonna sit here and interrogate you, so, why don't you tell me what makes you qualified to handle this job?" Carlos said to break the awkward moment.

"I'm a registered nurse, I'm very skilled in using over seventeen weapons, and I despise anyone trying to prey on the weak," Kadedra said, summing up her qualifications. "The specifics are in my file."

Handing Carlos the folder, she smiled shyly, and then she waited patiently for him to go over her paperwork. Once he had finished, he closed the folder and handed it to me.

"Tell me what you think, Dasio," Carlos requested, and then he made small talk with Kadedra.

The way they were flirting with one another had me a little leery, but after reading her qualifications, it really didn't matter. She was a perfect fit.

I cleared my throat to get Dasio's attention. "I say we go with this one, *primo*," I suggested when he looked over at me.

"Okay then," Carlos said. He turned his head to talk to Kadedra. "When can you start?"

"Tomorrow morning," she replied before standing to her feet while reaching out to shake Carlos's hand.

"Okay, I'll see you then. I'll give the agency a call right now, and they'll take care of everything else," Carlos assured Kadedra as he walked her to the front door.

When he came back in the den a few minutes later, he had a sneaky-ass grin on his face.

"Don't let ya lower head get ya upper head fucked up, boy," I teased. "We need her to be focused. When her job is done, then you can fuck her all you want."

"Whatever," Carlos sighed, waving me off.

"A'ight, so what you about to get into right now?" I asked him as I followed him into the kitchen.

"Nothin'. About to get some work done, I guess. I rescheduled my next two out-of-town gigs."

"Why did you do that, and you just hired someone to take care of Auntie May?"

"I don't wanna leave town until that muthafucka Harrison is behind bars or six feet under. I don't wish death on nobody, but that nigga done lost his damn mind. I don't trust his ass in the least bit. If you would've seen the way he came up in here acting like a man with nothing to lose, you would be saying the same shit."

"Yeah, those are the type of muthafuckas you have to look out for. They will take you out without thinking twice about it," I observed as I retrieved my car keys from the kitchen counter.

"You heading out?"

"Yeah. I'm about to go back and check on Constance."

"You like her, huh?"

"Yeah, I do," I admitted.

"You ain't wasting no time, are you?" he teased.

"Hell nah, I learned that shit a long time ago. I was really digging this one chick, but I didn't wanna sweat her. Well, I didn't really call her, because I expected her to call me. Long story short, she assumed I wasn't interested and started dating my homeboy, who decided to go ahead on and pursue her."

"Damn, did you let ole boy have it?"

"Hell yeah! That was my fault. I couldn't hate on him or the game," I admitted, laughing, as I headed to the front door. "I'm gone, Los. I'll check with you a little later."

"Hey, what's up with Lydia?"

"I saw her earlier at Constance's. Why? What's up?"

"Nothing. She's just cool people," Carlos answered, like there was something more to it.

"Okay, now, didn't you just listen to my story?"

“Go ahead on with that,” Carlos laughed. “But if you see her, tell her to call me.”

“Call her, man,” I suggested with a smirk.

“I told you I didn’t get her number,” he sighed.

“Damn, I ain’t the matchmaker, but I’ll see what I can do,” I replied, clowning, then made a mad dash out the door before Carlos could talk shit.

Smiling, I hopped in my ride, and as I drove, I briefly analyzed Carlos’s behavior. Yeah, my cousin was something else. If he wanted to just hit it and quit it, he had no problem stepping to a female, but if his feelings were involved, it was something different.

That shit right there made me decide that I wasn’t about to let that happen with Constance. I was ready to move forward with her, and I was going to tell her.

At the next red light, I dialed her number. I wanted to know if the tea had worked. Plus, I just wanted to hear her voice and see if she wanted me to come back over there.

Chapter 17

Constance ("Connie")

"Hey, Dasio," I said, then yawned. "I'm just waking up. What time is it? Is everything all right?"

"It's after five, and everything is cool."

"Are you coming back over?"

"Yeah, I'm on my way now. How are you feeling?"

"Believe it or not, I feel a whole lot better. I can actually breathe, and my throat is fine." I climbed out of bed. "Damn, what did you give me?" I wondered aloud, curious.

"My little secret," Dasio teased. "Do you have an appetite yet?"

"Yes! I'm starving," I replied as I rubbed my stomach, which was growling loudly. "I guess I can whip up some sandwiches or something."

"Nah, you ain't gotta do that. I'll stop by and get us something. What do you have a taste for?"

"Whatever you bring is fine," I answered honestly. "Some Chinese food sounds good, though."

"A'ight, I'll be there shortly," Dasio said before hanging up.

That gave me time to freshen up. I rushed to make myself presentable. I was back downstairs within twenty minutes. Just as the doorbell rang.

"Damn, that was fast," I whispered aloud to myself as I went to the door to peek out. "What the hell is she doing here?"

Not that I didn't want to see my bestie, Lydia . . . It was just that I wanted to spend some more alone time with Dasio. Not thinking twice about it, I let her in, a smile on my face.

"What's up?" she greeted. "Where are you about to go?"

"Nowhere. Dasio is supposed to be dropping back by. I'm feeling better, and I'm a little anxious to see him."

Blushing, I gently pushed my freshly colored, straightened hair out of my face and back to hang over my right shoulder. Looking up, I caught Lydia pouting.

"Well, I don't wanna be a third wheel."

"You don't have to leave," I rushed to say, not wanting to be mean. She was my friend, and the last thing I wanted to do was hurt her feelings.

I knew that she hadn't dated since dropping her last boyfriend of three years. She had caught him cheating more times than I could count. Last year she had finally got fed up and had kicked his broke ass to the curb. Ever since then, she had been just as cautious as I was when it came to getting into a relationship.

"Well, I'll just stay for a little while. If I start feeling out of place, then I will excuse myself. Cool?"

"Cool, but you have no reason to feel like that, girl. Dasio and I are just friends, Lydia."

As soon as I let those words drop, she was questioning me about Carlos. Keeping it real, I admitted that Dasio and I hadn't even spoken about them.

"Why don't you just ask Dasio yourself when he gets here?"

"No, Connie. I don't wanna act like some simpleminded groupie. I'm so much more than that, and if Carlos couldn't see that the night we spent together, then that's his loss."

"You are so right, girl!" I agreed, and we laughed loudly.

"Was that the doorbell?" Lydia asked while going over to the nearest window to look through the blinds. "Yes, that's him! That's Dasio! I still can't believe you let another man come over here, especially after that shit with Shorty! Hurry up and let his ass in! I gotta see just what y'all got going on over here!"

"Hush! And don't embarrass me please, girl!" I warned with a shake of the fist. "Behave!"

After quickly straightening myself out, I went to let him in. I had to subdue my undying grin before I opened the door. When I did, I instantly lost my breath.

Without allowing me a word, Dasio swept me off my feet and placed a sensual kiss on my lips before letting me back down. The look in his eyes told me that he genuinely cared for me. I was in fucking awe until Lydia snapped me back to reality with the clearing of her throat. Damn was her timing ugly.

"Hey, Dasio," she yelled, waving so that he was aware of her existence.

"Hey, Lydia," he greeted with a head nod as he passed by her in the living room and went into the dining room with the sack of food he had brought over. "I stopped at some place in the Old Town Chinatown neighborhood called Hung Far Low. The guy hooked me up with a little bit of everything."

"Are you hungry, Lydia?" I asked while dragging her up to join us.

"I wasn't until I saw this Mar Far Chicken," she teased as she snatched the box and ran to the other side of the dining room table.

"Don't even try it, heffa! You know that's my favorite! You can have everything else!" I exclaimed.

"Okay, I'm just gonna take two," she giggled before stuffing her mouth with one piece of chicken and holding the other in her hand. "Here, stingy."

Dasio just stood there and laughed at us. We didn't even notice until everything got quiet.

"What?" I uttered, my hand on my hip.

"Nothing," he said, smiling, as he made himself a plate.

After sitting down together, we ate and made small talk. The conversation didn't get interesting until Dasio asked Lydia if she had spoken to Carlos.

"No, we didn't get a chance to exchange numbers," she replied nonchalantly. I could tell that she was suppressing her excitement, but I took it easy on her and refrained from busting her ass up.

"Oh, yeah, that's what he said," Dasio replied with a sneaky grin. "He wanted me to get your number, but here you go."

Dasio pulled out his cell, hit a couple of buttons, and passed it to Lydia. She smiled and took it from his grasp.

"Hey, cuz!" Los yelled out through the speaker.

"No, this is Lydia," she giggled as she took the phone into the other room to have a conversation. That left me all alone with Dasio.

"So, you look like you feel a whole lot better," he said, flirting. "You got plans for tonight?"

"No, I'm just staying in. I need to go over a few contracts and do some promotional work, but I have until tomorrow at midnight to get it done. It won't take me but a few hours to do it. What about you?"

"I was hoping to spend some time with you. You cool with that?"

"Sure. We can stay here and chill, unless you wanna go somewhere."

"I'm gonna leave that totally up to you, but honestly, you're just getting over a little bug or whatever, so maybe we shouldn't go anywhere."

"That's cool," I agreed.

"Hey, y'all," Lydia interrupted. "Los wanted to know if you guys wanted to go to his show tomorrow night over the bridge in Vancouver."

Dasio and I looked at one another and shrugged.

"You wanna go?" he asked finally.

"Sure. That'll give me another day to regroup," I said, feeling excited about going on a real date with someone I actually liked. A whole lot at that.

Dasio glanced over at Lydia. "Tell him yeah, we'll be there."

Lydia's ass was over there on cloud nine, and that was the same place I was trying to get to. Only she was in my way.

"Carlos, let me dial you from my cell so I can give Dasio his phone back," Lydia giggled. She recited his number a couple of times, then dialed it.

"Here ya go," she said to Dasio, handing him his cell. She thanked him, then bid her farewells. "I'm about to go and give you two some privacy, but I'll call you later, Connie!"

"Maybe wait until the morning," I mumbled under my breath as I escorted her to the door. She was so busy already chatting it up with Carlos on the phone that she didn't pay me any attention anyhow.

"Oh, you don't have to do that," I whined when I turned around and saw Dasio cleaning up our mess.

"No, it's okay. Why don't you pick out a movie or turn on some music while I put this food up?"

"Okay," I replied, with not a clue as to what I was going to do next. My inner scary self was telling me to pick out an action flick, while my heart was urging me to turn on some nice mellow R & B. I was torn for a few. *Ugh!*

Choosing to follow my heart, I walked into my private den and turned on my digital stereo to play Pandora. I had used it only a couple of times, so it took a minute to get it going.

"Hey, this is a nice room," Dasio said when he walked in about ten minutes later. He scanned my many awards on the shelves on one wall. "You took martial arts?"

"Yeah, it was a stress reliever for me at first, but then it just got addicting," I confessed, not wanting to talk about that time in my life.

"You still take classes?"

"No, I pretty much took every one they offered at the gym, so now I just go to kickboxing classes a few times a week."

I had never thought it was a big deal, but obviously Dasio did. He was going on and on about how strong and smart I was. He was placing me on a pedestal, which I had no right to occupy. Not with my blemished past.

Sensing my uneasiness, Dasio motioned me to the oversize sofa and pulled me down onto it with him. "You amaze me."

"Why you say that?"

"Every time that I'm around you, I find out something else special about you."

"What do you mean?"

"I mean that you are definitely one of a kind."

"I am?" I blushed as he encouraged me to face him with a gentle hand on my chin.

"Yes, you are unique."

"So are you."

After I released the admission from my lips, I stared into Dasio's eyes. Surprisingly, he wasn't saying a word.

Chapter 18

Dasio Vazquez

While I was revealing my feelings to Constance, I never once thought that she would make me speechless. Her innocence was unreal, and her words touched me every time she spoke from her heart. I wanted her. Shit. Who was I fooling? I *needed* her in my life.

"Damn," I sighed, not knowing what to say next.

"What's wrong?"

"Nothing. That's what's got me tripping right now."

"What?"

"Everything is just right," I confessed as I continued to stare into her eyes. "Every time I'm with you, it's just—"

"Just what, Dasio?" she asked, interrupting.

Constance begged me for an answer, and I didn't know quite how to explain myself. The only way I knew how was to show her. It all began with a kiss.

The tender pecks that I continued spreading across her lips and neck had her body squirming. She was moving to a rhythm all her own, and I found myself getting wrapped right up in it. Her arms were around my neck, and mine around her waist. It made it a little difficult to calm my advances down a bit, but I tried.

Seeing that I was struggling, Constance backed up and allowed some space in between us. It was just enough for me to lower my head and place my mouth on the soft, lilac-scented skin in her cleavage area.

"Mmm."

The moans that Constance released only made me want her more. She was arousing every manly bone in my body, including the one between my legs. I could feel it swelling up by the second, but there wasn't a damn thing I could do about it. My dick was now hard as a rock, forcing me to reposition it in order to give it more room.

As I continued rubbing on her chest, I came across the front clasp on her bra. After hesitating a second or two, I clicked it open and released her perky breasts.

"*Shit*," she whispered, throwing her head backward while holding tightly onto my shoulders. Constance was beginning to loosen up, and I was helping her as much as I could without acting as desperate as I was feeling. Hell, she had me lusting for her ass.

Taking full advantage of the opportunity, I began massaging her breasts through her lightweight sweater until her nipples hardened. In order to get to them, I had to lift her shirt. I did it slowly and carefully. When her breasts were fully exposed, I took one in my hand as I ran my tongue across the other one. It caused her body to shiver and her back to arch. She began palming the back of my head to encourage me to lock on a little more. Once I had a mouthful, I applied a gentle amount of pressure as I caressed her backside. Instantly, her moans became gasps as I shifted one of my hands from her breast to between her thighs. The warmth made me rub more aggressively, with the side of my palm gracing her coochie with every stroke. It didn't take long for her to start grinding up against it.

"You feel so good," I whispered as I brought my head back up and kissed her lips once more before looking in her eyes. "I want you, but only if you're ready."

"I'm ready," she whispered. And then she permitted me to remove her clothing one garment at a time. Within two minutes she was standing in front of me totally nude.

"Damn, you're beautiful Constance," I complimented in a daze, not able to take my eyes off her flawless body.

She smiled shyly as she drew even closer to me and pulled me up to her. It was her turn to undress me, and let me tell you, she did that shit with precision and had me ready to get beside myself.

"Damn," I moaned as she brushed against my stiffened dick while removing my boxers. That muthafucka stood at attention and made Constance step back a little. She looked at me, then back down at my shaft before she began stroking it until the pre-cum started trickling out. Taking her finger, she swirled it around the head and used it as a lubricant while continuing to stroke me. Using her free hand, she fondled my nuts. That shit did it.

"Are you sure about this?" I whispered.

"I'm positive." She smiled as she gave a nod.

Laying her body down on the large sofa cushions, I took my time pleasing her with an oral assault to her pussy. She was releasing her first orgasm within seconds. I hurried to lick up every drop of her juices and held on to her ass tightly. I let my tongue dive in and out of her sweetness as I lifted her hips into the air until she released for the second time. Now she was shaking.

"Damn, I want you," I whispered as I dug into my pocket and drew out a condom.

Constance removed it from my hand, opened the package, and slid it on for me. My eyes watched intensely as she drew back and stared me in the face while pulling me on top of her. Lifting up a bit, I stroked my hardness as I fondled her clit with the tip of it until I felt her wetness drip. It was making a sloshing noise, which made my hair stand up on the back of my neck. I couldn't help but begin to insert it, but it wouldn't go in. I eased back a bit and tried it again, but her love hole wasn't budging. Constance must have become anxious, because the next thing I knew, she was twirling her hips until I got the head in.

"*Shit*," she groaned, as if she were in pain.

"You want me to stop?"

"No, I want you," she begged, still squirming in a sexual manner.

Relaxing a bit, I dug the head of my dick in and out until her box loosened just enough for me to get in the extremely tight fit. It was gripping my shit so hard that I found myself releasing prematurely. Shit, I couldn't help it.

Good thing my dick had a quick snap back. I was still hard and ready to go, but something wasn't right.

"What's wrong, baby?" I asked. I had noticed that she stopped all movement. "Are you okay?"

"Yes. It's just that I . . ."

"What? What is it?"

The first thing I thought about was her worrying about how serious my feelings were for her. Even though it was early in the relationship, I thought it was the perfect time to tell her.

"If you're wondering what my intentions are, I can admit I'm falling hard for you. I can see us being together for the long haul."

"What do you mean?" she asked, with tears in her eyes. "Are you saying that you wanna have a sexual relationship or a committed one?"

I scooted back and let my now-limp dick slide out of her warm, bomb-ass pussy. I didn't want to do it, but what Constance was saying was very important.

"I want it all, me and you too . . . exclusively. Can that happen?" I said, with a smile and a kiss.

"Yes, but I don't think we can go there until I share something with you that happened in my past."

Right away I thought of my deep dark secret. I didn't think I was ready, so I slid the thoughts to the back of my mind and decided to listen to her first.

"Remember when I told you I went to Catholic school?" Constance prompted.

"Yeah, you told me," I acknowledged while I got a little comfortable by propping up the pillows on the sofa and leaning her head on my chest.

"Well, my senior year I was seeing this older guy named Ricky . . ."

What Constance went on to tell me blew my mind. By the time she finished, we were both in tears.

"So where are the muthafuckas now?" I said, gritting my teeth, becoming madder by the damn second.

"Two of them are dead, and one is still out there somewhere," she told me, sniffling.

I hugged her closely and kissed her forehead. I tried my best to tell her everything would be all right, but I knew it wouldn't. Something like that had to have her head and her heart all fucked up.

"What's his name?" I asked, wanting to find the nigga and beat his ass until he couldn't breathe.

"I have never repeated his name, because it will give him the power. I promised myself I would never say it again until he was maggot food!"

I didn't want to rock the boat, so I let it ride and told her that I was there for her. Unconditionally.

"I'm sorry if it wasn't what you were expecting," Constance said, apologizing.

"What are you talking about?"

"Well, honestly, this is the first time I've made love with a man."

"Huh. So you have never . . . not since the—"

"No," she whispered and sniffled as she caught the tears with the back of her hand. "I was a virgin before the rape." That explained the tightness of her pussy and the tears that came after our lovemaking session.

"Why didn't you tell me? We could have waited. I would have waited," I said, feeling like a jerk.

"I didn't say anything, because I didn't want you to judge me and think that it was an excuse not to have sex with you."

"We made love, baby," I reminded her with a kiss. "It wasn't just sex."

"Huh? It wasn't?" she stuttered, in disbelief. "But you barely know me."

"I know you enough to see that you are beautiful both inside and out. Your kindness and thoughtfulness say a lot about your character."

"They do?"

"Yes, I have been checking you out. When I'm not with you, I wanna be. When I'm not talking to you, I wanna hear your voice. When you're not in my arms, I need to feel your heartbeat. So yes, I am falling in love with everything about you, baby."

I didn't expect Constance to say it back, so it caught me totally by surprise when she did. "I wouldn't have let you into my sanctuary if I didn't feel the same way, Dasio, but I'm scared."

"I know you've been hurt before, but you never had a love like this. This is different, *mamí*. The love I have for you makes me wanna be the man that you can see yourself with for years to come. I'm glad you took a chance on me. I promise you won't regret it. I'm here to stay, and I will protect you from all your demons until I can completely remove them from your world. Trust me, Constance. I'll be here until you say otherwise."

"But we don't even know each other," she insisted.

"I know more about you than I do about any other chick I've dated," I revealed. "And I've shared with you more about me than I have with anyone else. Maybe it is too early to be tossing around the L word, but I can't help how I feel, and all I can do is be honest about it."

"And I appreciate that, Dasio. I'm in this too, so let's just see where this goes."

Nodding my head, I grabbed the throw blanket that was on the arm of the chair and placed it over us. We held on to each other tightly and began to cuddle. It was a feeling like no other. Everything was just fine, but it wouldn't be perfect until I found the muthafucka who had damaged my girl and put his ass in the dirt. Constance may not have shared his identity with me that night, but I promised myself that I would find out. By any means necessary.

Chapter 19

Constance ("Connie")

I can't believe I just did that!

Suppressing my screams when I woke up in the den, on the sofa, in Dasio's arms the next morning, I couldn't help but smile. I had not one regret. Well, I did have just one. My Va-jay-jay was a little sore, but the tingling sensation eased the pain.

Everything had gone just as I had hoped. I'd been able to tear down all barriers and let myself be totally free. It was something that I had been dreaming about for years.

Lately I had found myself forcing things, but with Dasio, I didn't have to do that. That was what set him apart from the rest.

"Good morning, sleepyhead." He smiled and kissed me on the mouth. I instantly drew back and covered my lips.

"Constance, please," he said. "I don't give a damn about you having morning breath. You better give your man a kiss."

"My man?" I giggled playfully as I wiggled from out of his arms, so I could rush to the bathroom.

"Yes, your man," he repeated. "Now, where are you running off to?"

"To shower," I said, pointing upstairs.

"Wait for me. I'm coming."

"You are?" I replied shyly, knowing good and well he had already seen me naked.

Fully aware that getting into a relationship would make me vulnerable and open for heartbreak, I decided that I was ready to take that leap of faith. It was time. . . .

"I promise to be on my best behavior. I'll even wash your back."

"In that case, come on," I stated boldly.

Dasio was heaving me out of my shell, and I was enjoying the experience. He had me feeling totally comfortable in my own skin. It was refreshing, and I welcomed it freely.

After traveling upstairs, then through my bedroom, we entered my private bathroom and faced one another as we removed what little clothing we had on. I reached into the shower stall, turned on the water, and adjusted the temperature before l stepped in first.

Dasio came in right behind me and closed the glass door until the latch clicked. Then he backed up under the showerhead and allowed the water to massage his scalp.

"Come closer," he whispered as he licked his lips, then drew me near enough for our bodies to touch. Both of my breasts against his rock-hard abs were enough to perk up my nipples and have them craving attention. Needless to say, we were making love again.

This time it was more passionate. Dasio whispered his feelings to me throughout the shower session and had me in a space that I never wanted to leave.

When we finally stepped out of the shower and grabbed towels, I was still feeling euphoric. "Is this real?" I wondered aloud before I could catch myself. It was too late.

"You don't know?" Dasio teased as he towel dried my backside, then pinched my ass.

"Ouch!" I screamed.

"Did you feel that, *mamí*?"

"Yes!"

"Then know it's very real!" Dasio laughed before he gathered up his clothing and ran playfully out of the bathroom.

When I headed back into the bedroom, he was already dressed. He waved at me and walked out of the room. Soon as he got to the bottom of the stairs, he started yelling my name. "Constance! Constance!"

I stepped into the hallway. "What's wrong?" I called down the stairs.

"I'm hungry!"

"Okay. You want me to cook something?" I offered, really not wanting to.

"No, I was thinking about going out. You down?"

"Yeah, give me a few minutes to get dressed."

"A'ight. I'm gonna call and check on Carlos right quick while I'm waiting. Oh yeah. You got an extra toothbrush?"

"Yeah," I called. "There's a pack of them in the drawer down there in the guest bathroom."

"A'ight. Good looking out."

I stepped back into the bedroom and stood there, looking at myself in the mirror. That was the first time I ever actually liked what I saw. The reflection staring back at me was one of a strong, loving woman who was learning to accept herself, flaws and all.

Touching the wounds on my neck, I reflected on what took my innocence in the first place. That was a dark place that I never wanted to revisit, especially not now.

"Let me get ready," I sighed.

I took care of my personal business in a hurry and went downstairs to join Dasio. When I walked into the living room, he was on the sofa, dozing off. I didn't wanna disturb him, so I took the blanket and pulled it up over him.

"You ready?" he said, yawning, as he sat up. "That is, unless you wanna lay here and honey dip with me for a while."

"As much as I would love to, I'm starving. But can I get a rain check?"

"You don't even need one. I'll always be here for you, *mamí*."

His words melted my heart. They had me blushing so hard that I had to turn away from him.

"Come on with ya shy ass," Dasio teased as he took my hand and pulled me in for a kiss. "Damn, I can't get enough of them lips."

"Hush, and stop putting me on the spot," I whined, tired of hiding my face.

"So, you want me to stop complimenting you?"

"No, but when you do it and then look at me like that . . . damn!"

Now he was the one shying away. Yes, I took that opportunity to laugh at him.

"What? Did I get you with that one?" I asked him, chuckling.

"Yes, now come on," he laughed before dragging me out the door.

Breakfast was great, but the lovemaking when we got back to my place afterward was crazy. My body was finally loosening up, and I enjoyed every minute of it.

"It's five o'clock," I said and yawned as I hit the snooze on the alarm for the second time. "Your cell is going off too, Dasio."

He groaned. I shook him until he was fully coherent and got him to sit up and check his messages.

"It's Carlos. I have to meet him at the spot to help him with security."

"So, you won't be with me during the performance?" I asked as we left the bedroom.

"Nah, but you can stay backstage if you want. I'm sure you'll have a clear view of the musicians."

"Lydia too?" I asked as we walked down the stairs.

"Yeah, I'm sure it won't be a problem. This is my first time running his security staff, but you know Carlos won't mind. You and Lydia can meet us there. I'll make sure he puts your name on the list or leaves you guys some passes. However it works."

"Okay, then. I guess I'll see you there, then," I said, feeling a little down.

"Don't trip, *mamí*. I'll be near you the whole time."

"I don't wanna distract you," I answered as we headed toward the front door.

"You won't. I want you back there, so I can be your security too. You know I might have to beat some of your book fans off you."

"Stop playing, Dasio," I giggled.

"I'm serious. I'll see you tonight," he told me before opening the door, about to leave me all alone again.

"See you then," I said before he stepped outside and I closed the door behind him.

The moment he left, I snatched up my cell and dialed Lydia. She started in as soon as she answered.

"Girl, are you still with Dasio?"

"No, he just left."

"You mean he spent the night?"

"Yes." I giggled enough to make Lydia question me further.

"So, you're saying . . . ? No, I know you're not saying that, right, Connie?"

"What?"

"You know what I'm asking!" she cried happily.

"No," I lied with a sneaky giggle. "We just kicked it all night long."

"You love him, huh?"

"Yeah, I think I do," I confessed, butterflies fluttering in my stomach.

"Well, he better love you twice as much, because if he breaks your heart, I'm gonna break his fucking face!"

"Hush, heffa," I said jokingly.

"Hush hell! I'll fuck his little Puerto Rican fine ass up!"

"I think he loves me too."

"You think, or did he tell you?"

"He told me."

"Oh, bitch, shit! What the hell did I miss?"

Lydia sat on the phone for about ten minutes more, going on and on about what a cute couple Dasio and I made. She couldn't believe that I was in a real relationship. Quiet as I had kept it, neither could I.

"That's enough about me. What about you and Los?" I said, pivoting the conversation to her personal life.

When I asked her about it, she giggled but still insisted that they were just friends. I would just have to wait and see how that one played out.

"Okay, let me get the hell off the line and find me something to wear tonight," I announced.

"I'm about to come over and get dressed at your house. I'm too hyped to be by myself right now, and you know Mom is asking me a dozen questions about where we're going and who's gonna be there and how long we're gonna be out. I feel like a little-ass kid, knowing damn well we're grown-grown."

"Well, get your own place, Lydia. You have been working at the school district since you graduated high school. You make good money, and you need your space. You've been at your mom's since you and what's-his-face face broke up! What's the deal, boo?"

"I'm scared."

"You're *what*?"

"Hush! I'm scared! I don't wanna live alone."

"Shit, you are seriously tripping, Lydia! You just don't know the peace you get when you don't have to answer to anyone except to yourself. Just wait and see."

"Well, right now I'm not ready."

"Okay, I'm gonna leave ya ass alone for right now, but you need to think about it, girl. I mean seriously think about it."

I hung up with Lydia and chilled until she got here. I knew it was about to be a long night, and I was truly ready.

Chapter 20

Dasio Vazquez

The concert that night was crazy, and I had to chin check about four or five fools. By the time it was over, my fist was swollen, and I was tired as fuck.

"You look like you need a shower and some sleep," Constance observed as she palmed my head, then dropped her hand to my cheek. "I can see you tomorrow if you want."

"Hell, nah. We about to go eat and chill somewhere," I insisted. "Carlos should be out in a few. I already sent ya girl back there to check on him."

"For real?" Constance gasped, feeling happy for Lydia. "Will they let her back there?"

"Yeah, she has an all-access pass, just like the one I gave you."

"Does Carlos know?"

"Yeah, he gave it to me to give to y'all."

Constance couldn't even mask her excitement if she tried. I think she grinned so hard that her eyes began to water. Soon as I noticed, I teased her about it.

"I see when you love, you love hard. It doesn't matter if it's a friend or a lover."

"Yes, I do, but only those who are worthy." She winked at me.

"Oh, do I fit in that category?"

"Of course, Dasio," she said, flirting. "You're my man, ain't you? At least that's what you claimed to be."

"Damn straight, I'm yo' man," I boasted. "Now, let's get these muthafuckas up out of here so that we can bounce. I don't know where they're going, but they gotta get the hell up out of here."

Cal walked up behind us. "Don't worry about it, man," he said as he helped move the crowd. "We got it out here if y'all ready to roll."

My conscience was telling me to stay and help out, but once I saw Constance's sad eyes, I agreed to go ahead and leave after we rounded up Carlos and Lydia. "Come on."

After dapping up her brother Cal, who had come to work the gig, I laced my fingers with his sister's and went to the dressing room to check on my cousin. I had to clear the way just to make it to the door because the hall was thick with groupies. I kept Constance close. I could feel her clenching the waist of my jeans, making them sag more than they already were.

"I gotcha, *mamí*," I assured her as I reached behind me and pulled her closer. "Y'all need to clear out!"

I saw Chip, the big seven-foot bodyguard that was supposed to be keeping things under control. Shit, his ass was too busy trying to get some female's number.

"Ay, Chip!" I yelled, then whistled.

"What's up?"

"We ready to go, so these muthafuckas need to bounce!"

"I'm on it," he replied with a dumbass look on his face, then started ushering folks to the nearest exit.

When we reached Carlos's dressing room, I knocked, and then we must have waited a good five minutes while dude kept screaming, "Just a second!" before he finally opened the door. Instead of letting us in, he held his hand out and told us to give him five more minutes.

"Where's Lydia?" Constance asked just as Carlos closed the door. "Well, if she's not in there, where is she?"

After digging in her purse, Constance pulled out her cell and dialed Lydia. When Lydia didn't pick up, she dialed her again. This pattern continued as I just stood there and watched her, laughing to myself. I knew that her homegirl was in there with my cousin. I'd seen her ass run to the side when Carlos opened the door. I didn't say shit, though.

"Where is she, Dasio?" Constance asked, on the verge of tears.

I couldn't take the shit, so I was just about to tell her, but . . .

"Hey, y'all!" Lydia giggled as she came tiptoeing out of the dressing room, right behind Carlos. "He was trying to show me something. Gee whiz!"

Constance's expression went from surprised to happy. She eased on over to Lydia and nudged her, then whispered something in her ear.

"No!" Lydia laughed loudly. "You know better than that, girl!"

As we headed out to the car, I asked Constance about her plans for the night. Instead of her answering, her homegirl answered for her.

"We are going over to Connie's house to play some dominoes. What do y'all know about that? Dasio, they play dominoes over in Puerto Rico?"

"Girl, they play dominoes all over the world. That shit ain't just here on the mainland. I runs the table wherever I go!" I said, schooling her right quick.

"Yeah, let's go, so we can show them how the shit is done," Carlos interjected when we reached his ride.

"Wait! I drove my car," Lydia said, remembering at the last minute. "Connie rode with me."

"Just leave it here and I'll bring you back to get it in the morning." Carlos offered, causing us all to turn and look at him.

"In the morning, huh?" Lydia replied, clowning. "Oh, so where am I gonna be all night?"

"Don't worry about all that," Carlos laughed shamelessly. "Get ya ass in the car and ride."

"Oh, okay, then." Obeying, Lydia hopped in the passenger seat.

We bumped the music the entire ride to Constance's house. I scooted her close to me just so I could smell her sweet perfume. It was a scent that I wasn't familiar with, but that shit was intoxicating like a muthafucka. The more I inhaled, the more I wanted to be with her . . . alone.

That night we wound up kicking it hard at Constance's. Carlos and I ran them off the table after four games. After that, I was ready to chill with my girl. Carlos and Lydia were loud and were having a good time, but I wasn't feeling that shit. I was ready for some peace and quiet, so I was anxious to walk them out.

I finally started throwing hints at about 2:00 a.m., but it took until 4:00 a.m. for Carlos and Lydia to act like they were about to leave.

"I'll catch up with you tomorrow," I said while I gave my cousin some dap as we stood at the front door. Soon as I opened the door for him and Lydia, his cell began to go off.

"Who the hell is that at this time of morning?" I wondered out loud when my phone went off as well.

"It's Kadedra," Carlos and I both said in unison.

"It's gotta be Mom!" Carlos shouted, in a panic, and answered the call.

"I'm coming with you," I insisted as I grabbed my jacket. I gave Constance a kiss. "I'll call you as soon as I know what's going on."

"You two go," Lydia said. "I'll have Connie take me to my car later, but keep us posted, Los. I'll be praying that everything is okay."

The two of them hugged briefly, and we left. Carlos got off the phone but was still panicking, so I went ahead and drove to the house.

"What the fuck? I can't leave for a few hours without all hell breaking loose?" Carlos yelled.

"What did Kadedra say?"

"She said that someone was trying to come through Mom's window!"

"Did she see who it was?"

"From the description she gave, I'm sure it was Harrison! Let me catch that little muthafucka and it's on and crackin'!" he threatened. "She didn't go after him, because she didn't wanna leave Mom alone in the house by herself."

We couldn't get to my cousin's house fast enough! I was praying that we caught that muthafucka snooping around the property. I had something for his grimy ass. He just didn't know.

"You see that car creepin' with the lights off, cuz?" Carlos whispered as we parked across the street from his house.

I nodded.

We got out stealthily and sneaked up the driveway. When we got to the top of it, we bent down and peeked through the large bushes that ran along the side of the garage. It gave us a clear view of the back alley.

"Look. They parked, and someone just got out. You go around that side, and I'll go this way. If that's that nigga Harrison, I don't want his ass to get away!" Carlos huffed and got to moving.

I tried to be as quiet as I could be, but as soon as I stepped down on a branch, it cracked and made a loud sound. "Oh, shit!" I looked up and saw Harrison. Before he could flee, I caught his ass by the neck and threw him against the wall.

"Get the fuck off me!" he screamed like a little bitch.

"Carlos!" I yelled. "I got this muthafucka right here!"

As I held him, I punched him a couple of times in order to daze him a bit and calm him down.

"Get ya muthafuckin' hands off me, nigga!" he shouted.

"Settle ya punk ass down, before you get fucked up!" I threatened, getting more heated.

"You got that muthafucka?" Carlos yelled as he ran closer.

"Yeah!"

"Don't let him go!"

"I'm not."

Right then Harrison locked down on my arm with his teeth. The first thing that came to my mind was that he was infectious, so there was no way I was about to let him break the skin.

"Get the fuck off me, muthafucka!" I snarled, prying his mouth off my forearm while holding on to his shirt.

I instantly lost my grip, and his ass went running. While Carlos ran after him, I snatched my jacket off to check my arm. "Fuck!"

My ass was sweating bullets when I saw the teeth marks, but I quickly thanked God when I saw that his teeth hadn't penetrated my skin and caused it to bleed. I was ready to kill that muthafucka then.

Rushing to the street, I saw Carlos standing beside a red sedan. He was bending down, panting, like he was trying to catch his breath.

"That nigga got away! We gotta get that muthafucka before he does some more stupid shit. His ass is moving real reckless."

“Like biting a muthafucka!” I muttered.

“That nigga bit you?”

“Yeah, but I’m good. The skin didn’t break,” I explained as we ran back to the house to check on Auntie May. “I don’t know why he keeps coming around here. What the fuck does he want?”

“Money. That muthafucka needs some money to run. He ain’t got shit and don’ burnt every bridge the nigga don’ crossed,” my cousin replied while leading inside the house.

We into the kitchen.

“Look at this shit right here.” Carlos pointed to the broken glass. He began to clean it up. “Man, I’m not about to keep putting my mother through this shit. I was thinking about canceling all my shows and taking my mother to Puerto Rico to visit your mom. She’s been begging me to take her, and to be honest, I don’t know how much time she has left.”

Damn, I felt bad for my cousin, but I didn’t know what to say.

“I was thinking that we can all go and maybe even take Lydia and Constance. We need something to do while our moms are catching up and shit,” Carlos suggested, surprising the hell out of me. “I’ll pay for everything. You just run it by ya girl and her girl.”

I knew that the school Lydia worked at was on summer break, so she would be able to go, but I wasn’t so sure about Constance, though. Hell, I wasn’t so sure about going my damn self. I really didn’t want to deal with Carla. She was a bold bitch, and I knew she would start some shit with Constance on sight, and I wasn’t about to have that.

“Fuck it. I’ll call and run that shit by them now. How soon you talking about leaving?”

"I'm about to book that shit for tomorrow night. I'm gonna need a day to take care of all my business here. Is that cool?"

"Yeah, that's cool."

I left the kitchen and went to my room to dial Constance's number. "Damn. I hope she can go."

Chapter 21

Constance ("Connie")

"Heck, yeah! Are you serious?" I yelled into the phone at Dasio as I slapped Lydia on her arm.

"What?" she whispered. "What did he say? Can you let me in on the joy? Damn!"

"Hold on a sec," I whispered calmly into my cell and put it face down on my thigh. "They want us to go to Puerto Rico with them!"

"Who got money for that shit?"

"Carlos is paying for everything, girl! He wants you to come!"

"Are you fucking serious right now?" Lydia started crying real tears. "Hell yeah, I wanna go! When?"

I drew the phone back up to my ear, and before I could ask the question, Dasio was answering it. "Is tomorrow night too soon?"

"What?" I gasped. "Tomorrow night?" I repeated.

"Yes, let's go! You better not say no!" Lydia threatened with her fist. "I'm so not playin' with yo' ass right now!"

"I have to check my deadlines first, but I'm sure I can. The only catch is that I may have to take some editing work with me," I told Dasio. "Would that be a problem?"

"As long as you're there with me, I'm straight," Dasio replied, flirting. "Just pack your bag and be ready. You have today and tomorrow. I'm sure that's enough time to throw a few things in a suitcase, ain't it?"

"You are really funny, Dasio," I giggled. "I guess I'll see you tomorrow night, then."

"Wait, I'm gonna see you before then. I plan on taking you to dinner and a movie later. You know that flick with Taraji, *Acrimony*, started Friday."

I had honestly forgotten all about it, but I definitely wanted to see it. I quickly accepted the invitation and got off the line. I still had to take Lydia to get her car, come back, get some sleep, and then go back and pick her up to go shopping. I was getting tired just thinking about everything, but when I reminded myself that it was Puerto Rico we were visiting, I got pumped right back up.

"Passports!" I yelled. "How the hell are we gonna get one at the last minute?"

Lydia sank down into the sofa and began pouting. She was looking as if her whole world was crumbling around her. Her ass was on the verge of tears.

Then my cell went off. It was a text from Dasio, asking for our information for the plane tickets. Instead of returning his text, I called him back and explained my concerns about the passports. He told me that we didn't even need them. My forgetful ass hadn't remembered that Puerto Rico had been a territory of the United States since 1898!

"See? You have nothing to worry about," Dasio teased. "Just sit tight, and I'm about to send you all the info that you need."

I guessed it was meant to be. I guessed we were about to actually leave the US mainland. We were about to go to Puerto Rico.

Well, so much for the nap that I didn't get. Lydia was so damn amped that she was ready to go shopping right when the stores opened. We had been to ten stores already, and I was tired as hell and ready to go to bed.

"Damn. I gotta go pee!" I yelled as I pulled up to drop Lydia off at home.

"Well, I gotta go too, and you know we only have two bathrooms, and Mom ain't going for nobody using hers!" Lydia remarked as we raced up the stairs to her door.

Soon as she opened it, she nudged me and I bumped into the wall, just like when we were kids. My ass hit the floor so hard that I almost pissed my pants. I couldn't do shit but lie there and laugh at myself.

"Here y'all go!" Lydia's mother laughed as she helped me up. "Y'all so damn crazy!"

We both shook our heads and cracked up while we walked into the kitchen. Lydia's mother started in on me right away.

"I hear you're beginning to open up a bit, huh?"

"Whatcha mean?" I asked nonchalantly.

"Hush, child. You know exactly what I'm talking about. You know Lydia's ass can't hold water! Now, do you wanna share, or do I have to continue to pry?"

"No. I mean yeah. I mean, his name is Dasio," I replied shyly as I turned away.

"Dasio, huh? That sounds Hispanic or something. Is he from around here? Do I know his parents? How old is he? Does he have a job?"

"Whoa," I said and giggled.

"Well, forget all that. Does he love you? Better yet, do you love him?"

I took a deep breath and closed my eyes in order to allow my heart to speak. To my surprise, it was very easy to answer her.

"I feel like he loves me. He tells me as well as shows me."

"Do you love him, baby girl?"

"Yes, I truly do, ma'am, but we haven't known each other that long."

"Look at me for a second," she requested as she stepped closer. "You do, and you have!" Lydia's mom gasped suddenly and covered her mouth. When she dropped her hand, she whispered, "You have, and you did, didn't you?"

"What?" I stuttered, knowing good and damn well what she was asking me.

"Now, you are just like my daughter Connie. I have practically known you your whole life, and I have never ever seen that look on your face. If you don't wanna tell me, that's fine, but I know what I know."

"You know what? I know I didn't just hear what I thought I heard!" I exclaimed.

Lydia stared me down until I began laughing and crying at the same time. I hadn't really thought about letting Dasio into my heart, let alone my panties. It had just kind of happened. Thing was, I didn't regret it one bit. In fact, I was embracing it wholeheartedly.

"Mom, excuse us—"

"No, excuse *me*," I interrupted. "I gotta pee!"

I dashed off to the bathroom to handle my business. When I came out, Lydia's mother came over to me and hugged me tightly. "You deserve all the happiness coming your way, Connie."

"You're right, and I'm one hundred percent good with it. I promise," I whispered before releasing her.

"Well, that's all that matters," she replied, with a kiss to my cheek. "I love you, and I'll always be here for you. You remember that, baby girl."

"I will." I smiled and blew her a kiss while I walked to the door, with Lydia right on the back of my neck, damn near tripping me. "I love you too."

"Why didn't you tell me?" Lydia asked once we were outside.

"What?"

"Okay, here we go. I'm gonna let the shit ride for now, but when you get home and get settled, call me! I need to know the details!"

"A'ight." I nodded and then rushed to jump into my car.

"Yeah, don't forget we still have to go and get some swimsuits!" Lydia yelled. "I have to get at least three or so. I can't be on the beach or at the pool sporting the same shit every day. I gotta switch shit up, you know?"

Throwing my hand out of the car window, I bid my farewell and pulled onto the road. It was just starting to cool off, so I turned off the AC and enjoyed the night air.

Twisting the knob on the dash, I cut the radio on. "Oh, hell yeah," I screamed, then turned up the volume, so I could sing along with the lyrics of Monica.

"'Baby, that's just why I love you so much . . .'"

Singing loudly and not paying close attention to the road caused me to drive right by my turn. Now I had to go all the way to Lombard Street. I was mad at myself for being so careless, especially when I was exhausted and ready to get home.

"Who's this now?" I huffed when my cell rang. After picking it up off the passenger seat, I saw that it was Dasio calling.

"Hello?" I said.

"Did you forget about our dinner date, Constance?"

Actually, I had, but I wasn't about to miss out on a night with my bae. That right there was what I wasn't going to do.

Chapter 22

Dasio Vazquez

After all the bullshit, I was still about to make time to see Constance. She was the perfect distraction on a fucked-up day and the only thing that was keeping me sane.

I looked down at the floor as I stood in the middle of my room. "Damn, I can't believe I fell for her so fast! She done let me in on all her secrets, and she don't know shit about my past. I'm starting out all messed up! I killed a man! I killed my father, and I ain't told nobody," I uttered out loud, not knowing that my aunt was standing in the doorway.

"Boy, I know you're not in here beating yourself up about what happened in Puerto Rico!" she fussed, like she knew everything without me even telling her, as she came into my room and sat on the edge of the bed. "And before you even ask, yes, your mother told me all about it. It wasn't your fault, so stop blaming yourself."

"I can't help it. I took a life, Auntie May!" I replied, feeling even more upset. "That was a choice for God to make, not me. I could have gotten him up off her without killing him!"

"How do you know that? What if he would have shot and killed your mother? Would you feel better then?"

"No, but that was my father!"

"Ah, no, that wasn't your father! That man was no more your father than the man on the moon! That man you killed was a coldhearted son of a bitch that took your mother away from us and moved her way across the seas, where he could beat on her! I'm glad you killed him! I'm glad you killed that son of a bitch!" she screamed, with tears in her eyes.

Auntie May stumbled to her feet and fell into my arms. I held on to her as she cried on my chest.

"Your mother is all I have left, Dasio! I wanna see my sister!"

"Okay Auntie May, but what are you talking about? José wasn't my father? What do—"

"Yeah, Mom, what *are* you talking about?" Carlos interrupted. He was leaning against the doorframe.

"Well, I thought your mother would have told you by now, Dasio," Auntie May stammered, an "oops" look on her face, as she shrugged her shoulders.

I shook my head. "I have no idea what you're talking about."

Carlos and I sat his mother on the chair next to my bed and let her explain what she knew. By the expressions my cousin was displaying, I could tell he was just as shocked as I was.

"Your mother fell in love with Mason Crews when she was just a teenager. He was a handsome young man who swept her off her feet. Before we knew it, Mary was pregnant and so deeply in love that nothing else really mattered to her."

"So, what happened?" I asked, still in disbelief.

"Well, Dasio, that's when Mary found out that Mason was married and had a whole other family out in Beaverton."

"Say what?" I sputtered. "So, you're telling me that José isn't my father and my real father lives here?"

"Yes. Not only that, but you have two sisters and an older brother."

"Mom, why didn't you ever tell me about any of this?" Carlos huffed as he paced back and forth while I stood there in a daze.

"Because you have a big-ass mouth, that's why. Now, help me back to my room. I'm ready to go see my sister!"

"A'ight, Moms," Carlos replied. "We're leaving tomorrow night."

"Tomorrow night? You're taking me to see Mary?" she cried. "I get to see my sister?"

"Yes, Mom, we're going."

Their words trailed off in my mind while I tried to grasp everything that my aunt had told me. I really couldn't believe the shit. I had to call my mother.

When Carlos and my aunt left my room, I got my cell and had my mother on the line in a matter of seconds. "Mom, what's up?"

"Nothing. Dasio. How are you doing, baby?"

I dove right in. I had too many questions to play games and beat around the bush. "I'm good, Ma. I just wanna ask you about Mason Crews."

There was a brief silence, as I had expected there would be. I didn't push it, though. I waited for her explanation.

"I knew that May would tell you eventually, with her big mouth!"

"She shouldn't have had to, Mom. That's something you should have told me a long time ago."

"So, you hate me now, Dasio?" she asked and sniffled. "I love you, and I didn't know how to tell you! José was my only way out. I couldn't stand by and watch your father take care of another family and not claim you! I couldn't do it, Dasio, and I'm sorry!"

Tears rolled down my cheeks, and I didn't try to stop them. I really didn't know how I was feeling. I just knew the shit hurt, and I didn't blame my mother. My heart wouldn't let me.

"Ma, it's okay."

"No, it's not, Dasio! You're right! I should have told you, and I only pray that you can forgive me."

"I do, Ma, and I love you too."

After getting my mother to stop crying, I was able to hang up and pull my shit together. All the emotional shit was taking a toll on me, and I wasn't with it.

Right then I couldn't even think about finding my real father and confronting him. There was way too much on my plate, and with the attitude I had, I knew that the meeting would be nothing nice.

What I needed to do was clear my head. Hell, better yet, I needed to talk to Constance, so I dialed her up.

"Hey, *mamí*," I whispered into the phone as I tried desperately to erase from my mind what I had just learned. "Are you hungry?"

"You know I am, Dasio. Stop playing!" she giggled. "I'm starving."

I told Constance that I was feeling some type of way and didn't really want to go out. Right away she suggested that I come over to her house, but I had something different in mind. I wanted her to come over to my cousin's house.

The real reason why was to introduce her to my aunt. I knew that we were all about to go on a trip together, but I wanted them to meet beforehand. I honestly wanted to see how my aunt was going to take to her as well.

"So, you wanna come over here with me for a l'il while, baby?" I asked her.

"Okay, I was kind of tired, but—"

"You want me to pick you up? That way you don't have to drive, and I'll take you back home. If you feel uncomfortable at any time, we can leave. Deal?"

"Deal," Constance finally agreed.

"I'll be there in a few."

I set the phone down and listened to the voices in the other room. No one seemed to be yelling, so I took my time to go check shit out.

When I walked in, I saw Constance's brother Cal and a couple of other dudes in the kitchen, talking with Carlos. They were taking care of last-minute business before we left for Puerto Rico.

"Hey, what's up, Dasio?" Cal greeted me with a firm handshake and a pound, then pulled me aside. "I heard ya seeing my little sis. Is it serious?"

"I'm hella serious about her and hoping she's feeling the same way, bruh," I answered honestly.

"Well, you know how big brothers are about their little sisters, right?"

"Yeah, trust and believe I know," I replied, thinking about a few scuffles I had got in behind fucking with someone's little sister. "I ain't tryna go there. I love that girl."

"You what?" Cal choked on his drink, then quieted down. "You tell her that shit?"

"Yeah. What's wrong with that?"

"And she's cool with that shit . . . so soon?"

"Yeah. She says she loves me too," I answered hesitantly. I wasn't trying to start no shit, but when it came to Constance, things were a little different.

"Oh, hell nah!" Cal shouted with a big-ass grin. "Man, if you fuck this up! Man, if you fuck this up!"

Cal repeated himself a few more times before he gave me a hug. Right then I knew it had to be behind the tragedy that had happened with Constance. He just didn't know that I wasn't about to let shit happen to her. Shit, I would die trying to protect her.

Carlos hurried over to us to see what the commotion was. "Y'all straight?"

"Yeah, we're straight!" Cal assured me with a laugh. Then he joined the others back at the kitchen table, leaving me alone with my cousin.

"Damn. What was that about?" Carlos said, his voice barely above a whisper.

"Nothing . . . Just know that everything is cool."

"Are you sure? Because you know how I get down. I can handle shit right the fuck now!" Carlos whispered as he held his shirt up and revealed his chrome handgun tucked in his waistband.

"Nah," I told him emphatically. "Put that shit down. Everything is cool. Trust me, Los. Now I'm about to scoop Constance up and pick up some food. You want something?"

"Yeah, pick up Lydia too." He winked before running his ass back over to the kitchen table.

I swear he was a big-ass kid when it came to that chick. Damn, and to think I was sprung.

"I'm outside," I informed Constance through the cell as I sat in the car, trying to find the perfect song to play while I had her to myself.

"I'm coming," she sang before hanging up and prancing down the stairs, looking finer than a young Vanessa Williams.

Her hair was down and was all bouncing and shit. She had my third leg inflating, and I couldn't do a damn thing to stop it.

"Hey, beautiful," I greeted as I reached over and opened the car door for her.

"Hey, Dasio." She blushed.

"Why are you still acting shy around me, baby?"

"I don't know," she giggled as she climbed in the passenger seat. "Because I always feel like I'm on the spot."

"You are always on the spot when you're with me, *mamí*," I teased her, with a rub to her thigh. "My eye is always on you."

"Stop," she ordered, laughing.

After turning up the music in hopes of loosening her up, I held on to her hand and gave her a wink. "Let me stop messing with you. I see you can't take all the compliments."

"Whatever," she giggled and rolled her eyes. "Stop if you want to."

"Never that," I promised before I drew her hand to my mouth and kissed it while inhaling the fresh scent of the Nivea lotion that softened her skin. "Now, what do you have a taste for?"

"Huh?"

"I mean *food*," I said, putting Constance on the spot again.

"Real funny, Dasio!"

Once we stopped laughing, we decided on pizza and salad. I had Constance call and order delivery while we picked up her best friend. Then we drove to Carlos's.

"Who's over here?" Lydia asked me as we pulled up to my cousin's house.

"Oh, that's Cal!" Constance shouted when her brother came out the door with the other guys.

The second I stopped, she got out and rushed Cal. He met her halfway, and they hugged each other tightly. The way they interacted showed me that they were very close siblings, and I respected that. I respected anyone that had mad love for my girl.

"Well, I'll see you later, Cal," Constance yelled as we walked into the house. The pizza man was right behind us.

Carlos got the food and paid the man while I escorted Lydia and Constance into the kitchen. They both went and took a seat on the stools that were positioned at the faux-marble countertop.

"Where's the powder room?" Constance asked, talking all proper. "I want to wash my hands."

I walked her through the living room to the hallway and pointed it out. She stood there looking at me funny.

"You okay, or you want me to wait right here?" I teased her.

"You are real funny, Dasio!" she answered. "I think I can find my way back to the kitchen just fine."

Once I saw Constance hit the light and close the door behind her, I returned to the kitchen to find Lydia and Carlos already grubbing. "Y'all greedy asses couldn't even wait."

"Sho' couldn't!" Lydia replied, with a mouth full of salad.

I was going over to the cabinet to grab a couple of plates when all of a sudden I heard the sound of breaking glass and then Constance screaming. Carlos and I both jumped up, thinking that his dumbass cousin Harrison had broken into the house again, but when we got to the living room, it was something else entirely. It was Constance.

She was standing there with bloody hands, having broken a picture frame. I immediately rushed over to her, but she was shaking so hard and I couldn't comfort her.

Quickly jumping into action, Lydia pushed me out of the way, held on to her friend, and rocked her. "What is it? What is it, Connie?"

Constance cried and cried until finally she pointed down at the broken glass on the floor. "It's him! That's the one that raped me! That's Harrison!"

My nerves went from zero to a million as I pulled Constance away from Lydia and held on to her. "Don't worry about shit, baby! I won't let a damn thing happen to you!" I promised as I stood there, shedding tears with her. "This muthafucka will die, and I will see to it!"

Lydia and Carlos left the living room and gave us some time alone. That was all I needed to plan my next move.

Chapter 23

Constance ("Connie")

As soon as I got Dasio alone, I questioned him about Harrison. At that point, I didn't know who to trust.

"All this time that's the muthafucka you were talking about? Carlos's cousin? The one who has HIV?" I quizzed, sniffling.

"Yeah, I had no idea that was the dude from your past, Constance. That just makes me wanna fuck him up even more."

My stomach began turning with just the thought of Harrison having the virus. I was so scared to bring it up because I didn't know what the hell Dasio was thinking. Instead of delaying or beating around the bush, I decided to put it out there in the open.

"I don't know how you may be feeling about the whole situation, Dasio," I whispered as he stood there and held me in his arms.

"Whatcha mean?"

"About Harrison having the virus," I said.

Dasio pulled back a little and looked me right in the face, silently asking me if I was worried about this. I shook my head no. Then I confessed that I had taken medical tests seven years in a row to make sure I hadn't contracted any diseases during the rape.

"Well, if it makes you feel any better, I got checked too. I honestly hadn't thought about it until they made me get tested for the last real job I had right before I left Puerto Rico," Dasio revealed. "Even though it came back negative, that wait gave me a whole lot to think about."

"Yeah, when you sleep with one person unprotected, you're sleeping with everyone that person slept with unprotected. It just goes on and on."

"You're so right, but let's not talk about all that right now," Dasio suggested. "We have a trip to go on tomorrow night. You still feel like going?"

"Yes, we're going!" Auntie May shouted from the kitchen. "We're not gonna let that fool Harrison ruin a doggone thing! I'm going to see my sister! Hell, I'm going with you guys or without you! Kadedra will take me! Won't you, Kadedra?"

Dasio and I began to laugh at Auntie May. She was so funny and so full of spunk. I couldn't believe that her time on earth was limited. She seemed so healthy for her age. Her fair skin was barely wrinkled, and her hair was still medium brown, without a lick of gray. You could easily mistake her for someone in her forties.

"Yes, I still wanna go, especially since we don't need passports to travel there!" I smiled as I looked around the room. "But right now, I think . . . I think that I just wanna go home. I don't feel comfortable here with Harrison on the loose."

"I don't blame you." Dasio comforted me with a brief hug and grabbed his keys. "I'll take you right now."

I wanted to check on Lydia before I left, but by that time she and Carlos were shut in his bedroom. *Should I? Nah, they might be busy,* I thought. After debating for a few seconds more, instead of knocking on the bedroom door, I decided to hit her cell to tell her to come out for a minute.

Okay, Lydia quickly texted back.

Feeling satisfied, I put my phone in my handbag and walked behind Dasio to the kitchen. By then, everyone was there.

All eyes shifted to me immediately. I felt on the spot, so I began speaking.

"Hey, y'all. Sorry about that," I said, apologizing for my loud outburst.

"There ain't no need to be sorry! Shit, that fool Harrison needs to be the person sorry!" Auntie May fussed.

"Mom, calm down," Carlos said. "Kadedra, can you help her back into her bedroom?"

"I don't need help!" his mother barked, then cut her eyes sharply. "I'm going right now. All I need is a little rest before our big trip tomorrow! Y'all better be ready!"

We all laughed and waited for her to disappear before we began a conversation. Carlos spoke first.

"So, what's up?"

"I'm about to take Constance home," Dasio informed them.

"You want me to come with you, Connie?" Lydia offered.

"No, it's okay. Dasio is gonna stay with me. Ain't you?"

"You already know." He nodded, with a smile, then gently grabbed me by the hand. "I'm gonna take good care of her, Lydia."

"Maybe I should just stay here," Lydia mused, giving Kadedra the "stank face" as she came back into the kitchen.

Lydia then turned her cold stare on Carlos. He seemed to know what was up right away and insisted that Lydia stay with him.

Next thing I knew, Kadedra smirked, gave us all a dirty look, and drifted off to the back of the house. Now, I didn't quite understand what was going on, but I was damn sure going to ask Lydia about it as soon as I had the opportunity.

"Come on, *mamí*," Dasio urged.

He led me to the door after we said our farewells. After we went outside and walked to his ride, Dasio paused and gazed over me. I felt him staring, so I looked up over the top of his car at him.

"What is it?" I asked.

"You know I love you, girl." Dasio smiled bashfully. "This shit is like a whirlwind romance novel or some shit."

"I love you too, but tell me, how would you know about that?"

"Shit. I may not write, but I damn sho' read," he explained as he stared at me with passion in his eyes.

I loved witnessing such an expression on his face. It truly touched my heart.

Puckering up my lips, I blew him a kiss. "Muah."

"Nah, come here and give me the real thing."

"Nah, you come over here and get it," I insisted teasingly.

Dasio rushed around the car, embraced me, then picked me up off my feet before giving me a bomb-ass kiss that had me gasping. The way his tongue caressed mine while we engaged in a lip-lock had me shivering. I was ready to take his ass right there, and I probably would have if I hadn't heard footsteps approaching.

Dasio must have heard them, too, because like clockwork, he placed his body in front of mine and drew his gun. He immediately aimed it in the direction from which the noise came.

"Whoa!" the jogger yelled, throwing his hands in the air, hoping to avoid a possible piece of hot lead.

"Oh shit! My fault!" Dasio said, apologizing, and quickly placed his heater in the back of his waistband.

The distraught jogger nodded and sprinted off without a second thought. He left nothing but a trail of dust.

"Damn, I gotta put that nigga in the dirt! I'm not gonna be around here walking on fucking eggshells . . . looking over my shoulder every five seconds!" Dasio snapped.

"How the hell do you think I've felt all these years?" I asked in a low tone. "Now it's even worse, because he's *here*."

No matter how hard I tried to shake the terrified feeling that occupied my entire being, I couldn't. All the martial arts classes in the world couldn't prepare me to face Harrison again.

"I don't give a fuck where that nigga is! He just better know that when I catch his ass, it's over!"

"Let's just go, please," I begged, still feeling shaken up and a little on edge.

Dasio opened the car door and helped me in. Once I was situated, with my seat belt buckled, I noticed that he was still standing over me. "What is it?"

"You don't ever have to feel scared when you're with me. I'm not gonna let anybody fuck with you!"

"I know, Dasio, but all this just caught me totally off guard."

"Trust me, I'm just as surprised as you are."

After giving me another kiss, Dasio told me that he understood exactly where I was coming from. Although his words comforted me, they didn't stop me from worrying. The only thing that could do that was putting Harrison . . . six feet under!

Chapter 24

Dasio Vazquez

I hit the switch and cracked the window a bit to get some fresh air. It was warm but windy as we entered the highway. The gusts were powerful enough to rock the car a bit and shake my girl up even more.

To try to comfort her, I reached over and rubbed her shoulder, then touched her chin. Constance glanced at me and forced a grin.

The entire ride to her house, I paid close attention to the traffic in front and in back of us without being too obvious. From now on, I didn't put anything past Harrison. My shit was on "high alert" for real!

"Here we are," I sighed as I prepared to get out first and secure the perimeter.

Opening my door, I did a quick scan of the area. I hopped out, then went around to her side to let her out. With every step we took, I closely watched every angle up until we reached the entryway. I honestly didn't think Harrison knew where Constance lived, but I wasn't taking any chances with that shit.

"Lock that door behind you, *mamí*," I requested as I stepped inside her place.

I spent the next five minutes checking all the rooms. When I entered the living room, I found Constance seated on the sofa. I observed the funny look on her face.

“What? You think I’m overreacting, huh?” I asked.

“No, I think it’s rather sweet,” she replied, flirting with her eyes, as she stood up and came near me.

Slowly drawing her into my arms, I reminded her how much she meant to me. Even though it was out of my norm, it felt good to admit my feelings and be able to be real about them.

Rubbing my palms across her skin, I felt the goose bumps that were slowly rising. I caressed her shoulders, back, and arms until the goose bumps disappeared.

“I’m about to take a shower and get something comfortable on,” Constance informed me. “You think you can join me and maybe, uh, wash my back or something?”

Now, my girl knew good and damn well where that shit would lead, and I wasn’t sure about taking it there. With all the memories of the fucked-up shit that Harrison had done, I didn’t think that she was in a good headspace to engage in any sexual activities right then. Not that I would deny her, because if she asked, then she definitely would receive.

“Come on, bae,” she purred, then smiled seductively.

With no hesitation, I followed her into the bathroom and fulfilled her request, but when we got out of the shower and it came time to go all the way I paused that shit casually by taking the towel and drying her body.

To shift the mood a bit, I mentioned the trip. I wanted to know if she was really feeling up to going.

“So are you sure you want to go to Puerto Rico tomorrow, baby?” I asked as we held each other without a stitch of clothes on.

My shit was standing right up, poking her right in the gut. I was doing everything in my power to try to get that muthafucka to go down, including thinking about football.

There wasn't a distraction in the world that could keep Constance from noticing my erection. Shit, she hurried to take advantage of the situation and locked her warm palm right onto it and began to caress it.

"Damn!" I chanted.

"Yes, that's just what I need right now," she said, smiling. "Oh, and some of this right here too."

Gently easing her hand away, I tried to downplay it with a laugh. That shit did nothing but make her ass mad.

"What the hell is wrong, Dasio?" she snapped.

"What?"

"What my ass! Every time I touch you like that, you get to scooting your ass away! What the fuck is it?"

Constance's attitude threw me a bit, because I had never seen her act like that. I hurried up and tried to calm her ass down by holding on to her arms.

"It's just that —"

"It's just that what?" she barked, cutting me off. "Why? because Harrison raped me and now he has HIV? Is that why you don't wanna make love to me? I swear, I thought we already talked about that!"

Now she was crying, and it made me speechless. That shit was the last thing on my mind, but she wasn't trying to hear me.

"Fuck it! Fuck the trip, and you know what? Fuck you too, Dasio!"

Constance snatched away from me and rushed to the closet, butt naked. I followed her into the bedroom and headed over to the bed. Seconds later she stepped over to me and threw a document in my face.

"I already told you this shit, but here, here you go! I tested negative again for the shit just last month, and I haven't been with anyone, unprotected, since the rape, and that's been many years!"

Standing there fully exposed, I dropped the paper without even reading it. The fucked-up thing was that she actually had me in my damn feelings. No other woman had ever done that to me.

"What the fuck are you doing standing there, lookin' at me like that?" Constance snapped as she grabbed a thin light blue cotton T-shirt and pulled it up over her head. "Don't act like that wasn't exactly what you were thinking."

"Whoa! I don't know where the hell that shit came from, but it couldn't be further from the truth." I sighed and rubbed my head as I sat down on the edge of the bed and snatched up the sheet to cover my lower half. "To be honest, I was worried about you having that shit that Harrison did to you on your mind."

Freezing in her tracks, Constance dropped her jaw and covered her mouth. "I don't know what the hell is wrong with me."

I gestured her to me. When she reached me, I pulled her onto my lap.

"Just like I thought. The Harrison shit is bugging you more than you realize."

Constance squeezed me tightly as I held her. I could feel her warm tears trickling down my back, and my heart went out to her. That was my girl, and when she was hurting, I was hurting.

At that moment, I sat there and promised myself that I would lay Harrison down on sight. As soon as we got back from our trip, dude was as good as dead!

Chapter 25

Constance ("Connie")

My ears tingled as Dasio's cell continued to go off. While he slept peacefully, I forced my eyes open and slid my body upward into a seated position.

"Babe, you hear your phone?" I whispered as I reached my arm over him and grabbed it. "Babe, it's Carlos, and he's sent a bunch of text messages!"

"He's probably just bugging us about making it to the airport on time, *mamí*. Read the messages just to make sure, though."

Dasio rolled over and laid his head onto my lap as I scrolled through the first few texts. Each one was worse than the other.

"What the hell?" I muttered. My heart pounded heavily as I adjusted myself to get more comfortable. As I opened my mouth to speak, my voice failed me for a moment. I collected myself. "Dasio, babe, we have to get up and get dressed right now!" I said as calmly as possible.

"We're not gonna miss the flight, baby."

"Yes, yes, we are."

"No. it's still early."

"Dasio, babe, it's your aunt May . . . She's . . . she's . . ."

"What? She's what?"

I didn't answer him, because I was trying to read the rest of the messages so that I could get the whole story. I guess my silence threw Dasio into a panic.

He immediately sprang to his feet and started searching frantically for his clothes. He couldn't stop saying that it had something to do with Harrison.

"Wait!" I insisted as I scrolled through a couple more texts. "Carlos says they're all up at Emanuel Medical Center. Auntie May apparently had a stroke."

"Is she okay?"

Dasio shot me a dozen additional questions all in one breath. As I answered each of them, I threw on an item of clothing. I was trying to catch up with him.

"Constance, baby . . . are you ready?" he called a few minutes later.

I was in the bathroom. "Brushing my teeth!" I mumbled with a mouth full of toothpaste.

"I'll be out in the car, waiting. I need to get my cousin on the phone."

While Dasio called Carlos, I got Lydia on the line. I knew she had to know what was going on, and I couldn't wait to get the details from my man.

"Why haven't you called me!" I asked, feeling as if she was leaving me out of the loop.

"Girl," she whispered, so low that I could barely hear her, "I've been trying to help hold Carlos up. He's losing it, Connie! Him and his mom are really close."

"How is she?"

"She's stable now, but she gave us quite the fuckin' scare!"

"What happened?"

"Carlos and I went out for drinks and dancing last night. When we got back, he went in her room to check on her. Connie, I'm telling you, girl, when I heard that scream for help . . . ! My whole body locked up for about five seconds, and then I flew in there, right behind him."

"Where was Kadedra?"

"She was stuck in the damn bathroom! She didn't come out until we already had emergency services on the line. I was so irritated that I sent her ass on her way! What the hell do we need her for? Shit! She ain't never gotta come back!"

"Don't trip, boo, and tell Carlos we're on our way. I'll see you in a few minutes." I rushed my words as I hurried out of the bathroom.

When I hung up, I could hear Dasio shouting my name from outside. He had left the front door wide open, so his voice carried.

Snatching up my charger, I quickly stuffed it in my handbag before hurrying outside to the car. "Sorry it took me so long."

"It's okay. Carlos told me that Aunt May is awake now. He's in with her, and she's doing good."

Feeling relieved, I sighed, said a quick prayer, and gave thanks that Dasio's aunt was still with us. *Amen!*

We got to the hospital fairly swiftly. Dasio parked in the first available spot, and we went inside to find Carlos and Lydia.

"Hey, Los," Dasio said sadly when we hit the corner on our way to the waiting room and ran into him and Lydia. The guys embraced while my friend and I stepped to the side to give them some privacy.

"I'm so glad you're here, Connie!"

"Why? What's wrong?"

"Girl, I was stressed! I thought she was gonna die—"

"Hush, Lydia! Don't even say it! Carlos's mother is gonna be just fine! You see she's a feisty woman! She's much stronger than that stroke! Just wait and see!"

I comforted Lydia with words, then dried her tears best I could with a tissue, and before long, she was smiling again. It brought joy to my insides.

"Wait, where are the guys?" I wondered aloud when I realized that they had disappeared.

Lydia and I had been so engrossed in conversation that we didn't realize that Dasio and Carlos had gone in to see Auntie May. We headed into the waiting room and took a seat, and about ten minutes later, they both reentered the waiting room.

"What's up?" I asked first while rising to my feet.

"Mom is gonna be fine," Carlos announced.

"After she stops flipping out on the doctors and nurses about them making her miss her flight to see my mama!" Dasio interjected. "They had to kick us out to sedate her just to get her to calm down!"

"Wow, really?" I gasped as I envisioned Auntie May going off on the staff.

"She didn't flip the script until the doctor told her that she couldn't travel for at least several months," Carlos noted.

"What?" Lydia exclaimed. "I know she's upset! She really wants to see her sister!"

"Dasio, you think your mom can come here instead?" I suggested, unsure if I was overstepping my boundaries.

"Nah. I don't even wanna call her and get her upset. Besides, my mama ain't been here since I was a kid. She's stubborn."

"It's okay," Carlos said. "I'll just call and postpone our trip. Don't worry, though. We're going! My mother is gonna see her sister before she leaves this world, because this shit right here . . . this shit right here . . . is a fuckin' eye-opener for real! You never know when it's your time to go!"

Carlos's words had us all reflecting. We stood there in complete silence until a doctor approached our little group and confirmed May's condition.

Yes, she was expected to be okay, and no, she wouldn't be able to travel anytime soon. . . .

Chapter 26

Dasio Vazquez

The next several months went by faster than anticipated. During that period, not only did Auntie May's health improve drastically, but we didn't hear a peep from Harrison. That was a great thing.

As far as everyone else was concerned, we were all busy working. For every gig Carlos had, I brought home mad bank for just being head of security.

Constance had been busy signing two new authors while completing an Urban Romance trilogy in a short amount of time. I was truly proud of her.

Now, as far as slick-ass Carlos and Lydia went, they had been dating on the low. I didn't know how they thought they were under cover with their shit, but I knew. . . . Oh yeah, I knew!

I wasn't sure if Constance knew, because she hadn't been going over to Carlos's house much since we found out about her connection to Harrison. As for me, I spent all my nights with my girl, but I still went over to Carlos's at least once a day to check on Auntie May.

I swear, every time I went over there, Lydia was there. Just like she was when Constance and I got over to the house to get my suitcases for our trip to Puerto Rico, which we were finally about to go on.

“What’s up with you two?” I questioned as my eyes traveled from Carlos to Lydia.

My cousin just smiled as the women went into the den and we walked past them and headed to the kitchen. This dude didn’t say a word. Like, was he just going to ignore my question?

“Did you hear me, *primo*? What’s up with you and Lydia?”

“Whatcha mean?” Carlos laughed and bit into the apple he was holding.

“Damn! Is y’all together or what?”

“Well, she’s does stay over here all the time and helps me with Mom. And, uh, I’m really diggin’ having her around,” Carlos said, beating around the bush.

“Never mind. Damn, Los!” I smirked as Constance and Lydia joined us in the kitchen.

“What y’all talkin’ about?” Lydia asked Carlos while moving all up on him.

“We was talkin’ about you,” my cousin answered honestly and kissed her lips.

“What about me?”

“Dasio wanted to know what was up with us.”

“You do not have to answer that, Los! Dasio! Don’t be all up in their business like that!” Constance barked as she laced her arm with mine and tugged me closer to her side.

“There’s something really serious going on between those two!” Auntie May chimed in as she strolled slowly into the kitchen. She went to the fridge to get some orange juice. As she poured it into a glass, she enlightened us with her observations. “You know, I hear y’all laughing and playing all the time, but when either of you need something, the other is always there. You think I don’t see, Carlos?”

"What are you even talkin' 'bout, Mom?" he said, downplaying his mother's truths.

"You can act dumb all you want, but I know you're smart, son!" Auntie May remarked. She sipped her juice, making a slurping noise. "I just hope you were smart enough to schedule our flight to Puerto Rico! You know my doctor gave me the okay today at my appointment. Tell 'em, Lydia!"

"He did say we could leave as early as tomorrow. I knew you were gonna be busy, so I just went ahead and booked all the tickets with the credit we already had." Lydia smiled, then kissed Auntie May on the cheek. "You know I gotcha."

"See! That's my girl right there!" Auntie May laughed. "Now, when do we leave?"

"Tomorrow night," Lydia answered.

"Damn, how much notice was you gonna give us?" Constance muttered, her eyes bucked out.

"Well, Carlos doesn't have a show for another week. Connie, you can take your work with you," Lydia said. "And me, well, you know I'm my own boss now, with my new educational employment agency online business and all, so I can roll with it," she bragged as she sat down at the counter and swung her feet while twirling on the stool.

"You had that all figured out, huh?" Carlos smiled as he embraced Lydia and kissed her cheek.

"Yes, I even have your mother's bag packed, your bag packed, and mine too!"

"She's on it!" Constance giggled as she took me by the arm. "I guess we need to go to my house and get our things together, too, huh?"

"Yes!" I agreed.

We said our farewells and headed out the door. I was ready to make love to my girl and put her ass in a light coma while I took care of some last-minute shit.

Seeing that I stayed up all night putting it on Constance, I was exhausted when the morning came too quickly for my taste. I kept my eyes closed as I lay there listening to the birds chirping through the partially open window beside me. The birdsong was right in tune with the vibrations on the nightstand caused by my Note 8.

It was already ten o'clock, and Carlos had been blowing up my cell for hours. I was so out of it that I couldn't even budge to answer the call.

"Get up, sleepyhead," Constance ordered, razzing me, as she handed me a plate of fried potatoes, eggs, toast, and crispy bacon right along with my phone. "We have a long day ahead of us and an even longer flight tonight."

"Damn, I know." I yawned as I sat up. I checked my messages while eating at the same time.

The first texts were from Carlos. He wanted to make sure that Constance and I were still going to take the trip. I hit him back and told him that we would meet him at the airport.

Not only was Carlos's house out of the way in terms of the airport, but I was still trying to avoid taking Constance over there as much as possible given that Harrison was her perpetrator. It was apparent to me that the rape was fresh on Constance's mind every time we entered my cousin's house.

I wanted to do whatever I could to eradicate those memories and replace them with new ones. It may have sounded impossible to some, but deep down I knew that I had to try.

"Let me shoot this shit and get ready," I mumbled as I hit the keys on my cell.

We're coming, Los.

Carlos texted me right back. A'ight, cuz.

After I sent Carlos a final text, I saw that I had several text messages from Carla. She had been sweating me for months but had stopped after I cussed her ass out the last time. That was over three months prior.

"Now she wanna start up again?" I mumbled under my breath as I wondered what the hell she wanted. I open the first text.

Vas a ser papá!

"I'm going to be a father? What the hell? Damn!" I whispered when I read the message. "Is this bitch serious right now?"

Carla then sent me ultrasound pictures, saying that *we* were about to have a little girl. That bitch was crazier than I thought.

I placed my fingers on the screen and spread them apart to enlarge the photo I was staring at. I read the due date printed on the photo and calculated back in my head. "Oh, hell nah!"

"What's up, baby?" Constance asked, startling me enough to fumble my phone and drop it.

"Nothing. That nigga Carlos is crazy!" I laughed as I lied straight through my damn teeth.

"Oh, I can imagine. Lydia has called me twenty times to see if I'm going. They are too much!" Constance giggled and went toward the bedroom door. "I'm going downstairs to clean up. Do you need anything else, babe?"

"No, I'm good, *mamí*. Thanks."

When she left the room, I picked my cell back up and called Carla. That bitch answered on the first ring, as if she was sitting there waiting for me to call her trick ass back.

"I knew that would make you call me!"

"Miss me with all yo' bullshit, ma," I whispered. "I ain't fucked yo' ass raw since that pregnancy scare the last time, and that was nine months ago."

"I'm nine months! Due any day, *papí*!"

"Stop fucking lying, Carla! That ultrasound picture you sent me said your expected due date is in two months! That means you're only seven months. Damn, a nigga can count!"

"Fuck what you're talking about, *papí*! You and I are having a baby, and you are gonna take care of us!"

"Bitch, lose my number and forget you ever knew me!"

"Is that a fucking threat, Dasio?"

"No, that's a fuckin' promise!"

"Well, if you don't believe me, ask your mother!" she shouted. "Ask your mother! She believes me!"

"She betta not!"

I hung up and put the bitch on call block. I knew that would only delay shit for a minute. I would just wait and deal with her when I touched down in Puerto Rico. Not a second sooner.

Chapter 27

Constance ("Connie")

When Dasio's cell was going off nonstop, I let it get the best of me. At first, I figured it was just Carlos calling, but after I confirmed with Lydia that both Dasio and I were going on the trip, Dasio's phone was still vibrating.

Fuck it, I thought as I tiptoed my ass to go and take a peek at his cell, which he'd left on his nightstand.

Who the fuck is Carla?

Hurrying to exit the messenger app, I pressed the button twice and set Dasio's cell back on the nightstand. Curiosity was killing me, but I was able to refrain from taking a second peek until after breakfast. I waited for him to get in the shower.

"Sneaky ass," I mumbled when I noticed Carla's messages had been deleted but the one that he sent her hadn't. I read it slowly.

Bitch, it's over. Whatever bullshit ya tryna start, miss me with it and tell that to the next nigga. I moved on with my life, and I suggest you do the same. On the real.

Right then it clicked. I remembered who Carla was. Dasio had mentioned that he had an ex back home by that name. It had to be her ass.

"Oh, bitch, please don't start none," I sang softly to myself as I put Dasio's cell right back where I had got it.

I knew there was going to be some shit if I ran into her when I got to Puerto Rico. If so, I would be more than ready if she disrespected me. Whatever she had with Dasio didn't have shit to do with me, and I prayed the girl realized that before stepping to me sideways.

Damn, I should just ask him about it.

As I stood there thinking about it, I twisted my lips. I happened to turn around just in time to capture a vivid image of Dasio's banging-ass body through the shower door. Every muscle was well defined, even the one between his legs.

The temptation to join him was overwhelming. I tried to fight it, but as always . . . it got the best of me.

"Dasio, did you remind Carlos to grab the bag you left at his house?" I asked as we left the bedroom hours later.

"Yes, baby, everything is taken care of, luggage, airline tickets, rental car, and hotel reservations. Am I forgetting anything?" Dasio said before he kissed me and nearly dragged me to the front door. "Did you turn off everything and lock up?"

I didn't entertain his sarcastic question. Instead, I just gave up a little tongue action and pulled my keys out. After we stepped outside, I locked both the top and bottom locks. "There!"

As we got into the waiting rideshare, Dasio's cell chimed. He ignored it, but whoever it was called right back.

"Get it, bae. It might be important."

Yeah, I was fucking with him, because I had a good feeling it was his ex-girlfriend Carla calling. I was just hoping that Dasio would bite and answer the call in front of me.

"It's probably Carlos checking to see where we are," Carlos informed me.

"Why, when we're running an hour ahead of schedule?"

His cell rang again, and this time he retrieved it from his jacket pocket. After he looked at the screen, he showed it to me. "I forgot all about this gig I set up for Carlos while we're in Puerto Rico. That shit is gonna be a real payday. Those niggas jumped at the opportunity to have him as the main act for the Urban Music Festival, which is taking place while we're there."

"Oh, that's great, baby." I smiled and clenched his arm. "I hope we have something planned every day. I wanna see where you grew up, where you went to school and, of course, your old neighborhood," I said and watched his facial expressions.

"We can do whatever you want, *mamí*. This trip is for you too."

"What about Carlos and Auntie May?"

"Well, Auntie May is gonna be busy with my mother, and Carlos will have Lydia to keep him occupied. Trust me, we will do some family things together, but we will have plenty of alone time too. I will make sure of it," Dasio replied. "After these flights, though, your ass is gonna wanna spend the first day sleeping."

Oh, hell nah! So you can go see that Carla bitch! I hissed silently. I actually said, "I hope not. I can sleep when I get back home."

We began to talk about family, and that was when Carlos called Dasio. Right after his cell rang, mine did too.

"What, Lydia? We're already at the airport right now," I answered. We had arrived at PDX and were pulling into the extended-stay parking lot.

"Okay, I was just calling because Carlos is scaring me about getting on the plane. He's over here talking about Hurricane Harvey and Hurricane Irma! Shit, now he got me nervous about flying right along with his ass!" Lydia confessed in a whisper.

"Girl, didn't you think of that when we planned the trip?" I said as our driver pulled to a stop. "You know all those storms are over. Some of the island is without power, but not where we're going. Everything is gonna be fine."

"Are you sure?"

"Yes, and you knew all this before," I replied with a "duh" tone as Dasio and I got out of the vehicle.

"I guess I really hadn't had time to think about it," Lydia admitted.

"Well, I know you can't drink, girl, but when we get on this plane, I'm about to have a drink or two, and hopefully I can sleep all the way there. I don't wanna hear you and Carlos trippin' off being in the air! Both of you scary cats!"

"They'll be a'ight," Dasio teased as he gathered our bags. We headed to the courtesy shuttle bus that would take us to the terminal. Five minutes later we were seated on the bus, and ten minutes after that we arrived at our terminal.

As Dasio struggled with all the bags, I walked behind him, still holding my phone up to my ear with one hand, my purse in the other. "Girl, where are you guys?" I asked Lydia as Dasio and I entered the terminal.

Suddenly I felt a tap on my shoulder. I jumped, spun around, and was in the middle of swinging my arm when Lydia caught it in midair while she ducked. "Oh, hell nah! I was ready for you this time!"

"Why are you guys here so early?" I asked while Dasio checked in at the kiosk for both of us.

"We're here early because I didn't wanna be late," Auntie May said, giggling, as Carlos held on to her arm.

"Mom, are you sure you don't want a wheelchair?" Carlos asked.

"Boy, do I use a wheelchair at home?"

"No, but—"

"Okay then!" Auntie May exclaimed, cutting him off. "What makes you think I need one now? I'm going to see my sister standing on my own two feet. You got that?"

"Okay, okay, Mom," Carlos replied and shook his head. "Have it your way."

"Yeah, that's just what I'm gonna do. Have it my way," Auntie May went on. "Where's my nephew? See, now ask Dasio. He knows that I'm fine and don't need no wheelchair."

Auntie May fussed but quickly quieted down as soon as Dasio crept up and kissed her cheek. She was all smiles then. "Ain't that right, nephew?"

"Yes, that's right! Auntie May don't need no wheelchair!" Dasio answered as he laughed at Carlos behind his auntie's back.

"Damn. They play like little kids, huh?" Lydia whispered, a smile spread across her face.

"Yeah, I think it's kind of cute. They're all so close," I responded in a low tone.

"They are, Connie. You should see how Carlos's mother sings to him—" Lydia began, but Carlos cut her off.

"Stop telling all my secrets!" he chuckled as he took Lydia by the hands and twirled her around before hugging her.

"Whoa," she giggled as she dangled in Carlos's arms.

"Y'all stop playing and get me to the gate!" Auntie May demanded. "I'm not gonna miss this flight! I need to see my sister!"

Everyone laughed at once except for Auntie May.

Her expression was serious. "Come on!" she ordered.

We all started stepping without a word. We had a long flight ahead of us, and I was ready to get it moving as well. I was excited. We all were.

Chapter 28

Dasio Vazquez

"Constance," I whispered loudly in her ear. "Wake up, *mamí*. We're here."

"Ugh," she groaned, struggling to sit up straight.

My girl had slept through both flights and was still tired. I had to nearly carry her ass off the plane.

"You only had two glasses of wine," I reminded her. "Why are you so groggy?"

"I don't know, Dasio," Constance replied with a yawn, then looked around. "Where is everybody at?"

"They got off the plane already," I told her as I brushed the hair out of her face with my hand. "The guys who work for Carlos are getting all our luggage. Then they'll meet us curbside. You ready?"

Constance stretched one last time and hugged me tightly. "I'm glad I came, Dasio."

"Me too," I confessed with a smile. "Now let's get off this plane, go get checked into the hotel, and take Auntie May to my mom's."

"Okay, I'm ready. I'm hungry too."

"I kind of figured that," I teased. "We'll stop and get something on the way to the hotel."

Constance nodded and held on to me as we disembarked from the plane. She was so tired that I made sure not to let go of her arm.

After I had to nearly drag her down the concourse, we exited the terminal. That was where we found everyone waiting for us.

"Did you get everything?" I asked.

"Yep, we got everything! All twelve bags!" Lydia reported. "Are we going to the hotel first? I really wanna shower before we go out sightseeing."

"No, no, no," Auntie May fussed as we walked toward the waiting car. "I wanna see my sister first!"

"Mom, don't you wanna change into that pretty dress you bought for your trip?" Carlos coaxed. "I think Auntie Mary would love to see you in it."

"Oh yeah, you're right. I guess you are kind of smart up there in that big head of yours," Auntie May joked. "Looking just like your daddy!"

Tears formed in her eyes, but she didn't let them drop. She just kept on moving and climbed into the car first. We piled in behind her and set off to the hotel.

It was warm and the sun was out, but it was drizzling a bit. The breeze was just enough to keep the sweat from dripping.

Looking out the windows of the stretch town car, we all observed the damage the storms had left. It was pretty bad, but not bad enough to take away from the beauty of the island.

All our chatter was cut short when we arrived at the main building of the resort. Everyone got so excited about how nice it was, they forgot about all the tragedies from the hurricanes that they were just discussing and hopped out the vehicle. It was time to get ready for our first day on the island...

"I'm ready!" Auntie May yelled from the living room area of our penthouse suite about two hours later.

We all knew what that meant. That shit meant "Come the hell on!"

"You look so beautiful, Auntie May," Lydia complimented as she fixed her hair with a bobby pin. "Your sister is gonna be so happy to see you."

"Thank you so much, baby," Auntie May said with a smile. "I'm so glad you came with us. You're good for Carlos."

While Constance and I began laughing, Carlos nearly choked on the Pepsi he was drinking. "Mom . . . here you go."

"No, seriously, son. I think she's good for you. The only thing she has to work on is keeping you in line. You see, your father had that same problem."

We all shook our heads and laughed. Auntie May stayed having jokes.

Carlos was the funny one, though. His ass was blushing so hard that his face turned red. I started to clown his ass, but I gave him a pass when we left the suite, went outside, and climbed into the limo.

"Oh, did you hook up that gig that you were telling me about?" Carlos inquired after we gave the driver directions to my mother's house. "We're gonna be here a whole week! I'm gonna need something to do."

"Don't worry, Los," I assured him with a wink. "Everything is a go. We can go down to the arena tomorrow, around noon, so you can do a live rehearsal."

"Okay, cool," Carlos said with a nod of his head, then looked at Lydia.

"Here y'all go," I said, clowning. "Y'all are something else. Always trying to act like y'all not a couple but steady doing shit. Oops. I mean always doing things only couples do."

"Because they *are* a couple!" Auntie May chuckled. "I guess Carlos was the only one who didn't get the memo!"

"Mom, why?"

"Why what?"

"Why do you always have to clown me?" Carlos groaned.

"Because I love you, baby boy. You're my only child, and I wanna see you happy. I see how you guys act together, so what's the big deal?" Auntie May said. She opened a bottle of water and took a drink. "What do you think, Lydia?"

We all turned to Lydia and waited for an answer. Hell, even Carlos was staring her down.

"Well, we do spend a lot of time together . . . and . . . uh . . . ," she stuttered. "Oh, and we do have a lot in common."

"Girl, you know what I'm asking you, right? Do you love him? Do you love my son?" Auntie May quizzed.

Lydia's brown complexion turned bright red before she answered. "Yes, ma'am. I do love your son."

Nobody spoke, and every eye stayed glued on Carlos, including Lydia's. We were all waiting for a reaction from him.

Slowly reaching out his hand, Carlos took Lydia's and held it tightly. Then he looked over at her and began to speak. "I love you too," he whispered, as if he could hardly get it out. "You already knew that, though, huh?"

My cousin Carlos did everything in his power to suppress his emotions, but I could see straight through that shit. Priceless.

"No, I didn't know that, Carlos," Lydia answered truthfully. "I'm glad you told me, though."

"Oh, bull crap! He wouldn't have told you nothing if I wouldn't have had to push him," Auntie May joked. "You should never wait to tell someone something as important as that. You never know when it's gonna be time for you to go. Say it while you can, son. Say it while you can."

Feeling a bit overwhelmed by all the sentimental shit, I couldn't help but hold Constance and kiss her before reminding her that I loved her.

"I love you too, Dasio," she whispered as she turned to give me a wet one. "Mmm."

"Okay, cut that crap out!" Auntie May giggled. "Y'all wait to take your butt back to the room for all that. I'm staying with my sister, so you guys will have all the privacy you need!"

"Mom!" Carlos grumbled and frowned.

"I'm not gonna say another word. I'm just gonna look out the window and admire the beautiful scenery."

Auntie May stayed quiet for the next hour and didn't speak again until we pulled up on my old block.

"Shit. Ain't nothing changed," I commented.

I huffed as I helped Auntie May out of the car, and then I grabbed Constance's hand. "Let's go knock on the door."

Constance and I walked up onto the dirt porch and pounded on the screen.

"Who is it?" my mother called.

"*Mamá*, it's me."

"Dasio?"

Oh shit. I knew that voice, and it was not my mother's.

Carla opened the door. "Dasio, why didn't you tell me that you—" She stopped midsentence and ice grilled Constance.

"Dasio, baby, is that you?" my mother called out.

"Yeah, *mamá*, and I got a surprise for you!" I hollered back as I motioned everyone to go inside.

Shoving by Carla's huge belly, I led Constance to the back of the house to see what my mother was doing. We found her in the laundry room.

"Hey, *mamá*," I yelled before reaching her and greeting her with a warm embrace.

"Hey, son! I'm so happy to see you! I miss you! Why didn't you tell me you were coming?" she said before kissing me on the cheek. Then she turned to look at Constance. "Who is this lovely lady you have with you?"

My mom was giving me the stank eye, and I knew it was behind Carla. Obviously, she didn't have all the facts.

"This is Constance, *mamá*," I replied as we all walked toward the living room. Soon as we stepped in there, my mother and Auntie May began crying and hugging. I couldn't get wrapped up in that shit, because I was too anxious to kick my ex out.

"Look at y'all! How long has it been since y'all seen each other? Y'all see this?" Carla belted out all in one breath.

She was already in there, asking a million and one questions. I stopped her dead in her tracks. "Can I talk to you for a second?"

"Sure, what's up, *papí*?" Carla said flirtatiously as she batted her eyes, eased her big belly forward, and threw her wide hips to the side before sticking her hand on one.

I could have just slapped the shit out of that stupid broad, but I didn't. I spared her ass until we made it outside.

"What the fuck are you doing here, Carla?" I muttered in a low tone.

"Your mother invited me over."

"Why the fuck would she do some stupid shit like that?" I inquired, becoming more heated by the second.

"I told her that I was having your baby!" Carla taunted while she snaked her neck.

Just as I was about to respond, I looked up to see everyone standing at the front door. They had heard everything.

Chapter 29

Constance ("Connie")

If this girl was, in fact, his baby mama, he had some explaining to do. A whole lot of explaining.

"Carla, if you don't get out of my face with that bullshit!" Dasio spat angrily as he stepped closer to her.

"No, no, no, baby," his mother yelled as she flew out the door to get in between the two of them. "Don't do it! Don't you hit her!"

"*Mamá*, have I ever hit a woman?"

"No, but—"

"Have I ever lied to you?" Dasio interrupted, squinting as he looked directly at his mother.

"No, son," she confessed as she slid to the side. "You haven't."

"Okay, so listen, she's not pregnant by me. Her dates don't add up, and I was extra cautious with her."

"You know slipups happen sometime," his mother commented.

"Mom, it's not mine!"

"It is yours!" Carla insisted as she rubbed her extremely large stomach.

She was trying to get sympathy from Dasio's mother, but she wasn't quite buying it. "You gotta go with all this mess, Carla!"

"Yeah, get to steppin', trick! That ain't none of my damn baby!"

"Whatever, Dasio. You're just trying to show out in front of this little bitch you brought with you! What, you brought her to make me jealous?"

"No, I brought her because this is my woman. This is who I'm in love with."

I knew those words had to sting Carla's heart, because the next thing she did shocked us all.

"You said what?" Carla yelled as she drew down on Dasio with a nice-sized heater. "You said you're in love with her?"

"Put that gun down, girl! Are you crazy?" Auntie May said as she damn near broke her neck to get to Dasio. "This is my family, and you will not hurt na' one of them!"

Soon as Auntie May got closer, Carla shoved her into Dasio's mother and took a shot at Dasio. I couldn't get to that bitch fast enough.

"Whoa! What the fuck?" I shouted.

While I swiftly disarmed her, Lydia punched her dead in her grill. Blood spewed everywhere, and it was enough to stop her. At least for a couple of seconds. Then she got up pretty fast, despite being so big and pregnant. Wiping her mouth while seeing that she was outnumbered, she cursed loudly, and then she headed to her car, in shame.

"I'll be back! You can bet your ass on that shit! Y'all done assaulted a pregnant woman, and for that shit, y'all gonna pay!"

"Go run and call the cops! You need some protection!" Lydia yelled as she slapped me a high five.

"Ah, she wasn't talking about the police. Folks don't do that around here." Dasio sighed as he quickly ushered us all to the limo and got us inside. "She's gonna go run to her ruthless-ass cousins and overexaggerate shit so they will come by here, blasting. The shit is crazy."

"They really do shit like that around here?" Lydia gasped, understanding that the situation was much more serious than she had realized.

Dasio's mother and aunt shook their heads in disgust. They were beyond upset.

"Where in the hell did you find that one, nephew?" Auntie May asked as the limo driver veered off onto the main highway. "Wherever it was, you need to never shop for women there again."

"I got all I need right here, Auntie May," Dasio stated as he put his arm around me.

"That's good, nephew. That's what I like to hear."

"So much for that privacy . . . ," Carlos thought out loud as he looked back and forth between me, Lydia, and Dasio.

"Oh, no, me and my sister can get our own room. We're gonna get pampered and the whole nine!" Auntie May declared. "How does that sound, sis? Let's have us a spa day!"

Dasio's mother's face lit up so brightly that it truly touched me. The love between them was definitely visible. It was a beautiful thing.

"That sounds wonderful, sis." She smiled, her eyes teary. "I'm just so glad you're here, May."

"I'm glad to be here, sis," Auntie May replied.

"Dasio, I just want you to know that I already knew that Carla wasn't pregnant by you, baby," his mother announced. "When she called me with that mess, I dialed her auntie, and she confirmed it was by that guy she's been sneaking around with named Guano."

"You knew that, and you still let her clown me?" Dasio replied.

"I thought she was just gonna leave in peace. I had no idea she was gonna pull a gun out!"

"I know, Ma."

"I'm sorry."

I swear, as soon as she finished speaking, Dasio's cell started going off nonstop. He ignored it until we got back to the hotel and got his aunt and mother settled in their own suite. By then everyone was in an upbeat mood.

"Look at this shit!" Dasio gasped as he showed Lydia, Carlos, and me the video Carla had sent him after the four of us were back in our presidential suite.

"Did that bitch really just shoot your house up? Did they really just bust out all the windows?" Lydia snapped. "Are they that damn cold-blooded out here?"

Lydia was becoming more upset by the minute, and I was trying my damnedest to calm her down. Nothing was working.

"Yes, I can't tell my mother no shit like that!" Dasio sighed, then sat down on the sofa in the living room and placed his head in his hands. "That was all my mother had left. All she had was that raggedy old shack!"

"Don't let this woman ruin our trip," I declared as I rubbed Dasio's shoulders while Lydia took a seat on an armchair, and Carlos paced the room. "No one was there, and we're all safe. Plus, I'm sure your mother has insurance to cover all the damages."

Dasio appeared to be a little confused about why I wasn't tripping behind the shit that Carla was doing. "Are you sure you're not mad at me about that stupid chick?"

"No, you said that wasn't your baby, and I believe you."

"You do?" Dasio stammered, looking incredulous.

"Yes. Do you have any reason to tell me a lie?"

"Not one!"

I kissed him on his lips to hush him up. I no longer wanted to talk about Carla. I was ready to focus on us.

Sure, the shit that she said had touched a nerve, but I knew how females were, especially desperate ones. They would do whatever it took to try to keep a man. What she didn't comprehend was that you could never keep a man who didn't want to be kept. That was fact. A well-known fact.

"Dasio, I really think you should tell your mother about the house," Carlos blurted out. His concern was with what was going to happen next. "If she stooped that low to do that crazy shit, then what won't she do?"

"We're in the city, and she's probably laying low after that shit. Let's just go out and have a nice dinner and not worry about all that right now, a'ight?" Dasio responded.

Lydia gave me the side eye and frowned, as if she wasn't buying it. She didn't seem to trust the Carla chick, and I was right along with her.

"I'll watch your back, girl," Lydia whispered before we got in the car to leave for the restaurant. "If that bitch run up, I'm gonna just pound that ho in the face. So what she's pregnant? I'll just be defending myself. Now if she wanna bring the heat—"

"Then I got the heat!" Dasio interrupted, having overheard what Lydia was saying, and revealed both of the guns he had on him.

He handed one to Carlos and tucked the other one back in the side of his waistband before we left the hotel. "Don't nobody worry about shit."

Yeah, it's all easier said than done.

I couldn't stop thinking about how that chick had shot up Dasio's mother's house. The way she and her cousins had done it made it look like some shit you would see in a movie. That was how mind-blowing the shit was.

To get this off my mind temporarily, I began to think about food. That always helped.

"How far is the place we're eating at?" Lydia asked as she rubbed her belly. "I'm starving."

Obviously, I wasn't the only one who was hungry, because my homegirl was nearly ready to pass out. The look on her face displayed despair.

"Are you that hungry?" Carlos teased.

"Yes. Now how much longer before we get there?" Lydia whined.

"Here we are," Dasio announced as we arrived at the seafood restaurant and the driver pulled into the lot to park.

Grabbing me by the hand, Dasio helped me out of the car, and he and I led the way. The whole atmosphere felt so different than being back home on the mainland. Although the temperature was below eighty, the humidity was at an all-time high.

When we walked in, I wiped the sweat from my forehead and blinked my eyes a few times. They had to adjust to the darkness. The candles positioned on each table weren't giving off enough light for me. I damn near had to feel my way around.

"I need some eyes in the back of my damn head up in here," I announced in a low voice as I took in my surroundings.

After Dasio and I chose a table that was a bit more secluded, we all sat and ordered drinks while we decided what to eat. I opened the menu and began to browse. While I skimmed through the many selections, I tapped my foot to the music. A soft jazz song playing. It created a nice, relaxing ambience, and I was able to clear my mind. When I did, it took me straight to Dasio.

"Baby, what are you drinking?" I asked him before I ordered.

"I'm not." He smiled. "I need to focus. Shit, looking at you already got me distracted enough, with ya fine ass."

Dasio scooted closer to me and stole a couple of quick kisses. His public display of affection was off the chain. He was definitely "on me."

Lydia withheld her comments all through dinner. But as soon as Dasio and Carlos excused themselves to go to the bathroom and we got outside in the humid air to wait for them, she started in.

"Damn, y'all should've stayed in the room. We could've brought your ass some food back to the hotel!" Lydia pouted before her eyes got big.

Immediately turning around, I tried to see what had caught my friend's attention. "Is that Carla?" I whispered and covered my mouth.

"Yeah, and I bet that's the dude Dasio's mama was talking about!" Lydia spoke in a low tone and drew me back behind a bush with beautiful purple flowers.

"Baby, why we gotta stay at a hotel tonight and not your place?" We heard Guano complain. He clearly didn't like not being able to go to her house. Perhaps he felt like she was hiding something.

"Stop trippin'. We are about to have this baby and—"

"Oh, you about to have *his* baby?" Dasio snarled as he stepped through the restaurant's double glass doors, his cousin right behind him.

Lydia snatched me from behind the bush, and we eased a little closer. We wanted to see how shit was about to unfold.

"Who the fuck are you!" Guano barked, his hand on his gun, which was stuck in the back of his jeans.

"I'm the nigga that she's blaming that baby on too!" Dasio snapped with an attitude and displayed his weapon as well. "I ain't up for the beef, but ya girl is causing a lot of problems with the bullshit. I just wanna clear it up."

"You know this clown?" Guano frowned, forcing Carlos to become involved.

"Look, my cousin said he was comin' in peace!"

"Accusing my girl of some dumb shit—"

"Fuck all the bullshit and ask her!" Lydia screamed, cutting Guano off, as she stepped in front of Carlos, who now had his gun in his hand. "Bitch, tell yo' man the truth and squash this shit! We are out here trying to enjoy ourselves!"

"Bitch, shut up!" Carla snapped and pointed at Lydia. "That's the bitch that hit me earlier!"

"I thought you said that shit happened at the store?" Guano countered, probing, becoming skeptical.

"That's beside the point, *papí*," Carla insisted. "She hit me, and I'm pregnant!"

"With his baby, right?" Dasio rushed to ask.

Guano looked Carla dead in her eye and drew his gun on her. "Bitch, don't play with me. Is this my baby?"

"Yes, yes, you know it's yours, Guano!" Carla cried out of both fear and embarrassment. She had to be fearful and embarrassed. I know I would have been!

"Get yo' ass in the car, and I betta not hear shit else about this nigga!" Guano threatened as a brand-new money-green big-body Benz pulled up next to us.

The valet driver got out and rushed around to open the passenger door. Guano shoved Carla into the car and slammed the door before going around to the driver's side.

"Whatever shit you had with Carla is dust. She's my bitch now—" Guano began before Dasio cut him short.

"You ain't got shit to worry about."

Dasio threw his hands in the air as Guano smirked wickedly, then hopped in his ride. We all stood there, not saying a word.

"That bitch karma is faster than I thought!" I said, breaking the sudden silence.

"You sho' right, because that's the last thing I expected to happen! Where the hell did they come from?" Dasio wondered out loud as he drew his cell out and started dialing our driver.

Before he could key in all the digits, our town car arrived. We all hurried to get in.

Dasio turned to me and said, "*Mamí*, I'm sorry about all that drama—"

"I'm just glad it's over!" I huffed, interrupting him.

"But what about your mother's house, Dasio? You gonna let her get away with that shit?" Lydia asked angrily.

"Getting rid of her is worth it!" Dasio answered, then looked at me. "Now we can enjoy the rest of our time here in Puerto Rico."

"Yes, we can," I agreed happily.

We started as soon as we got back to the privacy of our suite. We didn't even get a chance to say good night to Carlos and Lydia.

Chapter 30

Dasio Vazquez

Once in the privacy of our room, Constance and I made love until neither of us could keep our eyes open. We must have drifted off sometime after the fourth or fifth round. I honestly didn't remember. All I knew was that I was in a deep sleep when I heard knocking at the door.

First, I thought I was dreaming. But when I sat up and focused, I realized someone was, indeed, pounding on the door.

Without thinking, I got up, half dressed, exited our room, ran through the living room, then peeked out of the peephole in the door to the suite. It was Auntie May.

"Shit!" I huffed and hurried my ass into the bedroom to throw on some shorts before I went back to open the door.

"What took you so long to answer the door?" Auntie May asked, barging her way into the suite. "What y'all doin' up in here?"

"No, what are you doing up at this time of night?" Carlos asked her after he emerged from his private bedroom on the other side of the suite. He helped his mother to the sofa. "Is everything okay?"

"Yeah, my sister is in there snoring, and I can't even hear the TV over that crap!"

We both laughed as Lydia and Constance joined us. Now it was a big party.

Lydia reached over the sofa and handed Auntie May the remote control to the TV. "Here you go. You can watch anything you want."

"Thank you, baby." Auntie May smiled. "Y'all can go on back to bed. I'll be fine out here by myself."

Taking a hint, we all took off to our separate bedrooms. I was already yawning by the time Constance and I closed ourselves in. "You still tired?"

"Yeah, I'm pretty exhausted, Dasio. You wore me out earlier," Constance confirmed with a stretch before undressing back down to her green lace panties.

Just the view of her body made my manhood damn near jump out of my shorts. I couldn't stop staring at her.

My gaze traveled up from her perfectly manicured feet and came to a halt as soon as it met her beautiful light brown eyes. She smiled and then shyly turned away. That shit just turned me on more.

After slowly drawing back the thick white comforter, Constance climbed between the cool light-print sheets. She gestured to me to join her by pulling back the comforter on my side and patting the bed.

"You know you are really about to start something, right?" I warned as I slid my body near hers.

I was so close that I could feel her heartbeat and smell the fruit on her breath from the candy she was sucking on. The sensual combination made my shit even harder.

I guessed that Constance felt it too. It was right on her thigh, throbbing for some attention.

"Mmm," she hummed as she began to grind up against it.

Her arms tightened around me, and she began to moan. That sent a nigga right over the edge. I had to back up and remove my shorts, plus my boxers.

"Damn," I gasped when I caught sight of Constance's nicely trimmed stash.

She had her legs open, like she was ready for me to bring it to her, but I had to hit her with a little foreplay first. Over the past several months, I had become very familiar with all her sensitive spots, and I graced every last one of them now. To enhance her pleasure, I saved the best lick for last.

"Oh, yeah, Dasio," Constance whispered as she rubbed the top of my head and twirled her hips. In turn, I gripped her waist and moved my lips from her clit to her slit, then penetrated it with my tongue.

That was it for her, and damn near for me too. The way I had her screaming almost made me bust on myself. Shit, everything about her was turning me on.

"Make love to me," Constance begged softly.

Shit, she didn't have to ask me twice.

That night I put it on Constance like never before. Even with everything that was going on in the outside world, we were still able to find a private place to escape to. There I was able to release with the one person I loved and trusted more than anyone. That was the most incredible feeling I had ever experienced.

Later, cuddling in one another's arms, we drifted back off again. It didn't take long.

Hours later, the sun rose over the horizon, and I woke up, refreshed. After easing out of bed, I showered, got partially dressed, then slid right back in between the sheets with my girl.

"Hey there, sleepyhead," I whispered as I leaned over and kissed Constance's lips.

"What time is it?" she asked, then yawned and tried to focus. "Where are you going?"

"It's almost noon, and Carlos and I are going to the arena to do a run-through of his show. He gotta give the band players the music and shit they need to back him up. You know he's gonna handle the keyboards, though. That nigga don't let nobody fuck with his keys," I told her.

"You didn't want me to go with you?" Constance yawned again before sitting all the way up in the bed.

"You're not even up and dressed, *mamí*! You know how long it takes you, and Carlos is already down there waiting on me. I stayed in bed with you all morning, but you've been knocked out."

"It's okay, bae." Constance sighed heavily. "I'll just stay here all day and be bored!"

"Stop trippin'! You don't have to stay in the room. You can get out and explore." I frowned. "Just don't go too far," I warned.

"Yeah, yeah . . ."

After giving my girl one last kiss to hush her complaining, I handed her my credit card and told her to make sure she went shopping to get her something nice to wear for the show the following night. I wanted to make sure she was looking extra special when I showed her off.

I knew niggas were about to be mad jealous! They had every right to be too. My girl was fine . . . one of a kind.

Chapter 31

Constance ("Connie")

When Dasio left me in the suite that morning, I huffed and puffed. I didn't feel like being cooped up in that room all day, and I figured Lydia had gone with Carlos and Dasio.

Since I hadn't got an invitation, I wasn't just going to invite myself, so I sucked it up and drew the covers over my head, then sighed a few times. Suddenly I heard a knock on my door. Instead of getting up to see who it was, I hollered, "Who is it?"

"It's me, Lydia." She let herself into my room. "The guys are gone. I'm bored already."

"I thought you went with them," I replied.

Lydia plopped her ass on my bed and began chatting it up. She was talking so damn fast that my mind couldn't keep up with the words that were coming out of her mouth.

Finally, after ten minutes of her nonstop complaining, I interrupted her. I couldn't take it. "So, I take it you wanna go somewhere?"

"Yes, I wanted to go to the arena!" Lydia said, pouting. "Don't you wanna go?"

"Why? It's not like we were gonna be able to spend time with them there. Carlos will be rehearsing, and Dasio will be taking care of things on the business side," I reminded her.

Lydia was quiet, as if she was thinking about what I had just told her. It seemed like she was finally getting it.

"You really like him, huh?" I teased her.

"More than you know, Connie," Lydia sighed as she rubbed her tummy.

"What's wrong? Are you hungry?" I asked as I got up to get some clothes out to wear.

"Yeah, we're starving," she told me, tears glistening in her eyes.

I didn't know if she was tripping or if she had just admitted to me that she was pregnant. Hell, I didn't even know that they had been getting down all like that.

"Are you . . . uh . . . are you—" I began, but she interrupted me.

"Yes, I got a bun in the oven."

Before I spoke again, I took a deep breath. Then I asked Lydia how she felt about this. She was truthful and told me that she was happy but was too scared to tell Carlos.

"You still have time," I said, comforting her by rubbing her shoulder. "Tell him when you're ready."

"What if he gets mad and accuses me of trapping him?"

"Then cuss his ass out!" I snapped, then instantly calmed down. "I don't think he would do that, though. He's too much of a gentleman to do some stupid shit like that."

"Well, I'm gonna wait at least until we get back home," Lydia told me.

I agreed, but I was still worried about the situation with Carla. Even though the truth was out about her baby, I knew she was a woman scorned. That made her reckless and an existing threat not only to all of us but also to my best friend's unborn baby. Shit, Carla had already destroyed Dasio's mother's house. At that moment, I didn't put a thing past her. As far as I was concerned, the bitch was labeled DANGEROUS until further notice. Therefore, we had to watch our backs while we were here on the island.

All that pouting and complaining Lydia and I were doing had me to the point where I needed some mental relief. With our men gone, the only thing to turn to was junk food to comfort us.

I quickly lifted the hotel phone, dialed, and ordered up room service. I'm talking about so much food that our stomachs were aching after an hour of grubbing. After we ate it all, we both felt guilty.

"You wanna go for a swim?" I suggested as I thumbed through the pamphlet that listed all the hotel amenities. "Or do you wanna go to the fitness room and get on the treadmill?"

"Let's go get in the pool!" Lydia shouted excitedly as she gazed at the picture in pamphlet of the pool's beautiful tropical setting.

We quickly packed tote bags and grabbed our cells before I called down and requested some help going to the pool. Meanwhile, Lydia went to check on Carlos's mother and auntie. I was hoping that they wanted to go with us.

Well, I got my answer fifteen minutes later, when Lydia came back into the room with Auntie May and Mary in tow. They were both dressed in the cutest swimsuits, with hats and cover-ups to match.

I began taking pictures of them with my cell. I wanted to get as many as possible.

"Come on!" Auntie May repeated several times before going to the door and opening it. Two big, buff guys were standing right there when she did.

"I almost forgot that we had these handsome men to watch over us while we're here," Auntie May said flirtatiously. "Are they included with the fancy suite?"

Lydia and I fell out laughing. That lady was something else!

"Yes, they are included Auntie May," I replied teasingly, then invited the two hotel security guys into the suite to pick up our tote bags. They gently took Auntie May and Mary by the hand after lifting all our tote bags. That put the biggest grin on both of their faces, and those grins stayed in place all the way to the pool.

"Wow! This is more beautiful than the picture," Lydia gasped as we checked out the pool scene.

The resort hotel had two pools, which were situated near each other. One was inside a glass structure, while the other one was outside and overlooked the ocean. The view was breathtaking. . . .

"Yes, take my picture over here!" Auntie May laughed as she stood in front of a tall statue of a nude guy. He was seriously "packing."

I began taking pics of everything and everyone. I didn't even get to enjoy myself until hotel security took Dasio's mom and her sister back to their suite.

"Good. Now I can kick back!" I sighed before I submerged myself in the shallow end of the outdoor pool.

Lydia was over on a lounge chair, sunbathing. I didn't know why, though. Her skin was already the perfect shade of light brown.

Turning onto my side, I stared over at the sun setting on the horizon. It was an incredible view over the ocean.

"That shit right there is dope, right?" I heard a male voice blurt out, ruining my moment.

"Yeah, it really is," I answered without looking back at whoever it was that was talking to me.

"This is my first time here. What about you?" He said with a deep voice.

"Yes, it's my first time too." I sighed, starting to feel annoyed.

"My name is Tiontay," he said, introducing himself. "I'm here on business. My company is hosting a conference. I usually don't go when the trip requires flying out of the continental US, but for some reason, I wanted to come this time. That's crazy, huh?"

The dude just kept on talking to me, and it must have caught Lydia's attention, because she sure came over there to bust shit up. "Who is your friend, Connie?"

"Yeah, who's your friend, Connie?" Dasio repeated as he stood right in front of Lydia, with his arms folded.

"Huh, huh?" I stuttered as I glanced back and came face-to-face with the stranger who had introduced himself as Tiontay. His whole being had me at a loss for words. He was like a linebacker and a model all in one. His looks alone had me drooling.

"You may wanna pick ya lip up, boo," Lydia whispered after she eased to the edge of the pool.

I ignored my friend's sarcastic remark and glanced over at Dasio. Damn. He didn't look too happy.

Chapter 32

Dasio Vazquez

I couldn't believe how that dude was all up on my girl like that. He just looked thirsty as hell and was eyeing the hell out of Constance.

Damn! Am I acting jealous? I asked myself silently as I helped my baby out of the water. My eyes immediately focused on her body. It was banging, and she was showing way too much of it with that little-ass bikini she was sporting. Shit, her caramel skin and long brown hair were glistening so brightly that all eyes were on her when she stepped onto the pool deck.

"What the hell do you have on?" I whispered as I wrapped her half-naked ass up in a towel.

"You don't like it, baby?" Constance teased, a flirtatious grin on her face. That shit made me forget all about the fool who had been all up on her moments before.

"Oh yeah, I love that shit!" I laughed as I led her over to join Carlos and Lydia, who were already heading inside the hotel.

On the way inside, I felt her up and down until I had her ass squirming and shit. She couldn't handle it.

"What took you guys so long at the arena?" Constance inquired when we got back to the suite and locked ourselves in our private room.

"We just had a lot of shit to take care of. You know, all this was at the last minute, and it's still all a little new to me. I'm still learning the ropes on some things."

"Oh, okay, then," Constance replied slyly. "Then why do you smell like Lily and Roses perfume?"

"Like what?" I played dumb as I sniffed my shirt in different spots, then thought back to the drinks we had had with a few groupies. "That's probably that shit I sprayed on me to mask the weed smell. You know me and Carlos had to sneak off a few times to puff and shit."

Constance looked at me, twisted her lips, and squinted. She wasn't buying it, but she wasn't pushing it, either, especially when I started nibbling at her titties. That right there had her going, and there was no stopping her.

She had me tapping that ass from the shower to the floor to the bed. By the time we were done, Constance was snoring, and my back was killing me.

The following morning, before the sun came up, I drew Constance into my arms. She immediately woke up and kissed me. As we lay there cupcaking, I thought about something.

"Are you taking some type of birth control?" I asked hesitantly to make sure I didn't offend my girl in any way.

With her being extra sensitive about certain things, I tried my best not to go there with her over nothing. It was just a thought.

"No, I really hadn't thought about it," she answered, looking up at me. "Why?"

"I was just thinking . . ."

"I know. Me too." She smiled.

"What?" I asked, to make sure that we were on the same page.

"What if I got pregnant?"

"Yeah, what if you did, *mamí*?" I asked.

"You tell me," she said, turning up her eyebrows.

"If you were pregnant, I would take care of you, and we would have a healthy little baby boy." I smiled at just the idea of having a baby with Constance. I knew that she would be a good mother.

"Hmm," she teased.

"Hmm what?" I said, thinking that she was trying to tell me something.

When I sat up and started smiling from ear to ear, Constance stopped me. "No, no, I'm not. At least not that I know of," she declared, but I could tell she still wanted to tell me something.

"What is it?"

"No, I promised not to tell."

"What?"

"Nah, I better not," Constance said while getting up out of the bed. She slipped her nightshirt on. "That's my friend, and I—"

"No, no!" I gasped, interrupting her, as I hopped up from the bed and got in her face. "Don't tell me that Lydia is pregnant!"

"No! I didn't say that!" Constance shouted and tried to hide her face. I saw straight through that shit and called her right out about it. She couldn't even lie good.

"Damn!"

I sat back down on the bed and shook my head in disbelief. I didn't know what to say, let alone what to think.

"What do you think Carlos is gonna say?" I asked, curious.

"I know that nigga is gonna be geeked!" I answered honestly. "One, he doesn't have kids. Two, he loves the fuck out of that girl. Three, that nigga don't believe in abortions, and neither do either of our mothers. We were all raised Catholic."

"Please don't say shit, Dasio!"

Constance made me promise, and I did! I absolutely had no intentions on breaking my word to her. Besides, it was only so long that Lydia could hide it. Her stomach would be getting big soon enough. I hoped she had enough sense to tell my cousin before then.

"There's something I wanna tell you too," I confessed.

"What's up?" she asked, at full attention.

"Carla called my cell. She's mad at me behind what her nigga did to her—"

"So, she's threatening you?" I asked, cutting him off.

"I wouldn't worry about the shit. Her nigga seemed to have her on a tight leash," I said jokingly.

Constance didn't find it funny. "I'm still gonna watch my back. That bitch already showed me she's crazy. Now I believe her, and you should too. She destroyed your mama's house, for Christ's sake!"

"Point taken, but let's not allow this shit to ruin our trip," I pleaded as I drew her back down on the bed and nudged her into a lying position.

"It won't, Dasio. I just wanna feel safe, and I'm cool." Constance spoke in a low tone and batted her eyes. "You know I can handle myself, 'cause these hands are lethal, but it feels so much better to know you have my back too."

"I got you," I promised and laughed.

We hugged, and when I released her, she smiled. Those pouty lips urged me to kiss them. I did.

"Mmm," she hummed and squeezed me tightly.

When she let me go, I assured her that I would take precautions whenever we left the hotel. I think that made her feel better.

"With all this shit going on, I want you to stay close to me," I said.

"I like that, bae," Constance responded as she snuggled up to my chest and played in my hair.

While we continued to honey dip in bed, I again thought of Constance getting pregnant. Before that ever happened, I wanted her to be my wife. I didn't want to wait until she got pregnant to ask for her hand in marriage, since then she might feel that I wanted to marry her out of a sense of obligation. I wanted her to know that I was doing it strictly out of love!

Yes, I knew it was way too soon to be thinking about marriage, but that was the way I wanted it. And I wanted to marry Constance.

I didn't bring the shit up right then. The reason being that I didn't even want to discuss it until we took care of the mess with Harrison.

"Have you thought about going to meet your father when we get back to Portland, bae?" Constance asked out of the blue, disrupting my thoughts.

"Why you ask me that?" I replied, curious. "Where did that even come from?"

"Well, with everything that's been going on, that might be a positive in your life," she answered as she sat on the edge of the bed and swung her legs off to the side.

"Yeah, but it could be a negative too," I smirked.

I didn't know exactly who Mason Crews was. The only thing my aunt had told me was that he was my biological father. I needed way more than that to step to him. Hell, especially since I had found out that I had two sisters and an older brother.

"Okay, don't be mad, but I did a little investigating."

"Oh yeah?" I said as I drew her ass right back into the middle of the bed. "What did you find out?"

"Well, your dad owns Maytex. It's that company downtown that makes all those electronic components," Constance explained.

"I've never heard of it," I admitted truthfully.

"It's a multimillion-dollar company, and they have factories all over the United States and overseas," Constance explained as she pulled out her cell and hit her Google app. She then entered *Mason Crews* into the search bar. Suddenly a bunch of pictures popped up of him and his family.

"Damn. It says right here that his wife died last year!" Constance gasped as she pointed to a photo of Mason and his late wife, Meagan. "She was pretty, and I hate to say this, but . . . she favors your mother a little."

Constance was right. She did look like my mother. That shit was tripping me the fuck out.

"Now check this shit out!" she yelled as she enlarged an older pic of Mason. "Damn, baby! You are dead-on him! This has to be your father!"

I took the phone from Constance's grip and took a closer look at the picture. The shit was eerie. Mason's skin was darker than mine, and my hair was finer, but other than that, the resemblance was strong.

"Yeah, you might be right, but first, let me talk to my mother about the shit. I need to know where her head is in the situation. The last thing I wanna do is offend her or bring up some fucked-up memories that make her feel all bad and shit. I don't wanna do that." I sighed as I handed my girl back her cell.

"Deal, but don't keep putting it off, Dasio," she said before she smiled and kissed my cheek. "I'd hate for you to wait, and you don't get the chance to meet your dad."

"I won't wait. I'll bring it up to my mother when I talk to her again about dude," I assured Constance. I began thinking about having another family out there that I didn't know. Shit, I didn't have the slightest idea if they even knew about me either.

Now I had something else on my mind. My fucking worries were endless. . . .

Chapter 33

Constance ("Connie")

Lydia and I were dressed and ready to head to the arena for the show. Since I hadn't had a chance to find something to wear for the show, Lydia and I had got up early this morning and run around shopping for hours. We must have come back to the hotel with at least ten bags each.

Since Carlos and Dasio were taking forever to get ready, Lydia and I went to Auntie May and Mary's and made sure they had everything they might need during our absence this evening. After taking care of all that, we met up with Carlos and Dasio in the lobby, and the four of us headed to the arena.

The ride was short, yet it was long enough for me and the guys to have a drink or two. Carlos really needed to loosen up, and Lydia wasn't making it any easier by making up excuses for why she couldn't indulge in alcohol. I thought she was more nervous than he was.

"What the hell?" Lydia shouted when our limo got within blocks of the venue.

There were so many people there that you would have thought it was a Bruno Mars concert or something. The crowd was overwhelming, and I couldn't believe it. Neither could Carlos.

"Nigga, you didn't say it was gonna be like this!" he shouted, holding his hand up to his mouth. "Shit! I ain't never performed for this many people!"

"Los, they know our mothers are Puerto Rican! They got mad love for their own! Obviously, you got plenty of fans out here! Just like I told you, *primo*!"

"But damn! Like this, cuz?"

Carlos was tripping, but not as hard as he did when the news crew, along with several broadcasters from various major cable networks, rushed him the second we got out of the car. Now all of us were in awe.

"Stand back! Give us some room!" the hired bodyguards demanded as they stood close to us to protect us from the crowd. The concertgoers were pretty rowdy.

"It's always like this when they have a concert here," Dasio explained, like it wasn't a big deal, as we entered the venue.

It was a real big deal to Carlos. That man was over there sweating bullets.

"Shit! Don't worry about these people, Los," Dasio laughed as security escorted us down the back hallway to the designated private room.

With the overwhelming crowd growing even larger by the second, Lydia and I opted to watch the show from the dressing room. There was no way that we were going to take the risk of being trampled.

"You sure you don't wanna watch from the side of the stage?" Carlos asked Lydia as he drew her in for a hug and a kiss. "Security will keep an eye on both of you, and I'm sure Dasio is gonna be right there. Ain't you, cuz?"

Strangely, the look on Carlos's face was telling me that Dasio had told him the secret that I had shared with him. I was almost positive he had.

"Don't let them out of your sight, Dasio," Carlos reminded him once more before they began calling him to the main stage.

The spectators were cheering so damn loud that I could barely hear Lydia when she told us she'd rather stay in the dressing room. I agreed.

"Well, I have to make my rounds and make sure the security team is in place. I'll leave Lionel and Terrell outside the room until I come back," Dasio announced before he followed Carlos out the door. He closed it behind him.

"I'm about to get fucked up!" I shouted as I went to pour one of the complimentary bottles of the finest champagne. Since my homegirl couldn't indulge, I helped myself to the alcohol and got her some apple juice.

"Oh, damn!" Lydia gasped after she watched me down two glasses of the smooth, sweet-tasting bubbly. That shit was so damn good, it tasted like a lightly sugared citrus soda with a twist.

As I continued to drink, we dove right into all the food and treats that they had supplied, then sat back and enjoyed Carlos's performance. I must say, it was off the hook.

He did a full set, and then he slowed it down for his final number. It was a mellow tune consisting strictly of keyboards. It was beautiful.

While the smooth melody played, Carlos spoke about falling in love. The way he expressed himself was crazy! He had Lydia over there in tears, and he hadn't even sung a note yet. I wasn't surprised, though. Lately she had been crying behind just about everything.

"This is for that special someone in my life. This is for you, Lydia. I love you, baby," Carlos chanted as he began to sing.

"Awww!" I shouted, about ready to burst into tears.

The lyrics of his song described how Lydia had come into his life and opened up his heart. He said that she had shown him how to love. Man, he was laying it on thick, with all the right words. I was even wrapped up in the shit and found myself being a crybaby right along with her.

"You never had a love like this," Carlos belted out with all his might, forcing more tears from our eyes.

"What the hell is wrong with you two?" Dasio asked when he walked in on the emotional moment.

We both pointed at the screen without speaking. We were too choked up.

"Oh, so he did sing that new joint?" Dasio grinned as he rubbed his hands together. "He just wrote that shit last night!"

"I'm going to the bathroom to get some more tissue," Lydia told us. Sniffling, she headed in the direction of the private powder room.

When she closed the powder-room door, I dried my tears and got right in Dasio's face about exposing the secret that I'd shared with him. That fool couldn't even lie! Ugh, he had me so damn heated.

"Why, bae? Why would you do that? Lydia trusted me with that info, and I trusted you! Why would you blab it before she could? Now she's never gonna speak to me again if he says something!" I whispered angrily.

"He's not . . . ," Dasio whispered, trying to hush me up before Lydia returned. "Just to let you know, though, my cousin is happier than a muthafucka!"

That was all good and dandy, but the fact still remained the same. Dasio had betrayed my trust, and I had a serious issue with that.

"We're gonna talk later!" I snapped in a low tone.

The loud cheers coming from the surround-sound disrupted our little spat, and right after that, Carlos came rushing into the dressing room. "They are mad crazy out there!"

"I know, right!" Dasio laughed as he pounded fists with his cousin. "You did ya thing out there tonight, fam."

As their conversation came to a halt, Lydia appeared from the back. She was glowing, and it was a beautiful thing.

"Thank you, Carlos," she giggled while hurrying to fold herself in his arms. "I love you too."

"We're gonna see just how much tomorrow night. I have something special planned for us."

I looked over at Dasio to see how he had reacted. Yep, he was smiling.

"Don't worry, *mamí*. You know I gotcha too. We're gonna have a ball," he assured me when he caught me staring at him.

"Are we all going together?" Lydia asked anxiously.

"Well, sorta," Dasio said, making a funny face at me. "We're gonna be at the same location, but in separate areas most of the time. You know, we're gonna need our privacy."

Dasio continued to tease me until there was banging at the dressing room door.

"The limo is ready! We need to go now!" Lionel, one of the private security guys, shouted loud enough for us to hear him clearly.

We all gathered our things and headed out into the hallway. We were shocked at the crowd, which all the strong security men were struggling to hold back.

"What the hell?" Dasio muttered.

Terrified of the crowd, I clenched Dasio's hand tightly and then grabbed Lydia's. We barely made it outside and into the car without getting our clothes ripped. Well, all of us except for Carlos. When we got in the limo, he didn't have his shirt!

Chapter 34

Dasio Vazquez

The night of the concert was insane, but not as crazy as when Constance flipped the hell out on me about running my damn mouth. How the fuck was I supposed to withhold some shit like that? I mean . . . I didn't mean to tell!

Truthfully, as soon as I saw Carlos, it just fell out of my mouth before I could stop it. I figured that he was going to find out anyway.

Well, now it was the following evening, and it was our last night in Puerto Rico. My mother and Auntie May had called a little family meeting before Carlos and I took the girls out.

"Okay, let me start by telling you that I know what I'm talking about when I say that I know that a baby is coming. I don't know which one of you it is, but I feel it strongly," My auntie began as she eyed both Lydia and Constance up and down. "I haven't heard of any weddings, let alone seen any type of ring, so now I wanna know what's going on!"

I had opened my mouth to quiet my auntie May down a bit, but my mother stopped me.

"May, cut it out, and stop being so damn old-fashioned!" my mother ordered.

"I'm not! That's the way it's supposed to be."

They went back and forth a few times before I cleared my throat and grabbed my jacket. It was time to bounce up out of there.

“Wait, I haven’t even shared my news,” my mother stated happily as she stood to her feet.

“What is it?” I asked, my curiosity piqued.

Everyone got quiet and focused all their attention on my mother, who was standing there grinning nervously. I couldn’t wait to hear the shit.

“Y’all know my house got shot up and totally wrecked?” she began.

All our mouths fell open, but none of us admitted a thing. We waited for her to continue to see how it was going to play out.

“Y’all don’t have to say a word or admit to anything, but just know my neighbor called me right after it happened,” she revealed, still smiling.

“So, why are you so happy about it?” I asked with a raised brow.

“Well, when I got word that my property was damaged beyond repair, I called the insurance company to see what they could do.”

“What they say, Ma?” I asked anxiously. “They couldn’t have offered you much for that shack.”

“Hush, boy! It’s not the structure that’s of value. It’s the land! They’ve been trying to buy everyone out in that area to build some shops for the tourists. Since that raggedy road and path lead right to the ocean, they want it!”

“Well, then, why didn’t you sell it a long time ago?” I asked, curious.

“I didn’t wanna move! I loved that house and the location. Remember we used to fish back down that secret path you found, Dasio? What did you name it?”

My mother started going back down memory lane, while I didn’t want to talk about it. I wanted to know what kind of money they were talking about giving her.

"Yes, I remember, Ma. It was called Dasio's Secret Passage. Now tell us . . . What did the insurance company say?" I said, pressing, as everyone else waited to hear what my mother was trying to tell us.

"Well, come to find out, everything was covered, and I have a buyer for the land. They will be mailing me a check to my sister's house within thirty days. It will be more than enough to buy another home somewhere real nice."

"Why would you get your check sent to the mainland?" I questioned, not quite understanding.

"Because, son, I'm going with you guys! I'm moving back to Portland!" she announced, with nothing but joy in her voice. "I never thought about it before, but ever since y'all got here and brought my sister, I realized that ain't nothin' more important than family."

Before any of us could react, Auntie May jumped up and went to hug her sister, then looked at us. "I'm so glad you guys brought us back together! I missed Mary, and we need each other right now."

We all understood why Auntie May wanted my mother there with her. None of us knew how much longer she had on earth due to her liver disease. That was probably the best medicine she could ever get, and we were happy for them.

The only downside was that my mother was about to live with Auntie May until she got her own spot. That place was about to get real crowded. Although I had been shacking up at Constance's house, it wasn't mine.

Yeah, now I had enough money to cop a spot, but the rent in Portland was fucking ridiculous. It was going to run me at least three grand to move into a little-ass one-bedroom. I may as well have considered buying.

"Y'all not ready yet?" I asked Constance as she stopped in front of me, wearing a head rag. Shit, she still looked finer than a runway model!

"We need another half hour, bae."

"A'ight, me and Carlos are gonna go down to the bar and have a drink while we're waiting on y'all. I know when you say a half hour, you mean an hour," I smirked. Then I smiled at my girl before I tasted those pouty lips.

Those shits right there always sent a little tingle to my stomach. That was the craziest shit ever. I had never felt that sensation before I started fucking with Constance.

"So, whatcha think about this shit right here, fam?" Carlos asked me, interrupting my revery, as he shoved a fat-ass diamond ring in my view as soon as the coast was clear. It was sitting nicely in a padded gold gift box that was neatly trimmed in silver.

"Oh, hell yeah!" I snatched it up out of my cousin's hand and began acting a damn fool. "You tryna make that girl have a heart attack, Los! Lydia is gonna fucking lose it!"

"Well, I guess I'll know in a few hours, huh?" Carlos smiled as he grabbed the box back from me and shoved it in his pocket. "I'm not gonna say shit about her being pregnant. I don't want her to think that I'm doing it because of that and start tripping. I need her to be on the same page as me."

"She will be, Los! She loves the hell outta ya crazy ass! Fuck that . . . Y'all both crazy!" I teased him as we went downstairs to the bar.

After taking a seat at one of the high tables, we ordered some shots. While we waited on them, we watched the big-screen television, which was showing the destructive path that Hurricane Harvey had taken through Houston, leaving thousands homeless. The shit was so sad, but so was Hurricane Irma when she swept through right after that.

Forcing myself to ignore the news, I began picking at Carlos about his proposal to Lydia. I knew that they were in love, but I, too, thought that he might be jumping the gun when it came to tying the knot. I knew a lot of couples that were raising their kids together and weren't married.

"Yeah, I'm positive, cuz!" Carlos replied, with a nod. "I have no idea what I'm doing, but I do know what my heart is telling me."

"Did you feel like that before I told you about her being pregnant?"

"I wasn't thinking about marrying her right away, but I knew that I wanted to be with her and nobody else. I know that she is that chick for me, fam, and I love that girl. I'm in love with everything about her. That shit I do know!"

That right there was the most confidence about a relationship I had ever seen Carlos show. It was enough to convince me that his decision to ask Lydia to marry him was sincere.

"I'm happy for you, and I'm down with y'all all the way. I think that y'all click good together. If you love her half as much as I see that shit in her eyes every time I see her look at you, Los, y'all will be straight."

"Well, shit, I guess we gonna be straight like a muthafucka!" Carlos said after downing his third shot.

"You feelin' it, and we ain't even got to the Villas on the Ocean yet," I joked, referring to the little bed-and-breakfast place that was right on the water.

Carlos and I had found that spot on the internet, and in the pictures, it looked all romantic and shit. I wasn't too good in that department, but I was about to take a shot at it. I had something real nice planned for Constance too.

"So right after you propose, hit my cell, so that we can meet you guys down on the water. I gotta eat first, though."

"I'm just gonna get the table on the beach, and before we order, I'm gonna ask her. Then I'll text you so that you and Connie can join us. I know she's gonna wanna tell her best friend right away."

Carlos laughed as both ladies came into the bar, attached at the hip. Their friendship was tight, and you didn't see that shit too often.

Hell, I knew plenty of backstabbing bitches. Carla was one of them. I had been fucking her sister for a long time before I hooked up with her. Those two bitches had fought for a month straight before her sister gave in and moved up out of their parents' house. They hadn't spoken since.

"We're ready," Lydia announced, interrupting our discussion. Then she greeted Carlos with a kiss.

Constance followed suit, and we were out.

Shit was about to get emotional . . . real emotional.

Chapter 35

Constance ("Connie")

Although I was upset with Dasio for running his mouth, he made up for it by offering to take me to a spot on the beach. It was a good way to start to make up.

"Are you hungry, *mamí*?" Dasio inquired while easing up behind me as I stood in the living room of our cottage at the bed-and-breakfast.

Slowly wrapping his strong arms around me, he kissed the back of my neck. His soft lips made a smacking noise that sparked a flame down below. Now he was starting some shit.

"Yes, I'm hungry, and we won't make it to dinner if you don't leave me alone, bae," I warned. Twirling up out of his grip, I faced him and asked him about the dinner on the beach.

"Take a look at these pictures right here." Dasio drew out his cell, handed it to me, and began scrolling though photos of outdoor beach dining at night. The more flicks I saw, the more anxious I became.

"Let's go!" I gasped as I stared down at his cell.

That was when a text message popped up from Carlos.

"It's on!" Dasio snatched the phone out of my hand and began grinning from ear to ear as he shouted, "Yes!"

"What? What happened?" I asked nosily, badgering him. "What does 'It's on' mean?"

My questions didn't faze him one bit! He kept it moving by escorting me outside and to the brick path that led to the ocean.

It was now dark out, but the path was well lit with solar lights. That was a great accent to the trees and flower bushes, which blew lightly in the wind.

When we got to the beach, we got a nice view of the ocean, lit by only the moonlight. Just the scenery alone was beyond beautiful. I couldn't take my eyes off it. It had stopped raining, but the wind was now picking up. It didn't bother me at all, because the breeze was warm.

As we neared the water, walking hand in hand, I heard screaming. It was Lydia!

"Come on!" I yelled as I let go of Dasio's hand and took off. I ran in the direction of her voice and her silhouette.

"Shit!"

My sandals were making it difficult to run on the sand. I quickly kicked them off, picked them up, and continued toward Lydia.

"Wait up!" Dasio laughed when he caught me right before I reached the secluded table that was set for four.

There were bottled candles everywhere, and that made it easy for me to see my best friend crying tears of joy. She rushed me and showed me her ring.

"I'm so happy for you two!" I replied with excitement. "I can't believe it!"

"Me either!" Lydia sobbed happily.

While Dasio went over to the other side of the table to congratulate his cousin Carlos, I whispered in Lydia's ear, "Did you tell him that you were . . . ?"

"No, but I'm about to tonight!"

Lydia hushed me and then ushered me over to the dinner table. We all sat down to enjoy the food that the line of waiters began to serve us. Nothing looked familiar, but it all smelled delicious. I was about to try a little of everything.

"Damn, ya piling your plate up, huh?" Dasio teased. "You must be hungry."

I didn't answer him, because I was too busy tasting the marinated beef with vegetables. It was so tender and sweet that it had my mouth watering.

For the next five minutes or so, I was so done. I think I ate too fast, because my chest was hurting, and I developed a bad case of heartburn immediately.

"Excuse me, sir." Dasio cleared his throat. "Could you please bring me a teaspoon of baking soda and a bottled water please?"

The waiter came right back with the items, and I consumed them immediately, praying for some type of relief. I was so uncomfortable, but the home remedy quickly did the trick.

"Let's go for a walk, Lydia" Carlos suggested. He took Lydia by the hand and was about to lead the way to the ocean when he turned to us and urged us to join them. "Y'all, come on."

Barefoot, with our shoes in our hands, we walked close to the water before putting our feet in. I was a little scared because I couldn't see what was under there. I kept shining the light from my cell at the water every time I felt something brush up against my foot.

"You are tripping, *mamí*," Dasio laughed as he tightened the grip he had on my hand. "Ain't nothing in this water gonna hurt you."

"I hope not."

As we continued to stroll down the shore, we happened upon a family. It was a mother and two kids. The little girl had to be about two. She suddenly took off running and headed straight to the water and jumped in. The mother had the infant in her arms and couldn't catch the older child.

"Help her!" Lydia and I screamed in unison.

"Get the little girl!" I yelled.

Carlos was the first one to take off. He reached the toddler right when she went under. He tried to grab her, but the current was too quick. Not hesitating, he dove under several times to search for her.

"*Ay, Dios mío*!" the young woman screamed.

Her piercing scream sent chills up my spine, and my heart went out to her. She even had the little baby hollering.

"Where's Carlos?" Dasio yelled right before he went in the water after his cousin.

He ran in a few feet and went right under. Seconds later he was heaving Carlos out of the water by his collar, but not without the little girl, who was secure in his cousin's arms. She was unresponsive, and that sent us all into a panic.

Dasio took the little girl, placed her on her back, and performed CPR on her tiny body. After three or four compressions, the small child began choking, then crying. It was music to our ears.

"*Gracias, gracias, señor*!" the young woman exclaimed before she took her daughter from Dasio and cuddled her little body.

The child was wet and shivering. I removed my sweater and quickly draped it around her.

"*Gracias*," the young woman repeated several more times.

The young woman must have thanked us a million times before heading off in the opposite direction. I could tell by her walk that she was still shaken up.

"Oh, baby, are you okay?" Lydia asked, sounding overly concerned. "We may as well go back to the room. You're soaking wet. Both of you are."

Heading back to the bed-and-breakfast, we all talked about our stay in Puerto Rico. We had had more action and drama there in just a few days than we had had in Portland in a lifetime.

"Well, I guess we'll see you two in the morning," I teased just before Dasio and I headed down the path that led to our private cottage. "Don't worry. I won't bug you two lovebirds until tomorrow."

The happy couple walked off, hand in hand, with big smiles on their faces. I knew in my heart that they were a match made in heaven. I just couldn't wait until Dasio and I got to that point in our relationship.

Well, not the pregnancy part. Not just yet at least.

"It's so nice out here," I said, gazing up in the sky, when we stopped before we reached the cottage.

Just as we did, it began pouring down raining. I screamed loudly and raced Dasio all the way to the door.

We both burst in and stripped out of our wet clothes. Standing there in the nude, admiring one another in our rarest form, we united in more than just a sexual way. Much more.

Chapter 36

Dasio Vazquez

That night on the beach was definitely one to remember. It was followed by hours of lovemaking. Still, I woke up at six the next morning. Surprisingly, I already had ten missed calls from my mother. I knew she wasn't worried about catching our flight, since it was scheduled to leave until around noon. Panic set in as I dialed her back. I didn't even want to think the worst as I waited for her to answer.

"Dasio, I need to go get my things that the church packed up for me from the house. There are only a few boxes, so it will only take a minute."

I arranged for the car service to take my mother and Aunt May to the house and sent two guys with them to watch their backs. Now that I had heard from Carla, I wasn't about to return to the house. I didn't want to take any chance of her coming at us on our last day.

I knew her sneaky ass was out there somewhere, lurking, just waiting to catch a fool slipping. Well, we weren't about to be those fools.

About two hours later Constance awoke. "Is everything okay?" She yawned and climbed out of bed.

"Yeah, that was Moms. She's cool."

"It's eight fifteen in the morning. What time do we leave?" Constance said after checking the time.

"Our flight isn't for several hours," I told her. "Is there anything you wanna do before we leave? Wanna take a short walk on the beach?" I asked as I got some clothes out to wear before climbing in the shower. She followed right behind me.

"No, I don't wanna do a thing. Shit, to be honest, I'm beyond tired. We've been kicking it so hard that I haven't had any time to sleep. I'm pooped."

I was feeling the same way and couldn't wait to get the fuck out of Puerto Rico. At least we had got a chance to enjoy it for a few days, but now I was ready to go.

For me, Puerto Rico didn't hold shit except for a whole bunch of bad memories for me. Personally, I was trying to create some new ones. All of them including Constance.

"Why don't you text Lydia and see if they wanna go get some breakfast before we head to the airport?" I suggested once we had showered, dried off, and begun to put our clothes on. "I'll get Mom and Auntie May from the resort, because I know they're gonna be hungry."

"Okay," Constance replied right before both of our phones went off with an emergency alert.

I grabbed my phone from the dresser. "Damn! A storm is headed this way!" I exclaimed, panicking. I grabbed my Nike running shoes. "The heavy rain is expected to hit tonight, so you know everyone is gonna rush the airport before then!"

"Will our flight be delayed? Will we be stuck here?" Constance cried, becoming upset.

"Don't trip. We'll be okay," I assured her.

"*Don't trip*? They said this storm is gonna be bad!" she yelled, shoving her cell in my face. "I'll call Lydia and Carlos and tell them to be ready and waiting outside their cottage in half an hour. Call for a car please, bae, please!"

Constance probably wasn't overreacting, but the last thing we needed to do was panic and freak everybody else out, especially my mother and my aunt. We needed to keep it cool.

"Calling the car service now," I assured her as I dialed the programmed number in my phone.

I got a driver on the line right away, and he informed me that he was already en route to the bed-and-breakfast. After thanking him, I grabbed our small bags, and Constance and I hurried to Lydia and Carlos's cottage.

The limo was pulling up to the main entrance of the bed-and-breakfast just as the four of us made it to the end of the pathway. We all jumped in the limo, and the driver hightailed it to the hotel.

While everyone went back to the presidential suite to pack when we made it back to the hotel, I took the stairs up to my mother and my aunt's suite. I was damn near out of breath when I reached the door.

After pounding on it three times, it finally swung open. I stepped inside. My mother and Auntie May had already retrieved the boxes from the house and had packed their bags.

"Boy, y'all ain't ready?" Auntie May fussed. "I know y'all done heard all about the storm coming! We gotta go!"

"If y'all already knew it was that bad, why didn't y'all tell us?" I asked, frowning up.

Neither of them paid any attention to me. They both just brushed by me and told me that a porter was on his way up to collect their bags and boxes and that I should meet them at the car.

"And hurry ya l'il ass up too!" my mother had the nerve to add.

I shook my head and went up to the presidential suite to get the bags, but when I got to the door, Lydia, Constance, and Carlos were all coming out. A look of fear was displayed on each of their faces.

"Come on, baby! We have to get to the airport!" Constance pleaded, grabbing me by the wrist. Then she practically dragged me down the hallway.

Lydia and Carlos were steps ahead of us, and Constance was still trying to make me walk faster. "*Mamí*, slow down. And where are the bags?"

"The guys came up and already took them to the car. Where's your mother and aunt?" she responded.

"They are already on their way to the car too," I explained when we got downstairs.

We hurried outside. Suddenly a siren sounded. It was so loud that Constance jumped into my arms and wrapped her legs around me. I damn near fell over before I gained my balance.

"What the fuck is that?" Lydia screamed as she held her ears.

"That's the storm warning!" the driver informed us as he rushed us into the limo with my mother and aunt waiting inside. They were both still fussing.

Once we were all in the limo, I laid my head back and I prayed silently as I held Constance's hand. Then I listened to my mother's stories about all the bad storms that we had had in the past. That did nothing but make Lydia and my girl more scared than before.

"Okay, listen, we're gonna check these bags and boxes curbside and go directly to the gate. If y'all have to use the bathroom, do it before we go through security," I announced when we approached the airport about a half an hour later.

When the limo driver reached our terminal, he pulled over to the curb. I helped him get the luggage out of the trunk.

"What the hell?" Constance hollered as rain began to pour down in buckets.

Powerful winds blew the precipitation sideways, and it was impossible to shield ourselves from becoming completely soaked. All I could do was move as fast as possible and help get everyone inside.

"No more flights will be leaving after noon. If you have a flight before then, then please report to your gate!" a man yelled over the intercom in both English and Spanish, then began repeating himself.

"What time does our flight leave?" Lydia gasped.

"At eleven fifty, and we start boarding soon! Let's hurry up!" Carlos replied. Then he helped his mother and fiancée through security.

As soon as we arrived at our gate, we heard a big commotion. Lydia's nosy ass was the first to go see what was happening. Carlos tried to stop her but wound up right behind her.

"Hey, check this shit out!" he yelled when he got a peek at what was going on.

I got my mom and auntie seated comfortably, and then Constance and I went over to the counter at the gate. All I heard was a familiar voice screaming.

"I need to get on the next flight out of here, and you're telling me that we don't have seats? I paid for the fuckin' tickets from my uncle that works for your fuckin' airlines!" I heard Carla scream. I knew that annoying voice from anywhere.

When I broke through the crowd, I saw her and Guano standing there, looking really upset. Carla was doing all the talking.

"What the fuck are you trying to tell me?"

"I'm telling you that you have standby tickets, and you are numbers nine and ten on the list," the ticket agent explained. "All the seats on this flight are reserved, so we have no standby seats available at this time. You may wanna check—"

"I don't wanna check shit!" Carla interrupted, continuing to show her ass.

Finally, Guano stepped in. "No, what you should've checked was the status of the tickets, Carla! I gave you money to get first-class tickets, and you undermine me and go back door to get them cheaper? See where the fuck that leaves us?" he snapped. He looked around the waiting area. "Who wants to sell their seats?" he yelled.

Nobody said shit until that nigga offered some money. As soon as he said, "I'll give you five thousand dollars for each seat!" folks start talking.

"I will sell mine!" a lady shouted. "I can stay at my aunt's on the hill. She has storm shutters and a concrete house!" She approached the counter.

"You only have one ticket?" Carla whined.

"Yes, but I will sell it for the cash," the lady replied.

Guano hurried to pull out money and purchased the lady's ticket. He then handed it to the ticket agent, and she began switching the info. All the while Carla was crying and making a scene.

"Go to your family's place and wait the storm out, baby," Guano whispered loudly before he gave her a kiss on the forehead.

"The storm is already here! What if I don't make it home? What if I go into labor in the middle of nowhere? Do you see how it's raining out there? It's probably already flooded!"

"Shut yo' ass up, Carla!" Guano threatened. "You are makin' a fuckin' scene!"

"Making a scene?" she gasped as tears rolled down her cheeks. "I'm pregnant with your fuckin' baby, and you are leaving me here for dead! Oh, and I'm trippin'?"

"Oh, I see ole boy is here!" Guano said as he pointed my way. "Didn't you tell him that it was his baby?"

"Are you seriously going there with me right now, Guano?" Carla stammered, continuing to cry.

"No, I'm not going *anywhere* with you. You don't have a ticket!" he replied, a malicious grin on his face.

"Are you serious?" she yelled and began stomping in place like a big-ass kid. I did feel sorry for her, but it was more funny than sad at the moment.

"I'm dead-ass serious, and my flight is boarding. I'll call and check on you when I land in Atlanta—"

Before he could get the rest of his words out, Carla charged at him, her fists swinging. Security got to her right as she threw her first punch. They had her handcuffed within seconds.

"So, you're just gonna let them arrest me? You want me to have our baby in jail, Guano?" Carla shouted, then gazed our way. "What the fuck are you guys lookin' at? Fuck all you dirty-ass bitches!"

Carla was so distraught that she began yelling in Spanish. I was glad that Constance couldn't understand her and was even happier that this was the last time we ever had to deal with her!

Chapter 37

Constance ("Connie")

The drama at the airport didn't have shit on our plane ride back to the US mainland. The turbulence was so bad that I nearly pissed myself. That mess had me so shaken that I literally kissed the ground when we made it home.

"We all may as well go to my house for the night," Auntie May suggested as we called for car service.

It was late, and all I could think about was sleep. The thought of Harrison never crossed my mind until we actually arrived at Auntie May's house. That was when I changed my mind and spoke up.

"I think I wanna go to my house," I whispered to Dasio.

"Okay. Let me help them in and get our bags in the car—"

"I don't wanna stay out here by myself!" I whispered and nudged Dasio in the arm with my elbow, then gave him the eye.

After dropping the two bags in his hands, he rushed over to me and held me closely as he swayed back and forth. His embrace caused me to shiver, and I nestled closer to his chest.

"Constance, I'm right here, *mamí*," Dasio reminded me before releasing me and taking me by the hand. "Help me get this stuff and we can leave."

After I lifted his mother's smaller bag, Dasio grabbed her large green suitcase and walked ahead of me. We dropped the luggage in the living room, and then he retrieved his mother's boxes. Finally, we said our goodbyes.

"Don't you stay here?" his mother quickly asked as we opened the front door to leave.

"Yeah, Ma, but I'm gonna stay with Constance tonight," Dasio responded. He burst out laughing, and then Carlos joined in on the joke.

"What you laughin' for, boy?" Auntie May chimed in. "You don' asked that girl to marry you, and you don't have a plan? What? What? Y'all gonna stay here with me and your auntie Mary?"

"They are gonna wanna move soon, because I think Lydia is who you had that dream about, sis," Dasio's mother said sneakily.

My heart dropped as I knew that I had betrayed my friend and leaked her secret. I was praying that Carlos hadn't given it away.

"Are you pregnant, Lydia, baby?" Auntie May asked, a hopeful grin spread across her face. "It's okay. You can tell us."

"Are you, baby?" Carlos asked genuinely, with tears in his eyes. Are we having a . . . ?"

"Yes, I wanted to wait to tell you," Lydia began before Carlos swooped her off her feet, then placed her down quickly before rubbing her stomach.

"I didn't hurt you, did I?" His face was full of worry.

"No, we're fine!" Lydia cried tears of joy.

"See, now y'all can't leave! We have to celebrate!" Carlos insisted.

There was no way that I wanted to stay there, so I hurried to speak up. "Okay, I wanna go home, shower, and change. Can we meet up down the street at that small café?"

"Yes! They have the best coffee cake!" Carlos's mother told her sister.

"Well, then, let's go there," she agreed.

Dasio waved and told them that we would meet them there in a couple of hours.

As we walked out to the car, Dasio slid his arm around my waist and matched my steps. Other than our heels clicking the pavement, there was silence until we reached the end of the driveway.

That was when a loud beeping suddenly sounded. It was a car horn. A driver was honking at a little boy riding his bike in the middle of the street.

To avoid hitting the child, the late-model gold Benz swerved and ran right into Dasio's car.

"Ain't this a bitch!" he yelled as he snatched me out of harm's way.

The woman who was driving the Benz got out and ran over to the little boy, who was now on the ground. "Are you okay?" she cried.

"I'm sorry! I'm okay! You didn't hit me." The small boy jumped up and got his bike, ready to ride off.

"But you're bleeding! Wait! Let me get a bandage or something!" the woman insisted, but the boy climbed on his bike and pedaled away.

Dasio and I stood there waiting for the lady to come and give us her insurance information, but when she turned around, we both were surprised.

"This is not the way I planned on meeting you," the woman said, apologizing. It was one of Mason Crews's daughters. We recognized her from the pictures online.

"How did you find me?" Dasio asked defensively as she approached us slowly.

A few shades lighter than her brother, she was slim and tall. All her hair was slicked up in a neat bun, and her attire was casual but all name brand, from her jewelry to her shoes.

"So, you know who I am?" she asked, with a surprised expression.

Dasio nodded. "I saw some pics of you online. Honestly, I'm just finding out about all this—"

"I'm Darlene. I'm your youngest sister," she interrupted, introducing herself.

"Okay, so you came to see me. What, you just wanted to see me face-to-face or . . . ?"

"You're my brother, and I wanna be in your life! When my mother died, Dad didn't let us touch her stuff. Recently, he decided we could take a look. That's when I found the paperwork and the copy of your birth certificate. I asked Dad about it, and he claimed he didn't know where you were. He said the last thing he knew, you were in Puerto Rico. But when I did some research, I found your mother's sister. That's why I was coming over here, to see if she could help me find you."

"So, Mason doesn't know I'm here?"

"Dad wants to see you, Dasio! Dolly and Manuel wanna see you too," Darlene said.

"Are you the only one who has looked for me?" Dasio asked, one brow raised.

"No, Dolly got me this address, and Manuel let me borrow his car. Oh, by the way, sorry again! He's gonna kill me!" Darlene laughed nervously as she looked back at the crushed front end of the shiny Benz. "I'm gonna have the tow truck come and get it and take it directly to the shop. I don't feel like hearing Manuel's mouth." She held up a finger to indicate she was going to handle this business right now.

Meanwhile, Dasio was huffing.

Picking his brain, I asked, "Are you okay, bae?"

"I'm straight, but this is the last thing I needed right now."

"The wreck or meeting your sister?" I inquired, with a smile, hoping to make him smile back. It didn't work, though.

Suddenly Carlos, Lydia, May, and Mary came flying out the door, all of them looking concerned. They surrounded us, and they all began asking questions at once.

Dasio's mother held her hands up and hushed everyone. "Who are you again?" Mary directed her words toward Darlene. "You say you're Mason's daughter?"

Being the overprotective son Dasio was, he went and comforted his mother. Thing was, she didn't need it.

"Yes, I'm the youngest. I'm Darlene," she said, politely introducing herself. "I hope I'm not being rude, but you are so beautiful and look so much like my mother."

"You know she passed away, Ma?" Dasio hurried to add before his mother could respond rudely.

"No, I didn't know," Mary said sadly and then expressed her condolences.

"Thanks, and I'm so sorry about all this," Darlene replied, then repeated this several more times.

"So, does this mean we're not celebrating tonight?" Lydia asked, pouting. "If not, I need to go get me something to eat now. I'm hungry."

"I don't mean to impose. The tow truck should be here any minute," Darlene explained. "You guys can go right ahead with your plans."

"We weren't going for a couple of hours. My car is barely damaged compared to yours. I'll take care of it tomorrow," Dasio informed everyone as he helped me into his ride.

As we pulled off, I looked back to watch as Darlene and Dasio's mother began to talk while the others went inside. I silently wondered what they were chatting about.

"Your mom seemed cool with Darlene, huh?" I asked, probing.

"Yeah, I was surprised," Dasio admitted. "I just wanna see how all this shit is gonna play out."

"Me too, baby. Me too."

Chapter 38

Dasio Vazquez

It seemed like too much of a coincidence to me that Darlene showed up right when we got back from Puerto Rico. I wasn't sure if her timing was good or if she had seriously been tracking me. Either way, the shit had me tripping.

"Wow, I can't believe that your sister came looking for you," Constance said out of the blue once we made it to her house.

"Damn, I was just thinking about that shit," I answered honestly. "I really don't know what to make out of it. I guess we'll just have to wait and see about that one. Right now, we gotta get ready to go."

Checking the square modern-style clock with the brushed brass–like finish, Constance told me the time, then reminded me that we had only an hour to get ready. That left us with little time to chill before we left, but I was able to squeeze in a short but satisfying round of making love and a quick shower.

"Did you call Lydia and tell her we were running a l'il late?" I yelled as I slapped on some aftershave.

That shit always stung, but it smelled good and prevented razor bumps. My face stayed smooth.

"She told me to take my time," Constance said, approaching me from the back.

Taking a towel, she wiped the shaving cream off my ear, then kissed it. To get me started, she took her warm palm and caressed my dick until it woke up.

"Stop that, *mamí*!" I gasped, shooing her hand away.

"I know, I know, we don't have time," she said, pouting, then smiled. "Rain check on round two, though."

"Soon as we get home," I promised, then thought about us moving into our own place together, with both of our names on the deed.

"Bet."

"Speaking of home, tomorrow we need to go house hunting. I wanna move up out of my auntie's as soon as possible," I informed Constance as I clasped the back of her dress.

"We do, huh?"

"Yes," I said in a whisper while I rubbed the smooth material, which hugged her hips perfectly. I almost told her to take it off and change, but like she'd said, we didn't have time for all that.

"You don't like?" Constance teased as she bent down to strap up her high-heeled sandals while keeping her eyes on me.

Meanwhile my stare was on her ass, which she had all tooted up in the air. I, being horny as usual, moved right up on her, gripped her hips, and pumped up against her.

"Whoo," she gasped loudly, thinking I was going to drop her, but I had her.

"Girl, you know I ain't gonna drop you," I assured her as I pulled her all the way to me and spun her around. "Give me a kiss and let's go, because if we stay in here any longer, I'm gonna have you out this tight-ass dress!"

"It's too tight?" Constance displayed a worried expression and darted to the nearest mirror.

"It's a l'il snug, baby, but in all the right places!" I replied with a wink and licked my lip before biting down on it.

"Stop playin', then, and come on!" she huffed before shooing me through the front door.

I laughed as I headed outside. Right away I noticed that my car was gone.

"*Mamí*, where the fuck is my car?"

"Dasio, you had the tow truck come and get it!" Constance reminded me as we got in her ride. "You called on the way here. You don't remember?"

With so much going on, I had totally forgot that damn fast. I guess I was too busy thinking about getting a house with Constance.

It was funny how I had noticed that she kind of downplayed the proposal before we left the house, but I brought that shit right back up soon as we hopped on the main road. "So, you heard what I said about going house hunting, right?" I declared after turning down Beyoncé and Jay-Z's new jam, which she had been blasting while singing along to it.

"That was my part, bae!" she screamed and tried to turn the music back up.

"Are you avoiding my question?"

Now I was beginning to think something was wrong. Seriously, I was getting a knot in my stomach and everything.

"No, Dasio, I heard you, and we can definitely do that soon," she replied with a slight giggle.

"Then why you take so long to answer me?" I wondered aloud.

"I just wanted to make sure that's what you wanted to do. You know, sometimes you bring shit up, and then we never talk about it again."

Yes, she was definitely going somewhere with her spill, and I knew exactly where it was coming from. Her ass was tripping off Lydia and Carlos having a baby and getting married.

"Okay, if I have, then I apologize," I said sincerely and patted her thigh as she turned down the road that led to the diner. "Just know that this shit I'm saying right here is from the heart."

"Okay." She smiled, glancing at me for a quick moment.

I waited for her to turn into the crowded parking lot and find a spot. Once she had parked, she killed the engine and faced me.

"Constance, I love you with all my heart, and there is no one I'd rather be with. I know that it's not a wedding proposal, but I do promise to love you forever. I just don't wanna dampen Carlos and Lydia's shine. They're experiencing new beginnings, just like us. They just beat us to the punch. So, I'll tell you what . . . Let's just support them through this, and then we can have our time, *mamí*. Are you cool with that?"

"Dasio, that's all I needed to hear right now." Constance reached over and hugged me tight. "I'm sorry for pouting. I guess I was feeling a little left out, and I wanna thank you for reminding me of what's important."

"It's cool." I smiled, then gave her a kiss before getting out of the car. "Just know it's always gonna be me and you."

Grinning from ear to ear, my girl rushed out of the car and ran to me before jumping in my arms. She couldn't even straddle me, because her dress was too damn tight!

I silently laughed and escorted her into the unusually crowded diner. The short blond waitress came right over to us as we entered.

"Are you here with the Crews family?" she asked, causing me to look at her strangely.

Before I could respond, Lydia was rushing over to us. She was smiling and shaking her hands in the air.

"Dasio, your sister brought yo' whole damn family! You see all these folks? These yo' peoples!" Lydia exclaimed, pointing around the room, which was full of beautiful faces. They were all smiling.

"Damn! What the hell?" I whispered, holding on to Constance even tighter.

Leading the way, Lydia grabbed my girl's free hand and dragged us both toward the large tables that had been pushed together to form one long table. At the head of the table sat Mason Crews. I knew his face right away.

Stopping in my tracks, I began feeling hesitant. There I was, just a simple assistant for my cousin. My accomplishments were cool on a street level, but compared to those of Mason Crews's family, they were probably a damn joke.

"Fuck this shit!" I muttered lowly as I tried to build my confidence.

Hell, I was a grown-ass man who could take care of himself. Shit! It ain't like I needed this muthafucka!

"Dasio!" Darlene shouted, disrupting my mental rant. "Come meet everybody!"

"I'm your sister Dolly!" a friendly female shouted as she hopped up and hugged me. She favored Darlene a lot, but her eyes were slanted, and she was a few inches taller.

Next was Manuel. He was much shorter than I was, but he was just as muscular. I could see some similarities between us, but not as many as I shared with Mason Crews.

"I know the circumstances probably ain't the greatest, and I know we have a whole hell of a lot to talk about, but right now I just wanna do something I haven't ever done," Mason Crews said as he rose from his seat, stood to his full height of at least six feet four, and walked toward me with tears in his eyes.

My heart started pounding hard, and the anticipation was killing me. I knew that I had to be looking all nervous and shit.

"Dasio, it's good to finally meet you," he said, sniffling, as he bent down a bit to give me an embrace.

Reflexes caused me to respond naturally, and before I knew it, everyone was cheering and crying. They were just as emotional as I was.

"Dasio," Darlene whispered to me as soon as Mason let me go, "you know, this is the first time we seen Dad cry! We didn't even see him cry at our mother's funeral!"

"Is he crying?" Dolly yelled before bursting into tears herself.

She, along with Darlene and Manuel, went to hug *our* father. Moments later a few other men and women came over to join in.

"Okay, break it up!" an elderly woman shouted as she wheeled her chair through the crowd. "Let me meet my grandson!"

Everyone cleared a path and let her through. She, too, was in tears.

"Dasio, I've prayed for this day since you were born. It wasn't my place to get involved back then, and I have regretted that day ever since! Forgive me as well, baby! I love you!" she said, motioning for me to bend down to hug her.

After slowly stepping to her, I took her in a gentle hold, not wanting to injure her frail body. She had to be about ninety years old!

"I'm Sarah, your father's mother. The head of this whole clan," she whispered, introducing herself while still holding on to me. "You can just call me Ya-Yo. That's what they all call me, baby."

When she whispered that name in my ear, my body relaxed. Strangely her name was comforting, and I didn't want to let her go.

“You need anything or wanna know anything, you come to me, Dasio. Ya-Yo is always here for you,” she whispered before finally releasing me. “I’m always here for you.”

I smiled at her, and she winked and asked about Constance. I hurried to introduce her to everyone, and of course, they all loved her.

Chapter 39

Constance ("Connie")

After the shocking reunion, we had all celebrated Lydia and Carlos's upcoming union, and by the end of the night, Dasio's dad had offered to pay for the venue. Of course, he owned the building, but nevertheless.

"That was so cool what your father . . . I mean Mason, did," I stuttered, not really knowing how to refer to him, as Dasio and I headed into the bedroom later that night.

"You're trippin' off what to call him, huh?" Dasio asked with a slight chuckle.

"Yeah," I sighed.

"Yeah, me too. I guess I believe he's my father, but I just can't start calling some strange muthafucka Dad! It just ain't setting right with me," he admitted as we got ready for bed.

"I heard him talking to Manuel about you coming to work with them—"

"I gotta job, and Carlos needs me," Dasio snapped, cutting me off. "It pays damn well. Matter of fact, my check just got deposited from the gig in Puerto Rico. My account is well over five figures. You know that's more than enough to move into our own place, right? Whatcha think?"

"I think that's a good idea, but nothing too big. Just a three-bedroom or something."

"We need a couple of guest rooms, and you need an office, so I was thinking more like a four-bedroom," Dasio countered and then looked at me, waiting for a response. Oh, he was so good at putting me on the damn spot!

"Fine, bae," I said, surrendering. "I'll look up some available properties, and you pick."

"No, I already found six properties near Auntie May. I'm shooting them to your email now. Check out the pics and let me know which ones you wanna go see. In the meantime, I'm gonna set up this gig for Carlos," Dasio told me. Then he went and got his laptop.

Those were the last words to spill out his mouth before he started working. I'm telling you we stayed up until three o'clock in the morning, but we did get everything done. Then we went straight to sleep!

We didn't get back up out of bed until noon the next day. By then we both had dozens of messages and unanswered calls. I didn't know whom to call back first, so I quickly dialed the last caller. It was Lydia.

"What's up, boo?" I sang out happily before Dasio kissed my lips and went to shower.

"Dang, I've been calling you since this morning! Y'all just getting up?" Lydia smacked her lips loudly.

"Yes, we were up late looking at houses," I told her.

She started screaming. "We are too! I wanted you to come with me to check some places out," she informed me.

"Okay, while Dasio and Carlos go check on this gig, you and I can roll the neighborhood and look at some houses," I suggested as I got up off the bed and walked into my closet. "I'll be by to swoop you up within the hour. Please be ready, Lydia!"

"Girl, you know I stay ready!" she laughed.

"You used to, but now that you've got you a real man, yo' ass stay in the bed!" I teased and giggled a bit.

"I know, and I need to get out of that habit. I need to start walking or exercising or something. I don't wanna get fat or not have enough energy to push this baby out when it's ready!"

"Thankfully, you have plenty of time before that happens!" I reminded her. "Now, let me get off here before Dasio comes out the bathroom butt naked—"

"Yeah, let you before you jump his damn bones, then take two damn hours to get here!" Lydia joked.

"Uh, look who's talking!" I shot back before getting off the phone.

A few minutes later Dasio walked into the bedroom. "What you and ya homegirl got planned?" he inquired, then dropped his towel on the floor, fully exposing himself.

I gasped and watched him slip his boxers on and adjust his manhood. When he lifted his head and busted me staring at him, he began to flirt.

"Oh, you want some of this before I go, *mamí*?" Dasio whispered, stepped up to me, and took me into a warm embrace.

I immediately felt his dick grow even more against my stomach. I had to admit, that shit got me horny, and all I could think about was having it all up in me.

"We don't have time," I whined.

"It won't take long," Dasio promised while standing back from me, far enough so that he could fondle himself.

Instead of answering him, I removed my tank top, then my shorts, and finally my panties. Within seconds, I was on top of my man, bucking wildly.

Three minutes of that shit, and I was exhausted. Hell, I had already climaxed about four or five times!

"Oh, no, I'm not done!" Dasio panted, a smile on his face. Then he flipped me on my back before gripping the bottom of my feet and drawing my legs up in the air.

After slowly entering me, Dasio probed in and out before he caught his rhythm. Then it was on. He was caressing my insides with his large, hardened shaft. It was a massage like no other, and it had me hollering his name at the top of my lungs.

"Dasio, oh, Dasio!"

"You comin', baby?" he huffed as I felt his dick pulsating.

I reached my hand down between his legs and touched his balls. They were all bunched up, which quickly confirmed that he was about to shoot a load.

"Wait! Let me get one more!" I pleaded as I began to match his every thrust.

Happily succeeding, I yelled out one last time, "Yes!" Dasio was right behind me, huffing and puffing as he let loose. Then he held me so tight that I couldn't wiggle out of his embrace.

"Where you think you goin'?" Dasio whispered as he struggled to catch his breath. "Can't a man just lie here and hold the love of his life?"

His question calmed my heart, and I looked up at him. His eyes were closed, but he was sporting a wide grin.

"Oh, I'm the love of your life, huh?" I teased, hoping that he would open up more and express his feelings.

"Yes, you are, and if you're patient, you'll see. I already have it all planned out."

"Our future?"

"Our future together," Dasio said softly before he kissed my forehead, then my lips. "I can't wait to move into our own house."

Easing out of bed, we both raced to the shower and got washed without giving in to our sexual cravings. We were able to wash up and get dressed in a matter of minutes. After that, we headed our separate ways.

Chapter 40

Dasio Vazquez

When I turned up Mississippi Avenue, I saw that there was limited parking near Miss Delta, a restaurant serving Southern food. I had to park three blocks away and walk. It wasn't bad, though. The temperature wasn't too low, and the crowd was festive, especially the two wearing plaid shirts and stripped pants who were so bold as to fire up a blunt of some dro right there on the street. *Yeah, keep Portland weird.*

As soon as I stepped inside, I spotted Carlos at a table in the middle of the restaurant. A guy was seated across from him.

"What took you so long?" Carlos asked me as he and the other guy stood up to greet me.

"Long story," I sighed as I shook the hand of the guy with Carlos.

Once we sat down, the guy removed his glasses, I knew exactly who he was. Beforehand, I had had only his real name . . . not his stage name.

"Damn!" I knew he was affiliated with the label and was from a popular group, but shit! I sure as hell didn't know that it was him that we were meeting with!

"So, let's get right down to business," he said. "I've been following you on YouTube for a minute now, Los, and I like your style. I have two tracks I want you to get on. I think you'd be perfect for both the hooks—"

"You from here?" Carlos interrupted.

"Yeah, and I just found out you were from here too!" he replied. "That's why I rushed to hit you up while I was in town, visiting my l'il shorty."

"Okay, well, I'm definitely interested in doing music with you," Carlos responded, with a big smile on his face.

My cousin had every reason to be happy because the deal was a huge one. I realized just how big, too, as soon as we all left the restaurant and Carlos walked me to my car.

"Los, I don't know why you needed me here. I could've told you over the phone to take that shit!" I laughed as we crossed the second intersection.

"Yeah, but then I would've had to wait to give you your cut," Carlos said as he placed a check in my face. "Plus, you're the one who set this shit up! Why didn't you know who ole boy was?"

"I didn't know him by his stage name . . . Plus, famous folks usually send their assistants or some shit to handle simple stuff like this . . ." My words trailed off as I stared at the seven figures that were printed on the check Carlos had just received. I couldn't believe it.

"Let me ride with you so we can go to the bank. That way I can give you your portion now."

I nodded, an excited grin on my face, and we headed to Bank of America over on MLK. It wasn't crowded at all, and there were only a few cars in the parking lot.

When we entered the bank, we were greeted by a nice young woman who was dressed conservatively. She was very polite and took care of us right away.

Once we were seated in front of her desk, the banker asked a series of questions, then had Carlos fill out some documents. Then came the last step.

"How would you like your funds?" she asked politely.

"All of it deposited into my savings except for three hundred thousand dollars. I want that in either a cashier's check . . . Or can you put that right in his account? He banks here too," Carlos said. "This is Dasio, my cousin, assistant, manager, and head of my security," he added, introducing me.

"Oh, yes," she replied, pulling out some more paperwork. "Just fill out the top section of both of these forms and we'll deposit the funds into your account. Your checking account?"

"Part of it in my savings and the rest in my checking," I responded.

"Okay, the second page will ask you for the specific amounts."

My hands were shaking nervously, for some reason. I couldn't believe that I had made that much fucking money just by setting a meeting! When I had done that shit, I had had no idea that it was that big!

A few minutes later, the young woman looked up and smiled. "Well, that's it. All the transactions are completed. Is there anything else that I can help you with?" she said as she gave us our receipts.

We both shook our head and stood, and she walked us to the door.

When I reached the door, I realized that there was one more thing I needed. "On second thought," I told the young woman, "can I have a financial portfolio drawn up? You know, just in case I wanna make a large purchase or investment or something like that."

Carlos thought this was an excellent idea and asked her to draw one up for him too.

The woman gladly ran off to take care of this. While we waited, a male banker stepped over to us and tried to talk us into some bullshit account. It wasn't anything either of us were interested in.

I was glad when the woman who was helping us showed back up about fifteen minutes later and saved us. I was just about to be rude to the male banker, who was still harassing my cousin and me.

"Here you go," she said, handing us the new documents. "Do you need me to go over these with you or to explain anything?"

"Nah. Thank you, though. We've been here long enough," I replied.

"Yes, we're all set," Carlos chimed in.

"Are you sure?"

I nodded affirmatively as I stared down at my deposit slip and documents. It was a proud moment. Then Carlos and I bade her goodbye and walked out of the bank.

"Stop trippin', cuz! This is just the beginning! I can feel it!" Carlos told me as we hopped back in my ride. "Don't take me to get my car. Let's go find some houses!"

"Right now?"

"Yeah!" he insisted.

"Ain't that where the girls are?" I questioned with a raised brow as I pulled away from the curb and veered off onto Mississippi, heading north.

"Yes, but they are looking for rentals. Let's look for some shit to buy! You down?" Carlos shouted loudly, a big smile on his face. "Let's surprise the ladies!"

Carlos got on his cell and pulled up three houses near his mother's. We went to the closest one first.

It was a huge Victorian-style house with plantation shutters. Although it was an older structure, it had been recently renovated and contained twelve rooms, including space for a studio. Carlos liked that shit more than I did, so he put his bid in right away.

Next house was a fixer-upper, and I passed without even going in. It was too damaged for my taste.

Now, the last property was right around the corner from Auntie May's, and they just happened to be hosting an open house. It was a new build but had an old-school feel. What sold me was the basement. It had been remodeled and was perfect for a family room.

"So, do you wanna go for this one?" the real estate agent asked, her eyes widen.

"Yes, I can give you a quarter mil, then make payments," I told her before handing her the portfolio I had had drawn up at the bank.

"You can put that much down without a loan?" she gasped and held her chest.

"Yes. Is that gonna be a problem?" I asked, feeling confused.

"No, no, not at all!" She grinned and placed her finger up before placing a call.

She got off the phone seconds later and told me that I could get the house and all I had to do was fill out the paperwork. She had approved me that fast! I guessed money, along with that portfolio, did talk!

Who would have thought that I would be a homeowner before the age of thirty? Not me! My life was turning around for the better, and I was truly grateful.

Spinning in my thoughts, I heard nothing Carlos was saying once we were back in my ride. All I knew was that he was going on and on about planning a wedding. I knew he was excited, but I was too wrapped up in my own happiness to share his.

"Okay, man, just keep me posted on the ceremony stuff and let me know what I can do," I told my cousin when I dropped him off at his own ride.

"Fo' sho', cuz!" Carlos exclaimed before he got in his car to leave. "I'll talk to you later."

After I left him there, I called Constance. She complained about being out all day and not finding one house. Boy, did I have a surprise for her!

Chapter 41

Constance ("Connie")

The next two months were hectic. Not only did we move into our new house, but we were also still planning Lydia and Carlos's wedding.

On top of that, Dasio and I had been getting to know Mason and his family. At first, it was awkward, but after a couple of get-togethers, everything was fine.

This particular night, Mason was throwing a party for his mother. It was her birthday, so he had gone all out to make it special, even renting a fancy banquet hall.

"You know your mother wants us to pick her up, right?" I reminded Dasio as I sprayed some perfume on my body.

"She's going?" he asked.

"I told you that, bae. We have to pick her up on the way," I yelled from the bedroom.

"Why would she be going?" Dasio asked while coming out of the bathroom, struggling to fix his tie.

"She's your mother. I'm sure she just wants to support you," I answered, without a clue.

We dropped the subject, headed out, and went around the corner to Auntie May's to pick up Mary. She was coming out before Dasio could go to the door and get her.

"Check yo' mama out!" I gasped, then placed my hands over my mouth. "Shit, she looks more like she could be yo' sister!"

"*Mamá*!" Dasio yelled through his open window. "You got that l'il ole dress on! It's huggin' all on yo' hips!"

"Hush, bae!" I fussed. "She looks amazing!"

"She don' died her hair and everything!" Dasio complained and shook his head.

I thought it was cute, and it also confirmed my suspicions that she and Mason were still sweet on one another. I couldn't wait to get there and see how they reacted when they saw each other. I was anxious all the way there.

Mary got in the back seat and closed the door, and Dasio pulled away from the house.

"Why are you two so quiet?" Dasio's mother inquired over the soft music that was playing on the car radio.

"No reason, Ma," Dasio sighed, not taking his eyes off the road.

I was certain that his mother felt the tension, but she sure was doing a good job of ignoring it. I swear, that smile did not leave her face. That was one happy woman!

"Well, here we are," I sang out when we arrived at the fancy venue downtown.

We all went in together, hand in hand, with Dasio in the middle. Darlene, as always, greeted us first.

Quickly approaching Dasio's mother, she began showering her with compliments. This had Mary blushing uncontrollably and giggling loudly.

"Yes, she certainly is beautiful. More amazing than the first time I laid eyes on her so many years ago," Mason declared when he joined us.

Looking over at Dasio, I watched his eyes tighten. I reached over to him and put his hand in mine, then patted it. When he glanced down at me, I smiled even harder, making a funny face at him. He couldn't take it and suddenly burst out laughing.

"So, Mary, can I talk to you for a second?" Mason requested after properly greeting me and Dasio.

Shyly accepting, Dasio's mother went with Mason, leaving us there with Darlene, who was watching them walk off. "I think they still love each other."

"Why you say that?" Dasio snapped before I could dig my elbow in his side. "That wouldn't bother you? Your mother ain't been gone that long."

"Dasio!" I huffed. "Stop that!"

I was beyond embarrassed, but Darlene wasn't. She kept it one hundred and told us how lonely her father had been.

"Up until he saw your mother that night, he had hardly smiled. Now he can't stop." Darlene took a deep breath. "Your mother did that, Dasio, and I see it as a blessing!" she insisted. "Don't you?"

"I don't know how I feel," he said, surprising even me. "Hell, I didn't even know you guys existed. I'm still getting used to all this."

"Well, just know ya baby sister is here, and I love you, bro!" Darlene said, becoming emotional.

"Love you, too, sis," Dasio replied as he hugged her.

The tears in his eyes were fighting to stay in, but I saw them. It showed me that he was beginning to let his shield down, and I loved it!

"Let me get a drink," Dasio quickly said, then sniffled.

I could see him out the corner of my eye as he wiped his face. It was so touching to see him that way.

"I got a bottle for us at our table, but first, we better get you over to Ya-Yo. She's been waiting for you two to get here!" Darlene informed us.

"Me too?" I asked.

"Yes. She's probably gonna bug you two about getting married. That's all she's been talking about," Darlene revealed.

Nervousness set in, and my palms began to sweat. I hated to be put on the spot, and I could see it coming.

I just prayed that Dasio would answer all the hard questions.

"So, have y'all set a date yet?" Ya-Yo asked as she motioned for us to bend down to her for hugs.

"You'll be the first to know," Dasio laughed as we sat beside her at the table.

We enjoyed ourselves for the next few hours; then everyone began to leave. While Dasio searched for his mother, I ran off to the powder room. I had had one too many shots of tequila. I swear, I must have drunk at least a pint.

"Whoa," I whispered to myself as I rushed toward the entrance to the hall, on my way to the powder room. When I made a turn outside the entrance, I almost ran right into Mason and Mary, who were engaged in serious lip-lock. I didn't interrupt. Instead, I kept on going.

When I came out of the powder room and headed back to the hall, they were gone. I didn't see Dasio's mother again until we all met a few hours later at the front door.

"So, did you have a good time, Ma?" Dasio asked as we drove her back to Auntie May's.

"Yes, a really good time," she answered with a giggle.

"So, you're really feeling Mason?" Dasio questioned, careful not to hurt his mother.

"And if I am?" she replied sarcastically. "Would it bother you?"

"No, you're grown. I guess you know what you're doing," Dasio sighed.

We arrived at Auntie May's, and he hopped out to accompany his mother inside. He left the car running so that I could listen to the music and have a little heat.

Meanwhile, I was texting Lydia to give her the scoop. I didn't pay attention to my surroundings until I heard a clicking noise. I glanced up to see the driver's car door open. I expected to see Dasio, but all I saw was red! It was Harrison.

"Get the fuck out!" I screamed as he put the car in gear. A split second later, he took off down the street. I couldn't even hop out, because my seat belt was holding me hostage. "What the fuck you want from me!"

"Yo' ass need to die!"

"Why? Why?"

"Because you had my boys killed over you givin' us some pussy! Plus, you still got that muthafucka after me! You think I don't know it was your brother, Cal? For what, though? Why you got him after me? I didn't do shit to you that you didn't have coming, and then you wanna run to the cops, talking about we raped you!"

"I didn't tell the cops that, but y'all did fuckin' rape me!" I yelled while trying to fight him.

The car was swerving, and he veered into oncoming traffic. Horns started honking. I couldn't even think straight. I was too worried about what Harrison was going to do to me, but I was even more terrified about the careless driving he was doing at over sixty miles per hour.

"Stop the fuckin' car! You're gonna kill us!" I hollered loud as I could.

"I'm already dead, baby! I'm already dead!" Harrison whispered, with a cold look in his eyes. "I'm not gonna let ya brother kill me, and I'm not gonna die by the hands of a white man! I'm goin' out the way I want to, and since you want me dead, you can go with me, bitch!"

Suddenly the tires screeched loudly, and the car shifted left before rising up on one side. Two of the tires lifted into the air, sending us up and over. We began tumbling and didn't stop until we landed in a ditch.

My airbag inflated and punched me in the face. The blow knocked me out instantly.

Chapter 42

Dasio Vazquez

When I heard my car door slam, I thought it was Constance getting out. That was up until I heard the screeching of tires, like when a vehicle peeled out of a lot. Then I knew something wasn't right.

"Why the fuck would I leave her out there by herself?" I snapped loudly, beating myself up about it.

Without saying a word to anyone, I reached over to the rack in the foyer and snatched the keys to Carlos's old ride. I rushed outside, hopped in it, and drove in the direction my car had gone. All the while I was dialing Constance's cell.

"Where is the car?" I yelled loudly, thinking the worst.

Stopping at a red light gave me a second to think. That was when I realized how much danger Constance could really be in. *Harrison!* Oh yeah, I was real scared from just the fucking thought!

After anxiously running the light, I quickly hit ten blocks before I heard sirens. Man, that familiar sound hurt me deeply. Just thinking that something bad had happened to Constance was killing me inside.

"Damn! Let me follow them!" I whispered to myself as I fell in line with the emergency vehicles, which were heading west.

Three blocks later I spotted a crowd near the road. My stomach knotted up as I parked, hopped out, and ran toward the commotion. I wasted no time pushing my way through the spectators until I got a clear view of the ditch. That was where my car was, lying upside down.

"No, no, no!" I shouted as I raced forward. Several officers grabbed me, but I was able to break loose from them. I ran as fast as I could and was able to make it over to the paramedics who were prying Constance from the passenger side.

"Who was driving?" I asked as I stood back a bit.

"The driver was ejected. His body is over there," said a bystander as he pointed over to a field, where Harrison was up against a tree, unresponsive. "They pronounced him dead."

That was the least of my worries at the moment. I needed to know that Constance was okay.

"Can I ride with you?" I asked an officer as the paramedics took my girl away on a stretcher.

"No, we don't know what went on here, so I think it will be better if you just meet us at the hospital," the officer barked at me, being rude as hell. I started to cuss his ass out, but I didn't want my temper to interfere with me getting to see Constance once we got to the hospital.

"A'ight. I'm following right behind you," I snapped, with a big attitude, and hurried to my car.

That fool pulled off before I could even rev my engine, but that was all right. I caught up to him after running another light. I didn't give a damn. They weren't about to leave me.

My phone rang, and I saw that it was my mother calling. She must've seen me when I shot out of the house without a goodbye or an explanation, so I had to answer to keep her from worrying.

"Are you okay? You ran up out of here and ain't said a word. You didn't even check on your auntie!"

"Sorry, Ma, and yes, I'm okay," I assured her, and then I gave her all the details.

My mother didn't do nothing but hang up and call everyone. I knew this because twenty minutes after I made it up to the hospital, Lydia and Carlos appeared there, and Mason's whole family came in right behind them. There were at least twenty of us.

"So, did anyone come out and tell you what's going on with Constance?" Lydia asked me, panic in her voice.

"Nah, they said that they would come get me in a few minutes. They had to run some tests to find out why she is still unconscious," I explained.

"She's unconscious?" Lydia screamed. "What happened?"

Now everyone's eyes were on me. I didn't know where to start, so I started at the beginning and told them what I knew, without going into any details about Constance's rape. When I finished, Darlene was madder than anyone. She was even crying.

"What's wrong with her?" I asked Mason.

"She went through something similar. Maybe she can help Constance heal from this," Mason replied. Then he added in a low tone, "Thank God that bastard is dead. Now I won't have to have his maggot ass taken out!"

My eyes bucked, and I realized that Mason was more hood than I had thought. He really shocked me with that shit.

"I was thinking the same thing," I confessed shamelessly.

"Glad we're on the same page, Dasio, and if you ever have any issues like this, bring them to me. That's what family is for. We stick together," Mason said.

As he walked away to comfort Darlene, a sense of peace came over me. It was the first time I felt that Mason was family. It kind of felt good.

"Dasio Vazquez?" the nurse sang out in the waiting room.

"Yeah," I answered, at full attention, as I hurried over to her.

"Constance is asking for you," she said, smiling, and then led the way.

"What about me? Can I see her?" Lydia hollered behind us.

The nurse stopped and turned around. "One visitor at a time for now," she replied nicely. Then we disappeared down the hallway.

On the way to see Constance, I must have asked the nurse a million questions. I needed to know what to expect when I walked into Constance's room.

"She's actually doing pretty good for someone who has just been in a bad auto accident," she answered before swinging open the door to Constance's room for me to enter. "Here. See for yourself."

Rushing in, I found Constance sitting up in bed with a black eye, a knot on her forehead, and plenty of scrapes and bruises. At first, I started to get upset, but when I drew near to her, she smiled widely.

I'm telling you, that muthafucka lit up the whole room and made me grin right along with her.

"You okay, *mamí*?"

"I am now that they told me that Harrison is dead. It is true, ain't it?" Constance said, an expression of hope on her face.

"Yes . . . yes, he's gone," I assured her before I kissed her busted lip. It was swollen on the left side, so I pecked the right side.

"I know I probably look a hot mess, but I feel fine. Just a l'il sore, that's all."

"Well, everyone is here—"

"*Everyone* like who?" she asked, cutting me off.

"Like us," Lydia cried out as she burst into the room, with everyone else in tow.

"You're gonna get us kicked out," Constance laughed. Then she started to cry.

"What's wrong?" I asked her, bringing the room to silence.

"It's just that I'm so blessed to have so many people to care about me!" She sniffled. "Thank you, guys, so much!"

"Yeah, Ya-Yo would have been here too, but she is at home with the nurse," Darlene explained.

"Yeah, she tried to push her out of the way and follow us in her wheelchair, but we were too fast," Dolly added causing everyone to chuckle.

"Y'all laughing now, but when we get home, she's gonna go off," Mason alerted them. "Y'all gonna stop playin' with Ya-Yo!"

Now we all laughed louder. A minute later the doctor came in and broke it up. He wasn't mean or rude about it, though.

"She'll be fine. We're just going to keep her overnight for observation. So, you all can visit her tomorrow in the comfort of your own home," he informed us, then escorted everyone out but me.

Shit, I wasn't going anywhere.

Chapter 43

Constance ("Connie")

After the accident, I was in better spirits, but it did take a few weeks for my body to heal. That was just in time for Carlos and Lydia's wedding.

I would never forget that very odd morning a few days before the wedding. It all started with a knock at the door. I looked through the peephole and saw a strange woman holding a manila envelope. When I opened the door, she said she was looking for me.

When I stepped aside for her to enter, the average-size blond lady smiled and told me she had some important news for me. Then she requested my identification. Before I made a move, I asked her for hers, and she flashed a work badge, which said she was from some legal office.

I reached for my handbag, which was dangling from the coat rack. Digging into the side pocket, I retrieved my driver's license and gave it to her. Once she verified my name, she held up the envelope.

"Are those court papers?" I huffed, thinking the worst.

She shook her head. "We got your name from the HIV database—"

"What? Are you saying that I have . . . ?" I interrupted and then burst into tears.

"No, not at all! But when you were tested, you filled out documents. When you put down the partner or partners that may have exposed you, it goes on a list," the woman explained.

"So, so, what are you trying to tell me?" I trembled with every word I spoke.

"I'm saying that six women who were infected by—"

"Harrison?" I interrupted.

"Yes, and even though you weren't infected, you are entitled to part of the lawsuit filed against him."

"Wait, he had some money?" I asked, feeling more confused than ever.

"The lawsuit is against his mother, as well, and she just collected his life insurance. It will be split four ways," she continued.

"Why only four? I thought you said there were six of us?"

"Sorry to say, two young ladies lost the battle with the deadly virus. Neither of them had immediate family that came forward, so the judge ruled them out of the lawsuit."

With no more questions for her, I signed for the envelope and opened it right away. Before I could read the letter inside it, a check dropped to the floor.

As I bent down to pick it up, I noticed the amount. I couldn't believe it!

"Two hundred fifty thousand dollars!" I screeched.

Upon witnessing my reaction, the woman smiled. "Well, I should get going. I wish you well," she said.

"Thank you. You too," I told her.

Then she turned and walked out of the house.

A few minutes later, Dasio came downstairs.

At the same time a large shadow darkened my doorstep, then knocked. I went over to the door and peeked through the peephole. Out of nowhere, my brother, Cal, appeared. I hadn't seen him in months.

"Where have you been?" I questioned him with a hug when I opened the door.

"Why? You miss me, sis?" Cal teased as he followed me into the house. "Hey, Dasio."

The three of us stepped into the den and maneuvered around the boxes. Dasio and I were still unpacking and decorating, so shit was a mess.

"Shit! Is that someone else at the door?" I mumbled after hearing yet another knock.

We all got quiet, and Cal went to check. I crept right behind him, while Dasio ran ahead of me.

"Ah, hi. Ah, is Dasio here?" I could hear Darlene stuttering.

"Who the hell are you?" Cal gasped.

"That's my sister," Dasio announced, and he stepped forward and let Darlene in.

Her eyes were glued to my brother the entire time. Oh, he was checking her out too.

"Stop staring!" I teased him as we all headed back to the den.

"Am I interrupting something?" Darlene asked as she set down two bags, which I didn't even notice her carrying.

"No, we were just making sure that it wasn't an unwanted guest. That's why I sent Cal to answer the door, just in case he had to take care of it," I told her, laughing.

"Yes, he is pretty big and looks pretty strong," Darlene commented shyly.

Cal took it all in and grinned. He had already taken a liking to Dasio's sister, and I thought this was adorable.

"So, I just wanted to drop by to bring you these pics of us. I got coordinating frames that would go perfect in here," Darlene said as she drew five or six photos from the bags.

"Thanks, sis," Dasio replied as he helped her line them up on the two empty hanging shelves.

As they chatted, I spoke to Cal about his whereabouts. He told me that he had a bunch of things lined up and was anxious to get Carlos and Dasio involved.

I got my man's attention, and he and my brother went into another room, while Darlene and I sat down in the den and chatted. The first thing she brought up was the incident with Harrison. I didn't think she was pressing me. It was more like she wanted to talk about her own tragedy.

After getting comfortable, Darlene told me all about how her mother's brother used to watch the kids while her parents worked. She said it started out with a little touching, but after a few months he took it all the way and put her in the hospital at twelve years old. The whole story made me sick to my stomach. Tears were running down Darlene's cheeks.

"Did you tell?" I gasped.

"Yes! I finally told my dad after a few months, and he took care of it," Darlene explained as she dried her tears.

"What did he do?" I whispered.

"He sent that muthafucka straight to hell!" Darlene snapped and rolled her eyes. "We never spoke about it again."

"That's why you were so emotional at the hospital?"

"Yes, it brought back the old memories," Darlene replied, frowning. "Now it's over for me and for you, because both of those bastards are dead. I never really fully healed. I think it's due to me not having anyone who could relate, and I wasn't going to those group meetings or to a shrink. Just talking about it now has me feeling a lot better."

I understood just what Darlene meant, since I was glad to have someone to talk to also. Someone who truly understood what I had gone through.

Once we were done sharing our horrible experiences, Darlene and I dried our tears, then joined the guys in the kitchen. Dasio was whipping up some breakfast burritos, and Cal was helping him.

"Don't tell me you cook too?" Darlene said, flirting with my brother.

Meanwhile, I set the kitchen table and got a chilled bottle of champagne and some orange juice out of the refrigerator and poured the four of us a glass of each.

Soon breakfast was ready, and we all took a seat around the table. As we ate, we discussed the Carlos and Lydia's wedding, to be held later today. By the second bottle of champagne, Darlene managed to invite Cal to be her date at the wedding. My brother jumped right on it.

"Sure. I wouldn't mind escorting you," he said.

"You see this shit?" Dasio whispered loudly.

"What?" Darlene said, giggling.

"My sister and my girl's brother," Dasio laughed. "Ain't that some shit?"

"Don't worry, bruh. She'll be in good hands," Cal promised while taking a quick glance at Darlene to see her response.

"Yes, Dasio, and like I said . . . he looks pretty damn strong. I don't think anyone will wanna mess with us!" Darlene teased as she eased her chair closer to Cal.

"Okay, enough of that!" I exclaimed, intervening. "Let's keep eating!"

"Your sister is always hungry!" Dasio told Cal, and he agreed.

"It's okay. Food is my best friend!" I said in a sassy tone.

"Yeah, and the gym is gonna have to be your best friend if those hips keep spreading!" Cal noted.

"For real?" I gasped loudly. "Are they, babe?" I whined to Dasio.

"They are getting a l'il wide, *mamí*," he said like it was killing him to admit it.

"Bae!" I whined. Then I began pouting.

Dasio rose from his chair, rushed right on over to me, and placed his arms around me from behind. "It looks damn good on you. Shit, yo' ass is sexier than ever!"

My man chose the right words, and they comforted me enough to pile another breakfast burrito on my plate, along with a handful of Tater Tots. Yes, I ate it all!

"Oh, yeah. Who was that lady that was leaving when I got here?" Cal asked as we continued to eat.

"What lady?" Dasio questioned, looking at me for answers.

"The lady that came over here and gave me something," I began. I ran to the foyer to get the check and the letter, which I had shoved into my handbag.

When I stepped back to the table, I handed the letter to Dasio. He scanned it and then started to interrogate me. But to stop him, I passed the check to him.

"What the fuck? Is this real? Are they serious?" Dasio gasped and nearly choked on his Tater Tots.

"Are you okay?" I said as I patted his back.

"Yes, but damn! If I'd known they were gonna give you a quarter of a million dollars, then I would've offed that son of a bitch a lot quicker!" Dasio said angrily. "At least something good came out of it."

"Not for the two women who died before they could collect," I told him.

After sharing with them what the lady had told me, Darlene went straight into prayer. When she finished, she came over to me and gave me a hug.

While she held on to me, I thanked the Lord above for sparing my life. I didn't know what I did to deserve this, but I was going to do right by Him from then on. I had to.

"Well, it's almost noon, and we've just been sitting here drinking and kicking it," I told everyone. "We all have to be at the wedding venue by six o'clock, so, I think we all better start getting ready soon."

Darlene double-checked the time before she got up from her seat. Cal did the same.

"Walk me to my car?" Darlene asked him.

"Sure," Cal replied politely as he reached out for her hand.

Darlene must've gotten a big kick out of that, because I heard her laughing all the way out the door.

Chapter 44

Dasio Vazquez

Mason had gone all out for Carlos and Lydia's wedding. I couldn't believe that he had dished out dough for some folks whom he didn't really know. I just had to ask him about it before we left the venue.

"Hey, I just wanna say thank you for all this. My cousin and all of us really appreciate it," I told him as we stood by the exit. "I just wanted to know—"

"Dasio, your family is my family," Mason interrupted. "I missed your entire childhood because of my selfish ways. After losing my wife and then finding you and your mother, my eyes and heart are wide open. I promise you, son, I will always be here for both of you. I only pray that you can forgive me."

"That's all in the past," I told him to keep myself from getting emotional, especially when I looked to his side and saw that my mother was in tears. "Let's just focus on the future and make the most of what we have left."

"Oh, Dasio, baby, I'm so sorry about all of this. I should've told you . . . ," my mother stated quietly.

"*Mamá*, please, it's all water under the bridge. Like I said, it's all in the past, and there's no need for any apologies," I assured her as I stepped up to her and embraced her. Mason joined us.

As we broke apart, all our family and friends had their eyes on us. Most of them were just as emotional as we were.

"Bae, are you okay?" Constance asked. She was right there for me, as always, and I was grateful.

"I'm cool. Let's just get up out of here. I need some alone time with you," I responded with a wink and gave her a quick kiss.

Before we could escape, we noticed that nobody was ready to leave but us.

"I'm really tired," Constance whispered to me. Then she yawned and leaned her head on my arm as she held it firmly. Everyone got the hint real fast, and we were on our way out. Shit, I was ready to get my girl home and in bed . . . literally.

While I had nothing but sex on the brain, Constance's mind was somewhere else. She was worried about her best friend, who had left the celebration over an hour before with her new husband, Carlos. They had a honeymoon to go on.

"So, you think I should call Lydia and check on them? She hasn't even sent me a text, and their flight to Miami just left. You think they made it to the airport on time?" Constance said the second we got in the car.

"Baby, they're fine—" I was telling her when her phone rang and interrupted me. "See? I bet that's her now."

"Yes, it's her!" Constance yelled happily as she read the text message. "They made their flight, and they'll check in once they get settled in their hotel on the beach. Oh . . . bae! Doesn't that sound so romantic?" Constance exclaimed, with a hand on her chest.

I stared at my girl. I could see it in her eyes. She was truly happy for her friend. Shit, I wanted to make her that happy, too, but marriage was a huge step.

I couldn't lie. The main reason I hadn't asked was that I was scared. Yeah, I was afraid she would turn me down or tell me to wait. I wasn't cool with that. Just the thought of rejection turned my stomach.

"So, you over there feelin' all dreamy and shit . . . You wanna do something?" I asked while thinking of a plan.

"Something like what?" she asked me as her eyes lit up and sparkled.

"I don't know. Maybe drive down to the coast."

"It's kind of cold."

"I'll keep you warm. I promise."

"We don't have no clothes with us, bae."

"Let's go to the house and pack a bag. Then we can roll out to Seaside. Let me check and see what's available."

When we pulled up to the house, I parked in the garage. I asked Constance to go inside start packing while I used my cell to set up a few things. She got out of the car, but then she turned around and leaned in to talk to me.

"Dasio, how long will we be gone?"

"Pack for a few days. If we need more clothes, we can buy some down there."

Smiling from ear to ear, Constance pranced into the house and closed the door. Damn, she was beautiful.

My attention went back to my phone and I checked the time-share availability in Seaside. I saw that the beach house was vacant for the next week. I booked it and paid extra for them to have fresh flowers, chocolates, and champagne waiting for us.

Next, I checked the weather. It was currently forty-eight degrees on the coast, and it was almost ten at night. We could make it there in just a little over an hour, and by then it would be much colder. Perfect for my idea.

"You rented a house?" Constance asked as I drove down the hill and turned into the long driveway of the two-story home.

"Yeah, it's a time-share that I bought into with Carlos. I almost forgot about it. They tricked us into it a few months ago, when me and my cousin went to that business meeting at the Marriott downtown. Remember?"

"Yeah, but I didn't quite understand what a time-share was," Constance admitted before we hopped out of the car and went in to check it out.

"Damn, I didn't know it was this big!" she exclaimed when we stepped inside.

We walked around and checked things out. There were three bedrooms, two baths, a kitchen, a den, and a rec room that had video games, a pool table, a ping-pong table as well as an air hockey table.

"This master bedroom is on point!" Constance gasped when we entered the large room at the back of the house. She spotted the roses, candy, and bubbly. "Do they always have all this?"

"No, *mamí*. I ordered that special just for you." I took advantage of the moment and laid a luscious kiss on Constance's lips. They were soft and sweet.

"Mmm," she purred as she backed up a bit. "I see you're tryna start something, Dasio."

Taking off my clothes, I gestured to her to do the same. She laughed but followed my lead.

"Right to it, huh?" she giggled as she stripped down to her sexy-ass royal-blue panty and bra set.

Taking her by the hand, I led her out to the back deck. Soon as we got to the door, she snatched me back.

"Are you crazy? Do you feel how cold it is outside? What kind of kinky shit are we gonna do out there in this weather?"

"Didn't I say I was gonna keep you warm?"

"Well, yes, but don't you think I need a coat and some shoes at least?"

"No, I got these," I told her, and then I went and grabbed the towels out of the bathroom.

"What the hell are those gonna do?"

Shaking my head, I grinned and told her to trust me.

"I do," she giggled as she nestled close to me.

Upon opening the deck door, I felt the cold breeze. We both shivered and latched on to one another.

"Is that a hot tub over there?" Constance asked as she pulled me outside. She dashed over to the hot tub and dipped her hand in. "Yes!"

We both rushed to get in. She beat me to it and submerged herself up to her neck. "You should've brought the champagne, bae."

I jumped out of the hot tub, and freezing my ass off in just my boxers, I hurried inside the bedroom. Then I grabbed the bottle, opened it with the opener that had been provided, and ran back outside to join Constance. She was smiling and holding her bra in the air.

Twirling it around before tossing it on the ground, she stood up a bit and gave me a little tease. It was just enough to get my dick rising to the occasion.

I carefully stepped into the hot tub, bottle in hand. I took a swig, then passed the bubbly to her.

"So, you like?" I asked once she had taken a swig from the bottle.

"Yes. Look at the moonlight hitting the ocean!" she said, pointing to the beach. "It's so beautiful!"

"Just like you are," I told her as I took the bottle from her and placed it on the deck.

That was the most romantic night ever. Well, at least so far.

Chapter 45

Constance ("Connie")

Oh, my fucking goodness! Dasio had my ass wide open to the point that I totally forgot about Lydia and Carlos the very first night we were in Seaside.

It was like Dasio and I were on a honeymoon all our own. Only we skipped the marriage part, and that was okay with me. As long as we were together, a little piece of paper was not going to make me feel some type of way. Instead of sulking, I enjoyed myself that night, and the next morning I slept until the early afternoon. I must have been really tired.

"Are you gonna get up and get something to eat, or are you gonna sleep all day?" Dasio asked as he played in my hair with one hand and traced my naked spine with the other.

The stimulation was so relaxing that I didn't want to budge. Not even to answer him.

"Constance, do you hear me? It's past lunchtime."

"What?" I gasped as I slowly rose.

"Yes, I ordered a pizza. There's a couple of slices left. Shit, I fucked most of it up! I was starving after all that good lovin' you put on me last night!" Dasio teased as he held on to my hips and drew me nearer.

"Will you get it for me, bae? I just wanna lie here."

Dasio went and heated up the pizza and brought it to me. I practically inhaled both slices and then drifted right back to sleep. I didn't get up again until he began shaking my body.

"Come on now, Constance. It's about to get dark out! I have everything already down there!"

"Down where?" I inquired as I got up and stretched.

"On the beach. We can go right out the back gate. We gotta hurry, though!" Dasio insisted as he tossed me some warm clothes and a blanket.

"What's the rush?" I asked as he damn near dragged me outside once I was dressed.

"Look, the sun is setting!"

"It is!" I gasped as I watched Dasio struggle with a bundle of wood and several bags. I followed behind him.

Once we got halfway to the water, I stood looking at the ocean, in a trance. I could see the sun slowly disappear.

"It's so fucking amazing!" I whispered as I sat on the large thick blanket that Dasio had spread out. I wrapped the smaller one around me.

After joining me, he held me close until we were in darkness.

"What now?" I giggled.

"Now to get this fire started!"

Dasio put his skills to work while I pulled out my Bluetooth speaker and synced it to Pandora on my phone. We had the mellow music going and the romantic fire. It was perfect, until I heard my stomach rumble.

"Are you hungry, *mamí*?"

"Yes, but I can wait," I lied.

"No, wait a sec."

Dasio ran off to gather some sticks, and when he came back, he pulled some hot links and chips out of one of the bags. "I'm gonna roast us up some of these bad boys. I even got some potato salad and wine."

"When did you have time to do all that?"

"You were the one sleeping. I couldn't. I was too ready to be with you," he said as skewered some of the hot links and put them over the fire.

Dasio had me blushing, as usual. He knew just how to get me in the mood.

"After this, we can catch a movie or something if you want to. I just wanna make sure you enjoy yourself," he told me.

"Oh, I'm having a ball. As long as I'm with you, bae, I'm cool."

"So, you plan on staying with me for a long time, huh?" he said, hinting around. I caught on really quick.

"For as long as you'll have me," I said, giggling.

"What if I said I want you forever?" he asked, pressing.

"Then we'll be together forever, babe."

"Remember you said that."

"I will!" I assured him with a wink.

Dasio finished roasting the links, and we laughed, drank, and ate until our hormones got out of control. Now, it was time to go inside. . . . It was definitely getting too cold outside.

As we entered the beach house, a series of alerts went off. We both checked our phones, only to find out that there was an emergency back at home. It was Auntie May.

"I hope she's all right We should go!" I cried as I started throwing my things in the bag. "Hurry, Dasio!"

When he didn't respond, I turned around to find him standing there staring at his phone. I went to him and asked what was wrong.

After slowly handing me the phone, he showed me the text from Carlos. It said that he needed him and that his mother was gone.

Tears flowed from Dasio's eyes, but he didn't budge. It was like he was in shock.

"Baby, come on. We have to leave. I'll drive."

While Dasio stood there, I packed everything in the car, then went back inside to get him. I held on to his arm and helped him in the car, then hopped in and sped off.

The entire ride, Dasio stared out the window. I was worried about him.

The only thing that I could do was pray, especially for Dasio's mom and Carlos. They had to be just as torn as he was.

Allowing my man all the space he needed, I didn't bother him until we got back to town and made it to his cousin's and parked in the driveway. Surprisingly, there were several cars out front, including Mason's.

"Come on, baby. I know your mother needs you."

After a few minutes, we both got out of the car and went to the door. Darlene greeted us there.

"I'm so sorry, Dasio," she cried as she fell into his arms. He hugged her and told her thanks.

When they released their hold on each other, we all walked into the kitchen, where Mason was comforting Dasio's mother. I immediately looked at him to try to read his facial expressions.

"Hey, y'all. What happened?" Dasio said, raising his voice a bit, as he fought off tears.

"Well . . . she went in her room earlier. She said she was tired and wanted to take a nap," his mother explained while trying to stop crying. "I had cooked and went to check on her to see if she was hungry, and she didn't answer me!"

Becoming overwhelmed with emotion, Mary stood up from the kitchen table and began shouting. "She was gone, baby! She was gone!"

Mason got to her before Dasio, and he backed off. I could tell Dasio needed comforting, too, by the lost look on his face.

Rushing over to his side, I held him, then escorted him to the den, where we could sit more comfortably. Moments later, Darlene joined us.

"Carlos and Lydia won't be here until the morning. That was the first flight they could get out of Miami. We were all gonna stay here with your mom. You guys should too. I know your cousin is gonna want you here when he gets here," Darlene said in a sad voice. "We will be here for all of you. Just let us know if you need anything."

"Thanks, sis," Dasio replied, surprising us both.

"Always, bro!" she responded with tears and a smile. "I'll be in the kitchen if you need me."

Darlene left us alone, and Dasio began to speak. His voice was so low that I could barely hear him.

"Constance, life is too short. We don't know when our time is gonna be up . . . when our number will be called. Look at all the shit we've been through. One of us could've easily lost our life behind bullshit."

"I know, Dasio."

"No, you don't understand."

"What, what is it?"

"After all this, we're gonna get married. We don't have to have a big ceremony or anything. I just need to know you're mine. We can have all that commercial shit later."

"What?" I gasped loudly. "Are you asking me to marry you, Dasio?"

"I'm telling you that we need to be official. If anything happens to either one of us, I don't want there to be any confusion."

"Any confusion?"

"No, and I need you to tell me you're on board."

"Yes, bae, yes!" I sang happily before we shared a kiss.

"Don't go telling everyone, Constance. I don't want Mason and all them making a big deal out of it until things settle down a bit," Dasio said with a forced grin. "I love you and want you to be mine forever . . . remember?"

I giggled and nodded before getting him into another lip-lock. It became so intense that my mind flew a million miles away, but Darlene brought us right back to reality.

"Excuse me," she laughed once she saw that she was interrupting. "Would you guys like something to eat?"

"No, I'm good," I replied.

"Me too," Dasio answered as he took me by the hand and stood up. "We're just gonna stay in my old room. I need to lie down and get my mind right."

I followed behind Dasio until we were closed in his room. That was when he used my body as a pillow and just held me. I didn't mind. . . . I didn't mind at all.

Chapter 46

Dasio Vazquez

That incredible night of getting closer to one another was just what I needed. I slept better than ever, but then morning came. That was when the harsh reality kicked in again. My auntie May was gone.

"What the hell happened? Where did they take her?" I heard Carlos yell from the other room.

After getting dressed as fast as I could, I burst out of the room to get to my cousin. He came to me and grabbed me as soon as he saw me.

"Dasio! Man, she's gone! I wasn't even here!" he cried. "I wasn't here for her!"

My mother and Mason came out of a back room. I ignored the strange feeling I had and focused on our loss.

"Carlos, baby, don't cry. She got to see you fall in love and get married. She was so proud of you—" my mother began.

"She's not even gonna be here to see my baby!" he cried, interrupting, as Lydia held on to him.

"Carlos, she's gonna always be with us. She's a part of our baby." Lydia tried to comfort him with her words. Nothing was working.

"Yes, but I'm not gonna get to see her again! I'm not gonna get to fuss at her and give her a hard time . . ."

Carlos was taking it so badly that he had us all in tears. Even Mason . . .

"You and Dasio, go down to the hospital and take care of all the paperwork, and we'll make all the funeral arrangements. Don't worry about anything but getting yourself together," Mason insisted.

Carlos thanked him, and we all went into the den.

"Lydia, you and Connie stay here. We'll be right back," Carlos announced.

"Okay, baby. I'm here if you need me," Lydia replied and gave her husband a kiss.

We left to handle business. Carlos stayed calm the whole time, until he viewed his mother's body. I had tried to talk him out of it and had told him to just remember the way she looked the last time he saw her, but he hadn't listened. I knew he was sorry afterward.

"Damn, Dasio. Why didn't I listen to you?" he yelled and hit the wall several times. "She don't even look like herself! She's pale, and why is her hair all over the place? They got her all fucked up!"

Someone heard him yelling and came out to see what was going on. He went right in on the poor elderly guy.

"Why the fuck y'all got my mama looking like that?" Carlos hollered. "What the fuck kind of place are you running?"

"I'm so sorry, sir," the elderly man said, apologizing, and patted Dasio on the shoulder as he called someone on his cell and asked them to come down.

As we waited, the man tried to calm my cousin down. I was thinking security was about to show up. That was why I was shocked to see a priest approach us.

"Can I escort you two upstairs so that we can talk?" the priest requested.

"No. I want someone to tell me why the hell they got my mother looking all messed up!" Carlos muttered, sniffling. Now he was calming down, and his tears were flowing again.

"The funeral home will take care of all that," the priest assured him. "The hospital is not allowed to alter a body without consent. Did you take care of all the paperwork to have her released?"

"Yes. And how long is that gonna take?" Dasio mumbled.

"I'm sure it will be soon," he assured him, and then he escorted us to the chapel.

I left them there to pray and chat while I went out into the hallway and checked on the girls. I needed a break from the emotional stuff. It was fucking my mental all the way up.

"Hey, Dasio. Are you guys all right?" Constance asked as soon as she answered my call.

"We're cool. Carlos is in the chapel, and we'll be there in a few."

"I love you, bae."

"I love you too, *mamí*," I told her before we disconnected our call.

Hanging out in the hallway for the next twenty minutes gave me time to reflect on all the tragedies. But just as I began to wrap myself up in the ill feelings, a sense of peace came over me. I was instantly reminded of the blessings that had been bestowed on all of us.

Sure, it hurt like hell to lose my auntie, but I convinced myself that she was in a much happier place. That thought alone brought me peace.

"Are you okay, cuz?" Carlos asked from behind me. I hadn't even noticed him standing there.

"Yeah, yeah, I'm cool."

"Well, I did my part here. Let's go check on Auntie Mary."

I nodded and followed him to the car. It was another long ride . . . a quiet one.

When we got there, it began pouring down rain. I'm talking about buckets.

"I'm gonna sit here for a bit. I need to pull it together before I go in there," Carlos whispered as he dried his face with the sleeve of his hoodie.

Instead of responding, I sat there silently and waited with my cousin.

About ten minutes later, he broke the silence. "I can't stop shakin'!"

"It's okay, Los. Let that shit out. It's just us here," I urged.

Carlos let out a loud cry and began praying. He was asking for understanding.

"Why? Why did this happen to such a wonderful woman and beautiful mother? Just show me a sign, Lord! Let me know she's with you! Let me know that she's okay—"

In an instant, everything went silent again, and the rain slowly ceased. Suddenly the sun came out and brightened up the block. It was amazing, to the point where it kind of scared me. The shit was eerie.

"That's all I needed." Carlos smiled as he wiped his tears one last time before he climbed out the car.

Closing my eyes, in total shock and gratitude, I thanked the man above for giving us the sign. It gave comfort not only to Carlos but to me as well.

"Carlos! Baby, is that you?" Lydia cried out as soon as we made it through the door good.

"Yes, it's me."

Lydia came flying into the foyer, with Constance and Darlene in tow. They all wanted to make sure that we were okay.

"Let's just enjoy these last few days in this house, because after the funeral, I'm gonna put it up for sale.

There's too many memories," Carlos sighed when we all made it into the den.

"Well, if you don't mind, nephew, I would like to buy the house. I'll keep it up and take care of everything. I just wanna feel close to her. I missed so much time with my sister."

"Of course, Auntie Mary! You don't have to buy it! Mom would've wanted you to have it."

"No, I have the money from the house coming."

"Use that to fix this place up a bit. Mom had been wanting to do it for some time." Carlos smiled. "That's settled."

We all laughed as Mason scooted closer to my mother on the sofa and wrapped his arm around her. When he glanced up, he caught me staring him down.

"Dasio, can I talk to you for a minute?" Mason requested before kissing my mother's cheek and releasing her.

"Yeah." I shrugged.

We stepped into the kitchen, where no one was for the moment. Mason wasted no time getting to the point.

"I just wanted to talk to you about what's been going on between your me and your mother."

"Yeah?"

"Yeah. I'm gonna be honest and tell you that I love your mother. I have always loved her, but as always, I made the wrong choice and let her get away."

"Yeah, that shit was a long time ago."

"It was, but when I saw your mother that first night, it brought back all the feelings I had for her before. It was like the first time I met her and fell for her. It happened all over again, and before I knew it, I was telling her—"

"Is she good with it?" I asked, cutting him off.

"Yes, she is, but she doesn't want it to interfere with us."

"Us?" I asked, flaring my nose while frowning.

"Yes, I'm just now meeting you and trying to get in your life. If my relationship with your mother is gonna bother you—" Mason explained before I cut him off again.

"If you guys want to be together, I'm with that. I just want everyone to be happy," I told him honestly. "Besides, I'm trying to figure out how to marry Constance without making a big deal out of it. I don't want folks to think it's bad timing, what with everything else that's going on."

"What?" Mason whispered loudly, a big-ass grin on his face.

"Why make a big deal?"

"Well, not only are you marrying one hell of a woman, but you will also be my first child to get married!" he bragged happily.

"Dolly's not married?"

"Nah, that girl can't keep a man!" Mason said with a chuckle.

"Well, damn."

"It's cool. We can wait until after the funeral to plan things."

"We?"

"Yeah, you know I'm gonna be as much of a part of this as I possibly can. I couldn't be prouder of you!" Mason confessed while taking me into a big bear hug. "I'm very proud of you, Dasio."

Damn! Nobody had ever told me no shit like that! I had been a two-bit hustler most of my life. I was raised in the slums by an abusive father and a loving mother. The combination had kept me balanced just enough to keep my sanity.

Now, there I was, and someone was telling me that they had noticed the good things I did. It was a feeling that I embraced quickly.

"Thanks, Pops," I blurted out. I didn't mean to call him that, but the title had been lingering in my head for a while. Today it just kind of popped out naturally.

"Pops, huh?" Mason smiled. "I like that, son. I like that."

After he wrapped his arm around my shoulder, we walked back into the den and joined the others. They were going back down memory lane. Talking about all the funny shit Auntie May used to say and do. The laughs were endless. Damn . . . She was truly going to be missed.

Chapter 47

Constance ("Connie")

Auntie May's homegoing was absolutely beautiful and portrayed her as the queen she was. I was sure she was looking down from the heavens, smiling, because the sun was surely shining during the entire service and burial.

"I'm so glad that's over!" Dasio declared when we got to the narrow driving path, where the limo was parked.

"We still have to go to the dinner they're having back at the hall Mason rented. It's catered and everything. We don't have to lift a finger. Well, except for lifting that fork to my mouth."

"Yo' ass is always hungry!" he exclaimed with a smile as we got in the limo.

Dasio's mother, Lydia, and Carlos climbed in behind us. Everyone looked exhausted.

"Well, after this dinner, we can all relax a bit," Mary sighed as she sniffled, then forced a smile.

"Yeah, this has been a long day, and it's not over yet," Carlos said while Lydia rested her head on his shoulder.

"We don't have to stay long. Mason has transportation set up where we can leave whenever we're ready," Lydia explained.

"Yeah, I'm thankful for him right now, Auntie Mary. He really came through for us. I couldn't have pulled off something as extravagant as he did. It was really nice," Carlos said, expressing his gratitude.

Dasio smiled as he glanced over at his mother. She was staring out the window, as if her mind was a million miles away.

Funny thing, all that changed the minute we got inside the hall and Mason greeted us. Oh, Dasio's mother was in good spirits then. I was so happy for her.

After taking Mary by the hand, Mason led her to the back and made her a plate. I watched as he carefully picked out just what she wanted, then walked her over to the family table, where we were all seated. He pulled out her chair, got her situated, then set her plate in front of her.

"Thanks, Mason," she said. "You're not eating?"

"Yes. I was waiting for you. Now that you're settled, I'll go get my plate," he explained with a smile, then kissed her cheek. "I'll be right back."

"Aw, that was so sweet," I sang as I grabbed Dasio's arm and pointed at his mother.

"Here you go!" he uttered playfully. "Let's go get some grub so we can get up out of here. Half of these folks are from the church, and you know more are coming."

"Hush, bae!" I whispered as we went for plates.

Dasio just laughed at me and followed my lead. Within minutes we were sitting down and feeding our faces too. The food was amazing!

About an hour or so later, we were all ready to leave. All except for Dasio's mother. She wanted to stay with Mason, so we went ahead on without her.

"Yo' mom and pops make such a good couple!" Lydia told Dasio as we stepped outside and waited for our ride.

"Yeah, I guess they do."

Dasio shrugged, and then he and Carlos stepped over to the side for a smoke. That gave me time to talk to Lydia.

"Hey, can we go see your mother tomorrow?" I asked her.

"Sure. You know you never have to ask me that, and I do miss her mean ass," Lydia responded and nudged me.

"I know. It's just that . . . it's just that with all that's happened, you know . . . It kind of makes me miss my mother and Grandma Betsy," I confessed through tears.

Lydia immediately embraced me and patted my back. "Connie, you know my mother loves you just like you were her own! Shit, sometimes more than she loves me."

"Hush, heffa!" I sniffled.

"You know what I'm saying, though, Connie?" Lydia whispered as the limo pulled up and the guys stepped back over to us.

"Yes, I do, and thank you."

"No thanks needed, boo! My friend to the muthafuckin' end!" she giggled.

"What y'all over here getting' all teary eyed about?" Dasio inquired as we got in the car.

I downplayed his question and told him that it was nothing. The last thing I needed was for him to be worried about me again. The Harrison shit had been put to rest, and for once in my life, I was financially and mentally stable.

Together not only had Dasio and I had established an unbreakable bond, but we also had nearly a million dollars between us! That was more money than I could imagine receiving in a lifetime. We were truly blessed.

"What are you over there thinking about?" Dasio asked, prying, after the driver dropped Carlos and Lydia off at their new house.

"I'm feeling lonely." It sounded real crazy once I heard myself say it out loud. I tried to explain to Dasio what I meant, but he wasn't getting it.

"You have me, Lydia, Carlos, and my mama."

"And I love them all! It's just that you are always working, and Lydia is a newlywed . . ."

"I'm sorry, *mamí*," Dasio said, apologizing.

"It's not your fault. I'm probably feeling this way because I lost my mother and Grandma Betsy. The only mom I have had since then is Lydia's mother."

Dasio comforted me all the way home, into the house, and up to the bedroom. I was exhausted. My whole body was.

I sat down on the bed, and Dasio stood in front of me and began to take my shoes off. Once he got the first one off, his cell rang.

Glancing at his screen, he noticed it was Mason. He quickly pulled off my other shoe and held his finger up before rushing out of the room.

My nosy ass hopped right up and went to the open bedroom door to ear hustle. I couldn't hear anything at first, so I eased a little closer.

Plain as day, I heard Dasio talking about me. He was telling him my favorite foods, my favorite color, and my sizes for clothes as well as shoes. Hell, I didn't even know he knew all that!

"Well, I'll hit you back in the morning to discuss the details," I heard Dasio mumble loudly.

After quickly running into the closet, I began removing my clothes. I took off everything right on down to my red cotton thong.

My birthday is coming up! I wonder if he's planning a surprise party for me!

Feeling extra excited, I ran out of the closet and into the bedroom, butt naked, as soon as Dasio called out my name. Oh, he wasn't expecting that!

The cool breeze created by the ceiling fan set my nipples straight up. Dasio's eyes traveled down to them and rushed to give them attention.

"Mmm," I couldn't help but moan.

Not missing a beat, Dasio was fully undressed in less than thirty seconds and slowly led me to the bed. The back of my legs touched the edge of the comforter, signaling to me to lower my body into a lying position. Next, he gently eased me up until every inch of me was on the bed. Slowly lifting my thighs, Dasio crept closer until the tip of his member graced my lower opening. He rubbed it back and forth while staring down at me as he licked his lips. The more he stroked himself while teasing my clit, the more I jerked uncontrollably. The stimulation was so intense that I was climaxing back-to-back as I wildly bucked upward.

"Shit!" I screamed loudly as I clenched my legs around his waist and drew him closer to me. It forced his hardened shaft right up inside me.

Now I was the one doing all the work. Dasio didn't stand a chance. I was holding him so tight that I controlled the rhythm.

With each thrust, I kissed his neck and whispered his name. It drove him to pump back until we both exploded.

That shit was a serious stress reliever. . . .

Chapter 48

Dasio Vazquez

For the past three weeks, I had been touching basis with Mason about the surprise wedding but hadn't made any progress. Although he had all the pertinent information, he hadn't given me very many details. Shit. I was starting to feel nervous.

"What's the concerned look on your face for?" Constance asked as she snuck up behind me and politely took my coffee mug from my hand.

As she sipped my coffee, I told her about how Mason was thinking about taking my mother to Las Vegas. She had never been before, so she was excited.

"When are they leaving?"

"Tonight, I guess." I shrugged and sat at the kitchen table to check the weather on my cell.

"We all should go! It would be a nice getaway since everything has kinda settled down."

While it was raining in Portland, it was in the eighties in Vegas. Sunshine in the forecast sounded really good to me.

After Constance put the idea in my head, it was stuck there. If we joined Mason and my mom to Vegas, not only could I enjoy some great weather, but I could keep an eye on my mother too.

While I dialed Carlos to run the idea by him, Constance darted off to call Lydia. I wasn't sure if she was going to be down, because her belly was getting bigger each day. Plus, she couldn't drink and party like the rest of us.

"You know Kendrick Lamar is gonna be there tomorrow night?" Carlos reminded me. "You know Connie's brother Cal said if we wanted to go, he would hook it all up!"

"I'm down. Just talk to Lydia about it and let me know."

"Oh, we're going!" Lydia shouted in the background. "I need some sun in my life!"

"Well, let me check these flights," I told Carlos.

"Shit, the girls are already booking them for early evening. I guess we'll be swooping y'all up a l'il later, cuz," Carlos laughed.

"A'ight."

When we hung up, my calendar alert went off, reminding me that it was Constance's birthday the following week! Not only had I been slacking on the wedding plans, but I had also forgotten my girl's special day.

"Why didn't I remember that shit?" I mumbled as I got up to go to the home office so I could get Mason on the line and talk without Constance overhearing me.

After entering our home office, I began pacing the wooden floor, all the while wondering how the hell could I forget something so damn important. I dialed Mason.

"Hey, son. What's going on?" Mason said when he finally answered.

"Hey, Pops! I know you and mom are going to Vegas today. Well, I don't wanna just barge in on your plans, but I just found out it's Connie's birthday in a few days. See, I was thinking that we fly out to Vegas too."

After quickly running down the plan, I asked him what he thought of it. Surprisingly, he was beyond happy and jumped right on board. In fact, he even wanted to invite the whole family.

Damn, I went from having only my mother to having a bigger family than I could even imagine. What made it even better? The fact that they all showed so much love. That wasn't normal in any family I knew.

"So, everything cool?" Constance asked when she entered the office about ten minutes later.

"It sure is, *mamí*!"

I smiled as I embraced the love of my life. She was more amazing every day. Not just her looks either. It was more like her nurturing ways. She always wanted to help someone or fix something. She was truly a gem.

"How about we shoot down to the mall and get us some shorts and shit?" I proposed.

"When have you known me to turn down a shopping trip?" she giggled, gesturing for me to go back to the bedroom with her.

As she walked backward, she held on to my shirt and blew kisses at me. The way she was looking and licking her lips had my dick hard before we made it to the room.

I watched as Constance's eyes roamed from my mouth to my goods. That was where her eyes paused.

"Someone wants some attention, huh?" she teased as she sat on the bed and drew my shit out.

As she gently stroked it, she stared up at me and smiled while she whispered the words, "I love you." I repeated them, closed my eyes, and tilted my head back as she latched her warm mouth onto my hardness.

"Mmm," I hummed as I rocked forward and backward while softly palming the top of her head.

Suddenly, she unleashed my beast and began teasing my shaft, going up and down, until her tongue graced my nuts. My knees trembled as she guided her mouth across them over and over.

"Shit! What the fuck?" I shouted as she hurried to put my dick back in her mouth.

Her slurping and sucking while fondling my balls had me going crazy! Shit, there was no way I could hold that shit. Hell, I couldn't even warn her before I shot that shit straight into her mouth.

I swear, I thought she was about to go off, but she didn't. Instead, Constance let me finish shaking and shit before she released my stiffened dick. Then she went and spit it all out in the sink.

I couldn't help but apologize and laugh. It was funny to see her react like that.

"I'm sorry, but damn! That shit was feeling so fuckin' good. You had a nigga screaming and shit! A niggas toes was all curled up and getting cramps and shit!" I told her, not overexaggerating about how she had me feeling, as she came back over to me. This time she was butt naked!

No more needed to be said. We let our bodies do all the talking.

Constance and I really pressed our luck by trying to do too much over the next few hours. Two rounds of lovemaking, two showers, shopping, eating, packing, then making it to the airport. Yeah, we did that shit just in the nick of time!

"I thought you two were gonna miss the plane!" Lydia screamed as she came flying toward us when we reached the gate so that she could hug her best friend.

"Yeah, so did we!" Constance's brother, Cal, chimed in, my sister Darlene right behind him.

She was peeking around him, smiling. I could tell she was happy.

"I didn't know you were coming!" Constance told her brother.

"I invited him," Darlene confessed. "I hope you don't mind." She covered her mouth and gasped.

Constance hurried to clear the air before Darlene could feel some type of way. "Not at all! I think it's kinda cute!" she told Darlene, a smile plastered on her beautiful face.

"Cute, huh?" Cal smirked, causing his sister to giggle.

"Where's everyone else?" I asked, curious, after we had lined up to board the plane.

"They left earlier. They're all staying at Caesars Palace on the Strip. Where are you guys staying?" Darlene said as we headed down the Jetway.

"We're staying there too!" Lydia and Constance sang together as we all got comfortable in first class.

Carlos, Cal and I laughed at them and ordered some drinks. I knew my cousin had to get lit every time he flew. It was the only thing that helped him relax. Once the liquor kicked in, he was fine. Hell, we all were, except for Lydia, who couldn't drink. She was still high on love and life, though. She definitely had a glow.

We all continued to chat, and before I realized it, over two hours had passed, and we were descending into Las Vegas. Everyone's eyes were glued to the Strip, which wasn't lit up yet, because there was still daylight.

After getting off and retrieving our luggage, we caught a shuttle to the hotel. Everyone was so excited that there was no talking, only a bunch of gasps and a few exclamations, like "Look!" and "Oh, my God!' and "You see this shit?"

When we arrived at Caesars Palace, it only got worse. We had to stop every few feet to take pictures. It took us nearly half an hour to get to the check-in counter.

As I received our keys, I saw that Constance had booked the Julius Signature-Level Executive Suite. I didn't know what it was, but the shit sure sounded expensive.

"Y'all got suites too?" I asked.

"You know it!" Lydia and Darlene cheesed as they held their key cards in the air. "We're all on the same floor!"

Sure, we had dough, but I didn't want to waste it on some hotel room. Well, that was how I was feeling until we got inside the suite. Not only was it nice, but the hotel staff provided us excellent service, starting off with a complimentary bottle of some type of red wine in a fancy bottle.

Putting the bottle to the side for the moment, we decided to walk the Strip a bit to do a little sightseeing. That way we could get out and enjoy the scenery before having dinner with my folks.

Chapter 49

Constance ("Connie")

The Vegas Strip at night was fucking amazing! The lights were flashing, and music was playing. The weather was beautiful, and it wasn't too crowded. It was perfect.

"Lydia, did Carlos or Dasio mention anything about my birthday?" I asked my friend in a whisper as we ambled by Bellagio on our way to our hotel.

"No, they haven't said a word about it, but I'm sure Dasio hasn't forgotten your birthday!"

"What if he has?" I replied.

"If he doesn't mention it the night before, then I'll start throwing hints at Carlos. Is that cool?" Lydia whispered as we headed back into the hotel to meet Dasio's mom and dad at the buffet. "You know he can't hold water!"

I tried not to worry myself about it. I had never really made a big deal out of my birthday before. But then again, I had never had someone special in my life to share the occasion with. Now I did!

All through dinner, we talked about how Mason first met Dasio's mother. It was truly a love story that I could write about. Unfortunately, it ended on a sour note.

Maybe they'll have a second chance, I thought.

As I sat there and started to daydream, I pictured the two of them having a beautiful ceremony. It made my eyes water just thinking about the two of them reuniting.

"So, I was thinking that we could go over to Fremont Street and check out the band. I heard they were playing some old school. Anyone interested?" Mason asked as we finished up dinner.

"I'm game!"

"Me too!"

"Count me in!"

Everyone was down to go, so we headed there immediately after dinner. All the while, we carried our drinks around. It was legal, and I couldn't believe it. They didn't even have a cutoff time for serving alcohol.

At ten o'clock, we were still wandering around. We had left Fremont Street and had wound up by some office buildings in downtown Vegas.

"What's this place? Why is everyone lined up?" I asked.

"To get a license to get married. You and Dasio wanna get one? You know, just in case? I think it would be fun. You wanna get one too, Mary?" Mason proposed.

"Huh? Who, me?" Dasio's mother giggled, as if she was a little tipsy.

"Yes, of course you!" Mason laughed as they went and got in line.

"You two should just get one! You know . . . just for the hell of it! And if you decide to tie the knot here, you'll already be prepared!" Lydia explained to Dasio's mother, with Carlos standing right there, supporting her all the way.

"Yeah, *mamí*, let's do it!" Dasio suggested before kissing my lips.

I couldn't believe it! I knew it wasn't a wedding or anything, but shit! My ass was on cloud nine for real. Nobody could tell me a damn thing, especially when we waltzed out of there twenty minutes later with our license.

"Why didn't you and Darlene go in?" I teased as I waved my document in Cal's face.

“Whoa. Way too soon for that!” Darlene declared.

“It’s never too soon for true love, baby,” Cal said, sounding all sophisticated.

“Aww,” Darlene purred as she snuggled closer to him.

“You need to keep that one right there!” Mason teased his daughter. “He seems to have a nice head on his shoulders, and the street smarts to back it up.”

Cal looked at Mason and tightened his eyes. Not in a mean way, but out of curiosity.

“Yes, I did have you checked out as soon as you began seeing Darlene. Nothing personal, but you may not understand until you have kids of your own, especially a daughter!” Mason confessed.

“No disrespect taken, Mason. I totally understand, and you don’t have to worry about a thing. I’ll take good care of her,” Cal promised with a wink.

Mason in turn gave my brother a head nod and a smile. It was priceless!

“Okay, where’s the car at? Because I’m lit!” Carlos laughed as we walked along the north end of Las Vegas Boulevard.

“We took the limo, remember?” Mason told him. “I’ll call for it now.”

“I’m not ready to go in!” Dasio’s mother whined as she clenched Mason’s arm. “I wanna go on that Ferris wheel thing that we can have cocktails on. I wanna get some pictures from in the air.”

“Okay. I’ll let the kids take the limo, and we can get an Uber,” Mason suggested.

While they went on their late-night date, the rest of us headed back to Caesars Palace. Lydia and Carlos went up to their suite, and Dasio and I gambled a little.

We stayed down there for nearly five hours, until about five o’clock in the morning, but we went back to the room fourteen thousand dollars richer! Yes, we had both taken mad chances because we were drinking, but it all paid out in the end.

"Look, bae, we are having blessings on top of blessings!" I screamed as I threw the cash all over the suite as I spun around in circles.

When all the bills dropped to the floor, I thought of the marriage license. I didn't want to bring it up, so I just politely placed the document on the coffee table and smiled.

"My brother, Manuel, and my sister Dolly will be here later today. We should do something!" Dasio suggested, overlooking the hint I had placed in front of him. "Too bad Ya-Yo couldn't come."

"I know! I love her! She's a spunky l'il thang, Dasio!"

Feeling a bit frisky, I went over and poured myself a drink and climbed out of my clothes. Since it was now dawn, I closed the curtains to make it dark inside the suite.

Before I tripped over my own feet, I clicked the electric fireplace on. It was perfect.

To distract myself from thinking about my birthday or about getting married, I took my mind to another world. . . .

While Dasio took my body to that very same place . . .

Chapter 50

Dasio Vazquez

For the next two days in Vegas, I avoided any talk about marriage or birthdays. Instead, I went out and bought a three-carat solitaire wedding set. I planned on giving Constance the engagement portion of it. At least that would buy me some time.

"What do you think, Pops? Honestly?" I asked Mason as we left the jewelry store on the Strip.

"I think it's a fine-cut stone and an exquisite setting. It's very unique."

"I meant about giving her the ring without a date."

"Just give it to her today, at lunch. We're going to some fancy place your mother picked out. Make sure everyone dresses formally, because we're taking family pictures afterward."

"A'ight. Let me go get a fresh new suit, then, and make sure Constance has something to wear," I told him as we entered our hotel lobby.

"She went this morning with Lydia and your mother, so I'm sure they found something."

I nodded, said goodbye, and went up to my suite to change. There was only a couple of hours until lunch.

"Constance?" I yelled when I walked into the suite.

No answer.

I assumed that she was still out with the women, so I took advantage of the alone time and showered and shaved. By the time I was finished, my cell was ringing.

"Hey, *mamí*," I sang out after seeing it was Constance calling. "Where are you?"

"Over here at the MGM. We're all gonna get dressed over here. Dolly has a huge suite overlooking the Strip! Baby, it's so beautiful!" Constance gasped, like she was still amazed at Vegas.

"Okay, well, I'll meet you down in the lobby at noon. I don't wanna look all over for y'all, so could somebody be in front around that time, so a nigga won't look so lost?"

"Bae, of course! I love you and can't wait for you to come and see this place!"

"A'ight. I'll be there. Love you too!"

We hung up, and I was still laughing. I thought it was so fucking sexy how the littlest things made Constance happy. I loved that about her.

After checking the time, I went ahead and slid into my suit and dress shoes. Then I was out.

I swear, I couldn't make it to the elevator good before Mason called me on my cell.

"Hey, Pops!"

"Hey, son! I was just wondering if you could bring that marriage license. I wanted to take some pictures with it," Mason said.

"I'm already gone out the room, but I'll double back," I offered, hoping that he'd change his mind, but he didn't.

"Okay. Thanks, son. We're all here waiting on you. The photographer is gonna take a few pics until you get here."

"Okay. I'm on my way."

Fifteen minutes passed before I was walking up to the MGM. Darlene and my mother were standing out front to meet me.

“Where’s Constance?” I asked as I hugged my mom and sister.

“She’s inside. You know everyone is starving, so they’re already in the hall we have reserved,” Darlene announced as we turned to headed inside.

“Look at y’all! Everyone looks so nice!” I said, complimenting everyone, as I entered the hall.

Then suddenly I paused. My eyes landed upon the most amazing woman I had ever seen. I couldn’t believe how stunning Constance looked in this long peach-colored dress with a long split up the side, showing all that thick thigh. I couldn’t even tell if she was wearing any panties or not. Shit, I wanted to take her right there.

“What is all this?” she asked as she approached me. “I thought this was just a family luncheon.”

“Actually, this hall is set up for a ceremony . . . that is, if we have any takers!” Lydia said slyly.

I felt around in my pocket and drew out not only the license but the ring as well. “Lord, let this be a sign,” I whispered to myself.

My hand shook as I opened the little box and lowered myself down to one knee. Hell yeah, I got to stuttering and everything when I said a few words to Constance! My mama had to help me out.

“Chile, he’s trying to ask you to marry him!” my mother announced as she popped me in the back of my head.

“Yeah, Constance . . . Connie . . . *mamí*, would you marry me? Right here? Right now?” I begged.

“You had me from the moment you kneeled, baby!” Constance cried.

I rose and hugged her tightly.

Once again, everyone was in tears! My mom being the loudest!

I couldn’t believe what Mason and the rest had gone through to plan all that at the last minute! Everything was perfect, from the ceremony to the food to the honeymoon night! The shit was going down!

We snuck out of the hall around three in the afternoon and got a room right there in the MGM! We couldn't even wait to make it back to Caesars Palace. If I didn't do anything else that day, I was gonna put a baby up in my wife or kill myself trying!

The very next morning we got up and did everything Constance wanted. She was so damn happy that the smile never left her face the whole rest of the time we were in Las Vegas. The shit was amazing!

Then, when we got back to Portland, it was even better. I mean, the sex was better, our communication was in tune, and our finances were secure. The only thing we were missing was a baby. As much as we had made love without protection, it was baffling to me why she hadn't gotten knocked up yet. Damn. I was beginning to worry, but I definitely didn't stop trying.

Every single day I checked to see if she had gotten her period, but all the while I was making love to her every chance I got. I would pray immediately afterward, hoping that God would hear me.

Things went on that way for the next four weeks. Then it happened. Constance was only three days late, but I was so anxious, I practically forced her to go to the doctor.

"I'll go, but I think it's way too early!" she huffed as she grabbed her jacket and purse.

On the way out, we ran into my mother and Mason. You know they just had to ask where we were going. And Constance just had to spill the beans.

"Well, after you two are done, meet us at the diner. We have something to tell you," my mother announced happily as she followed Mason back to the car. He hadn't said a word.

"What was that all about? What do you think they have to tell us?" Constance questioned as we set off to the doctor's office.

When we got there, she was seen right away. She didn't let me go back with her. She said I was making her too nervous.

Shit, how the hell did she think I would feel waiting out in the lobby for the next hour? I was ready to go back there and get her.

To pass the time, I played games on my cell, checked my social network, and browsed the news. Nothing was taking my mind off what was going on with Constance.

"Was I long?" she whispered as she snuck up behind me.

I jumped and turned around to hug her. "I love you."

"We love you too!"

"See! See! I told you, *mamí*! I told you!" I cried and didn't care who saw or heard me. "I love you! I love you guys so much!"

The few people in the lobby were cheering and taking pictures. It didn't faze me. I was too busy hugging my girl!

"Come on! Let's go!" she screamed excitedly, and we rushed outside.

We couldn't get in the car good before she started spitting out girls' names for the baby. You know I came right back with some boys' names!

I was so excited that I nearly forgot that my moms and pops had something to tell us. I reminded Constance about it, then headed over to meet them at the diner.

When we got there, to our surprise, Lydia, Carlos, Cal, and Darlene were waiting there with my parents. I knew right away that something was up, especially when I noticed a new piece of jewelry on my mother's left hand.

She caught me staring, so she cut to the chase and blurted it out. “Me and your father got married the night before you did. We wanted to wait to tell you because we didn’t wanna dampen your incredibly beautiful union with Connie, son.”

“Damn, y’all sneaky as hell!” I laughed, and then I congratulated them both.

“I guess another congratulations is in order too,” Constance announced.

“What is that?” my mother asked excitedly.

“You and Mason are gonna be grandparents in less than eight months!”

My parents screamed and hollered like they were expecting a baby of their own. Thank God that wasn’t happening! I truly wasn’t ready for all that!

“Well, let God bless this day and every day after! Let us be grateful for all that He has done for us. Let us do it every day . . . in God’s name . . . Amen!” my mother prayed once we were all seated around a large table.

“Amen!” we all replied in unison and smiled. It was surely a great day. One that I would forever remember!

From all that had happened, we had learned how to heal from tragedies, and we had also realized how important it was to love and support one another, especially family.

“Remember, family over everything!” Mason chanted as he raised his glass.

We all did the same and repeated his words.

“Family over everything!”

Epilogue

Dasio Vazquez

One Year Later . . .

Our families may have begun this incredible journey with tragedies and heartbreak, but through it all, we remained vigilant and united. That was how we obtained our happily ever after. Hell, even Cal and Darlene got hitched. Constance couldn't believe it, and neither could I, but, hey . . . if a two-bit hustler like me could find love and turn my life around, and my parents could make it back to one another to rekindle what they had once had, anything was possible. Absolutely anything.

The growth we all had experienced so far was amazing, but not because my wife was carrying our second baby. At the rate we were going, we would have plenty more, and I couldn't be happier.

Now, for Lydia and Carlos, one child was enough, and I couldn't blame them, because Junior was a handful. He was already walking at nine months and, hell, the little boy couldn't even speak clearly, but he could hold a tune. That child mimicked every note his father belted out, and I knew that it wouldn't be long before he was a star, just like Los.

As for me, I continued to work with my cousin and also managed a few other artists. From up-and-coming soloists to well-known groups across the United States, I had them signed and taken care of. Only the best for mine, and that was how to get appreciated and to be in high demand.

Damn, who knew this shit could be so profitable? Definitely not me, and I enjoyed doing it. At this point in my life, I didn't want for a thing . . . and neither did my family!

Constance Vazquez

With a wrecked childhood and trust issues, I truly thought a real relationship would never be in the cards for me. That was up until I met Dasio. The love of my life.

I was not only grateful not only that he had swept me off my feet and taught me all about real love, but that he had also given me something that I didn't have. He gave me a family.

As my husband, the father of my child and the one on the way, he vowed to protect me. Just like he had with Harrison and just like he had with Shorty when he tried to release some material he had stolen from my computer. I swear, if Lydia hadn't read his new book, I probably wouldn't have ever found out. But once again, the Lord wasn't about to let that happen. Nope, he would expose the devils and make them pay.

It wasn't about karma, though. With me, it was all about the blessings, and God had definitely showered our extended family with quite a few. One of my favorites was the gift of Mary and Ya-Yo.

Although they couldn't replace my mother and my grandma, their love was more than I could ask for, and I greatly appreciated them. Just having them there to give me guidance and advice was a sacred present that I would always cherish.

With my plate now filled with teaching other authors how to be published independently and taking care of my family, I couldn't ask for much more. Only continued blessings from the good Lord above. The one who had put love back into my life. For that, I would be eternally grateful.

Always and forever.

Family over everything . . .